CHEMICAL BODIES

By

Ben Woodiwiss

For permissions contact:
lookthinkfilms@gmail.com

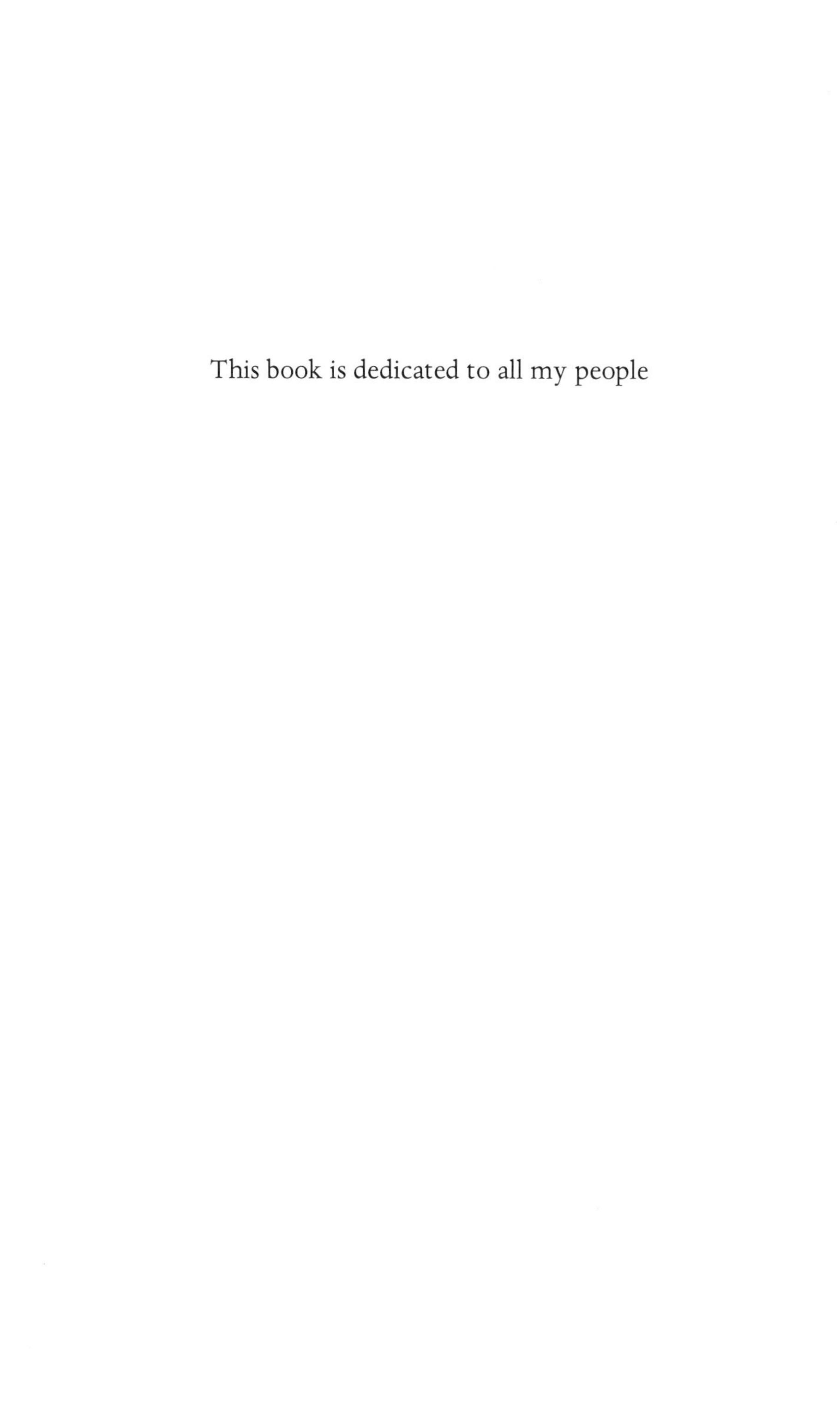

This book is dedicated to all my people

Time / Space map

I:	8th April, 1994 19.55	The City
II:	8th April, 1994 20:08	The Gallery
III:	3rd April, 1994 10.20	The City
IV:	3rd April, 1994 15.20	Above the ocean
V:	5th April, 1994 08.20	The Chelsea
VI:	5th April, 1994 16.20	One of Three
VII:	5th April, 1994 16.21	Cuir Absolue
VIII:	5th April, 1994 17.05	The Chelsea
IX:	4th April, 1994 19.12	(Serge's experience of) Berlin
X:	5th April, 1994 17.37	The Chelsea
XI:	5th April, 1994 21.12	Barnes & Noble
XII:	6th April, 1994 02.46	JFK
XIII:	6th April, 1994 09.39	Gare Saint-Lazare
XIV:	6th April, 1994 11:52	All known time – Two of three
XV:	6th April, 1994 11:52	The Musée d'Orsay
XVI:	6th April, 1994 14:13	The Hotel Opera
XVII:	8th April, 1994 20:45	The Gallery
XVIII:	All time	Three of Three - Everywhere
XIX:	8th April, 1994 21:40	The Gallery, and Beyond

I
8th April, 1994
19.55
The City

It's not easy to identify which scent hits her first. Maybe it's the swirling dust from the concrete streets, so acrid and dry. Or maybe it's the stench from the thick opaque liquid forming pools in the pavement, blending together notes of chalk, limestone, and petrol. Of course, it might be the car exhaust fumes, or the sour tang of fermented yeast that's coming from somewhere, or even the heady aroma of the white blossom on the trees. So hard to say. And then she opens her eyes.

Two words:

Heavy traffic.

That's what she thinks as she becomes aware of the steadily growing roar of white noise and turns her head to the right to see the road she's walking alongside. It's a big road. A main road. One of those things with two lanes of traffic going one way, and two going the opposite direction on the other side. But because she doesn't drive, she doesn't know the correct name for it, only that it's huge, aggressive, and loud.

As if that wasn't bad enough, Eldo's not entirely sure whether the world is moving unusually quickly, or this uncomfortable sense of urgency is emanating from inside her body, but either way something certainly seems amiss: jagged breath, pounding heart, frantic desperate eyes, and that relentless traffic, so loud, insistent, like the tape's on fast-forward. Even the birds in the trees offer no respite. All singing at once, as though the idea was not to be heard, not to communicate, it was simply to create noise, as much as possible.

And yeah, sure, this sensation could be stemming from the fact that she's running late, slightly panicking, but it's not like there's anything really wrong with being late, is there? Not these days, anyway. It's almost like people expect it of her now, like it's something she just has to do. But then it could be something to do with the half gram of pink champagne rolling around inside her. Yeah. Sure. Maybe. Perhaps. Whatever it is one thing's for certain, something in her internal locomotion system has been throwing more logs on the fire than usual, encouraging her to speed up and up and up.

It started gently, too slight to notice, a minuscule increase in pace stepping off a curb or something, so small she barely registered it, but, as Serge often says, once an increase has been made, it's all too easy to make another, and another, and another. And now she's racing along while the unseen hand of someone in charge of the city has been slowly turning the dial all the way to 11.

Take it easy.

She thinks.

Don't want to put yourself in a hole in the ground

She thinks.

And, breath by breath, she gets her body to ease its foot from the pedal. And instead of the breakneck pace she was going at, she now finds herself slowing, positively ambling behind two women who sashay with a ripe, hypnotic rhythm that moves like the ocean: left right, left right. Calming. Relaxing.

She needs these women right now. She needs a model of serenity. She blocks the external noise of the world out. Chooses one of the women and brings her vision down to a telescopic pinpoint that focuses on the swaying locus just below her centre. And slowly, but steadily, her heart rate relaxes, slows right the hell down, and the cacophony of sounds becomes bearable, and she looks to her right again and the passing traffic is far more like waves lapping against the shore now, then she turns back to the sight in front of her, and wonders whether this process of relaxation she's engaging in with these two female figures is based more on admiration or objectification, and then, just as she contemplates whether or not there really is any distinction between those two terms, whether you can have one without the other, her phone rings.

Mobile phones are still rare enough that the sound of the ringtone stops the two women in front of her dead in their tracks. Like Lot's wife they turn and look back. Eldo answers the phone as quickly and nonchalantly as she can, the voice on the other end speaks without saying who it is, but it sounds like Serge. It's just got to be Serge. Anyway, the voice-who-is-probably-Serge says something that Eldo doesn't quite catch, so she repeats what she thinks the words are.

Cut codeine is dead? Serge, is that you?

Serge corrects her.

Cobain. Kurt Cobain is dead. Nirvana is over.

It's at this point that Eldo is interrupted by one of the women in front of her who steps close, smiles, and husks.

Did you say you could get codeine?

Now Eldo can't deal with two things at the same time right now, so she mutters something into the phone before holding it down by her side, mouthpiece covered, just so that Serge will understand.

Give me a second …

And then she turns her attention to the young woman standing in front of her.

I, uh, don't feel totally comfortable talking about this kind of thing on the street.

So, does that mean you can get codeine, or you can't?

For a second her ego gets the better of her, instead of hearing this as a question Eldo hears it as a challenge. This brings out a rarely seen cocky side to her:

Don't be ridiculous, of course I can.

So…?

Eldo's not going to tell her what she's actually thinking, which is *Well… I normally deal in commercial quantities rather than handfuls,* because that is not the correct response for this situation. She has to say something though, so she looks around to make sure the coast is clear. And even though there's no one nearby, and the sound of the world roaring about its business is deafening, she still leans in a little closer, just in case, because, well, you never know.

You can't just walk up to anyone in the street to buy drugs. That's not safe.

Pffi. Look, safe doesn't get you drugs…

Well, I can't argue with that.

The woman pulls a flyer from her bag for a nightclub somewhere in the north of the city, produces a ballpoint pen from somewhere else, jots something down on the flyer. Meanwhile, Eldo gets a darkly floral hit from her that can only be rose, with something sweet and spicy underneath, like… cinnamon and vanilla maybe? And lying underneath both of those notes there's the unmistakable powdery kiss of sandalwood and, surprise surprise, patchouli. And even though *everyone* smells of patchouli these days there's something about this specific combination of scents that leaves her smelling like a Renoir nude. Anyway, she goes on with:

…here's my number. If you manage to pick anything up just give me a call.

Now before Eldo looks at the number, let's get some truths out of the way. Hand on heart, if Eldo were to find herself talking to this particular lady outside of this particular context there's no way she'd be able to play it cool. Not only is her paranoid head out to get her on the best of days, but on this particular day the pink champagne and the breakneck pace of the world are combining with her usual twitchiness to convince her that, without a shadow of a doubt, this woman can see through her head, as though it were made of crystal, with her idle erotic thoughts projected as a slideshow for the world to see, one embarrassing reveal after another. This fleshy paranoia is in conflict, however, with the fact that she has eyes which are singing an aria of seduction to Eldo. And as if that wasn't bad enough, she also has a piercing in her throat, a metal bar that tapers to a fine point at both ends: clearly signifying that she's hip, can be trusted, and is probably very good in bed.

Shut up, don't think that.

Her dumb brain thinks.

Anyway, the point being that all of these elements added together make this a woman that Eldo simply wouldn't have the nerve to talk to on a different occasion. But this thing right here, this interaction in the city by the side of a busy road? This is fine. This is drug stuff. Not people stuff.

Okay, look, I don't have anything on me right now, but when I get some, I'll give you a call. Cool?

Cool.

But I'm still going to say you shouldn't do this, giving your number out to strangers in...

And this is the part where Eldo looks at the number the woman wrote down for the very first time. She makes a face, narrows her eyes as though there were a bright light shining directly at her, her mouth forming something between a grimace and a smile, and that's the face she's wearing as she looks up from the number and into the eyes of the woman in front of her.

Are you messing with me?

She shakes her head, eyes lost.

No, why?

Eldo looks around, as though there were someone watching from a concealed position. As though this were a hidden camera setup. I mean, yeah, she gets this feeling most of the time, but this is just extra weird.

Your number. That's my birthday. With a '4' in front of it.

The woman (who Eldo is about to discover is called Naomi) cocks her head to one side in this darling coquettish fashion and gives a wry smile.

Now I'm getting the feeling that you're screwing with me.

Eldo can hear the faintest sound of Serge's voice on the phone muttering *I'm the one being screwed here,* but she ignores it. Despite the fact that Serge is a good guy, a really good guy, and probably deserves better. Probably? Definitely. Anyway, Eldo now takes a step she doesn't usually take, because she tends to think it's *skeezy*, and says:

What's your name?

Naomi.

Eldo raises her left hand, open, palm out, a gesture of welcome, or greeting, or meaning no harm, and says her name out loud, and the woman replies with:

Did you say Eldo?

To which Eldo, who has heard this response before, just nods.

Okay then. Well call me when you can help, Eldo.

There's the softest tail of a giggle as she says her name, and then Naomi walks off with her friend, whose name Eldo never learns. She brings the phone back up to her ear and speaks, quietly and apologetically.

Serge?

Yeah, I'm still here.

Sorry man, did you hear that? That was weird. That wasn't just me, right?

No, from what I heard that seemed like the lattice of coincidence was in full effect. That shit with your birthday, man. What was that? A trick? She playing you?

No, she felt real, genuine, straight up, that was just weird. Anyway, what were you saying about Kurt Cobain?

He's dead, man. Found earlier today. Shot his self in the head.

Shit. You're fucking with me?

Wish I was. It's true, I'm not fucking with you.

Damn.

I know, right? He was found in a greenhouse, surrounded by plants. Life surrounding death. End of an era. Times are changing, man. Mark my words.

And how was Berlin?

Berlin?

Yeah, you went on Monday, right?

There's a moment's silence before Serge speaks again:

Eldo, man. You went to Berlin on Monday. Remember?

I did?

Yeah. Today's the 8th, Friday, you went to Berlin on the 4th. Monday. I'm looking at the diary right here.

Eldo wracks her brain for any memories of this, any fragments: the airport, the flight, the meet, duty free, asking someone for a light, anything, anything at all, but there's nothing. Just a void. However, instead of letting Serge know she's drawing a blank on the Berlin deal she covers it all up by saying

Oh yeah, yeah. Of course. Sorry man. I don't know where my head's at.

What's up?

For a moment she gets the craziest uncanny feeling that someone unformed is watching her. She doesn't really understand what this feeling is, or what an unformed person is, but she looks all around her, pivoting on one heel to take in a 360 view of her surroundings.

Hey. Do you ever get the feeling that something bad's about to happen?

Let me guess, pink champagne, right?

No! Maybe. Yes?

She brings the phone ever so slightly closer to her mouth, lowers her voice.

How do you know?

You always get like this on speed. It's one of those, what you call them, eternal truths: Death, taxes, and Eldo will say some fucked up shit when she's on amphetamines.

You think? Yeah. It's just that, right? There's no conspiracy.

Of course not man. You should chill. Relax.

I'm actually on my way to the gallery to do just that, opening night, drinks and shit.

The gallery? What, is Annick going to be there?

Well, a lot of people might be there, guy…

A lot of people including Annick?

Dude.

See, I know this routine. I've heard it before. And you have this funny sound when you seeing Annick. Look, whatever man, chill, relax, have a blast, and call me tomorrow. We have a Geneva job next week and something to set up in Caracas.

Will do. Rough news about Cobain, man.

Truth. The roughest.

Eldo hangs up. She and Serge know each other well enough that they don't have to say *Goodbye* every time they speak on the phone. And she looks left just in time to see Naomi and the woman whose name she will never learn turning a distant corner, and she looks at her and smiles one last time before disappearing out of sight. She would never see either of them again.

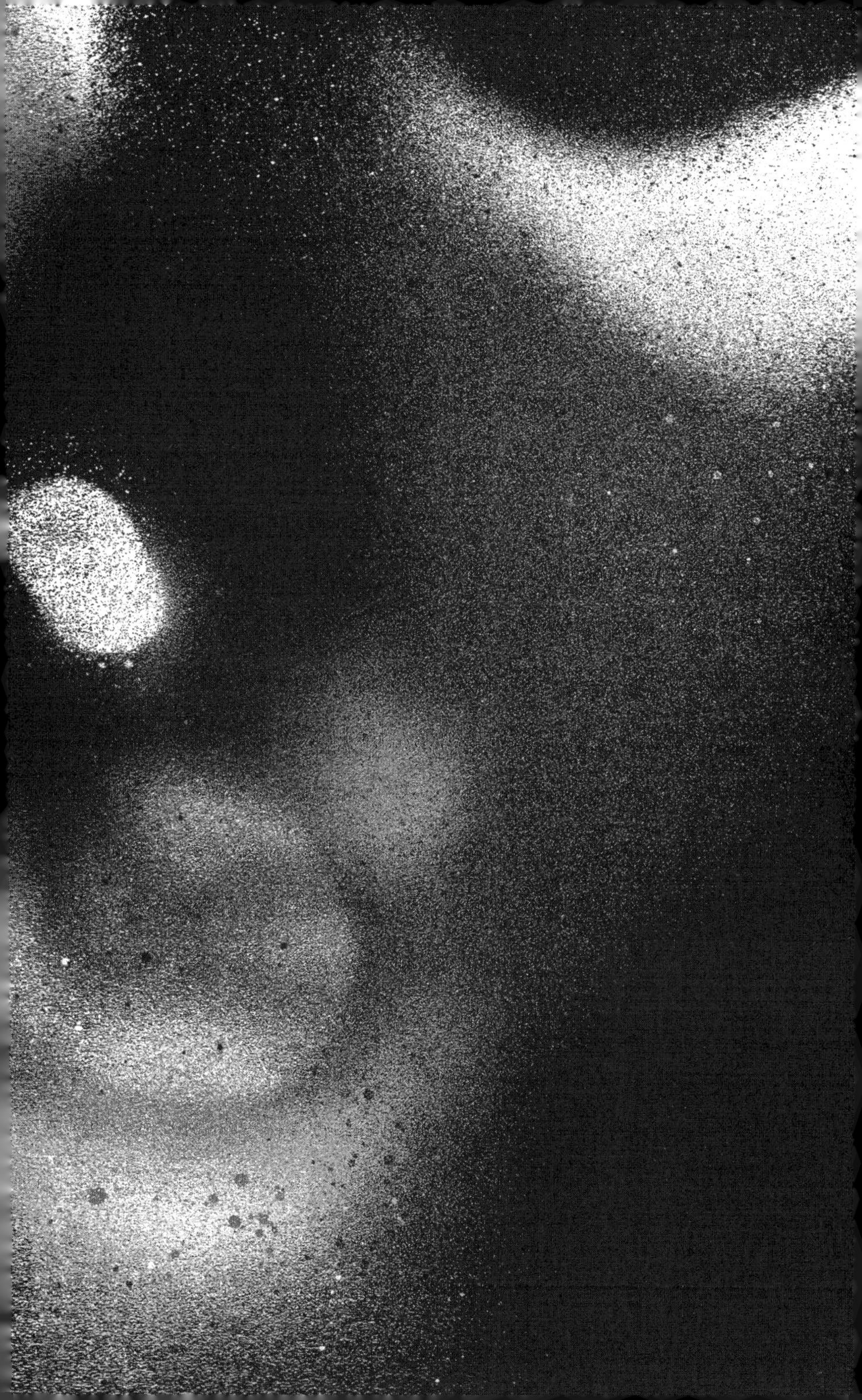

II
8th April, 1994
20:08
The Gallery

Herman is standing outside the gallery, as usual. Tired and irascible, with feet that are screaming at him, yelling that they've had enough of this standing shit. He gets a hit of cigarettes from his own breath, but not the good kind of tobacco scent, not the fresh, heady, intoxicating type. No, this is the old and stale and ashtray kind. And here's him without any gum, or mints or anything. Just then a weird feeling ripples through him like a wind, carrying the possibility that he's not the main character in this story, but rather that the protagonist is looking at the world through his eyes, seeing this moment from his perspective, but before he has time to study this uncomfortable sensation in detail Eldo appears round a corner and the idea melts away and the pain in his body lifts somehow, and a broad smile works its way across Herman's face.

Like most people, he knows Eldo well, or so he thinks. But one detail that Herman and most people are unaware of is that Eldo is actually her last name. Her first name is Jeanne. But no one calls her Jeanne. She got the moniker Eldo when she was at university and had fallen into the habit of calling herself and her colleagues by their surnames. Kind of a joke to begin with, like they were in a classic novel or something, but it stuck. Stuck so hard that now she's Eldo to everyone. Including Herman.

Eldo! How's it going?

My man Herman, always a pleasure. You hear about Cobain? Can you believe this shit?

And of course Herman's heard, it's all anyone's talking

about, so he shakes his head with the disbelief and motherfucking sadness of it all.

What kind of a world have you got where a kid of 27 kills himself? It's a disgrace, man. Un-fucking-believable. So much talent, gone.

Herman clicks his fingers on the word *gone*, emphasizing the brevity of Kurt Cobain's time on Earth.

Right? End of an era.

End of a fucking era. That's what they're all saying. Hey, Eldo, you don't happen to have any…

Eldo raises a finger and stops Herman in his tracks.

Herman, my man, I thought you might ask, so I just happened to bring a little pick-me-up, especially for you.

Eldo sings those last three words as she dances a hand into her pocket and then out again. She shakes hands with Herman, her right hand doing the shake, her left hand wrapped around Herman's to provide cover for the drop. The whole move is graceful, balletic, and conceals the handover beautifully.

That'll give you the pep you need.

Herman breaks the shake, draws his hand back, gently, and carefully opens his hand, cupping it so as not to drop anything expensive, glances at his palm, smiles. Eldo leans in close.

Now, about, this show…

But this time it's Herman who stops Eldo, because he gets what she's saying immediately.

You want to know what it's all about?

Eldo nods.

It's this artist called Fougére, French name but the guy has no accent, like you. And his whole artistic concept is to make love – yes, that's what he calls it - to different women on different canvases, covered in paint.

What, the canvases are covered in paint, or the bodies?

The bodies. And then the canvasses.

Wild concept. He actually calls it making love?

Straight up. Nothing but. He takes offense at the word fucking, but whatever. The crowd here are loving it.

If I wanted to say the whole thing reminded me of something, what might I say?

Pollock. It's obvious, but no one really talks about Pollock these days, so you'll sound insightful, like you considered it carefully. And hey, everyone loves the classics.

That's what I always say. Herman, my man, I can always rely on you.

Eldo takes a look at her watch, but the numbers don't seem to be legible. They're fluid, moving around, like a special effect.

Uhh... you wouldn't be able to read this for me, would you Herman?

Eldo extends her wrist, Herman peers, and then speaks.

It's a little after eight.

Eldo nods, brings her wrist back in front of her face, opens her eyes wide, then narrows them, trying to get a fix on the digit 8 now that she knows it's there, but it's no good, it's completely eluding her, so she gives up, lets her arm drop to her side and asks Herman a question.

You want me to send you out a drink?

Champagne if you see it, and you will. You're a good one, Eldo.

These words leave Eldo feeling a little awkward: *a good one*. Is she really? Just because she has the time of day for someone, can pass over a pinch of Bolivian marching powder if required – are these aspects that make someone good? Most people on the street wouldn't say that Eldo had any *good* qualities to her if they knew about all her curricular and extra-curricular activities. She could hardly talk about most of what she does if she were in, say, a church. Surely a 'good one' would do something that you could talk about anywhere, to anyone, no? And did she just think the words *Bolivian marching powder*? Jesus, who talks like that? Anyway, instead of saying all of this stuff Eldo simply points a finger at Herman and says *Sure am.* Later on she would remember this moment and wince and feel like an ass, but there you go.

And without really noticing the movement from outside to inside, Herman is gone and Eldo is suddenly protected from the chill April wind, and there's a lady in front of her and she's being asked if she'd like to check her coat. She declines. And it's not because she's cold, but rather a combination of preferring to keep everything close to hand, mixed with a deep distrust of cloakrooms, or rather, the kind of people who work in cloakrooms. She worked in one herself as a young lady and dear God, there was no coat or bag she didn't rifle through, playing it smart, looking for whatever she could get her hands on that wouldn't immediately draw attention (so for example: the wallet stays, but maybe a note or two disappears, it was all about the sly move, the drip drip drip, gaining in increments, little and often). And didn't Herman say Eldo was a good person just now? If he's right then all it would take is for someone in the cloakroom to be slightly less of a good person than Eldo and *bang*, everything's gone from her coat. And then where are you? Anarchy. That's where.

She's passed the cloakroom and is approached by a waitress with a silver platter of champagne flutes. Eldo takes one and smiles at the waitress.

Could you take one of these outside to Herman, the doorman? I promised him one.

She returns the smile with a professional seductiveness that Eldo feels is very well practiced and says

But of course, Miss.

As soon as she's passed her she inhales, takes in the cloud of scent she leaves in her wake, and studies her form as she sashays away like she's something from a 1940s movie. The perfume is nothing special, and includes patchouli (naturally), iris, and some kind of white musk. All pretty basic. But that wriggle she's got is either something that one is born with or has spent years mastering. And that, either way, spells molto class.

Eldo turns her attention to the champagne. As a rule, she doesn't drink, but because she's infrequently (okay, let's be honest here, *never*) sober it helps if she has the scent of alcohol on her, stops people from asking questions about a glassy stare or dilated pupils. So, she takes the smallest sip of bubbles, swills it around her mouth, and then swallows. The next time she finds herself talking to someone who notices her pallor, her glazed eyes, the gentle sway of her body as she tries (and fails) to stay standing upright, they'll simply put it down to the smell of the alcohol. That's the plan, anyway.

Despite what people might think, Eldo knows better than to introduce alcohol into the heady combinations she plays with, that's just asking for trouble. Alcohol is the real killer. She knows this for a fact. Just look at what happened to Steve. And all of a sudden, a huge well of sadness builds up inside her and she finds herself deeply missing the rich timbre of Steve's voice, and the pleasure of his company.

Eldo shakes off the bad vibes and closes her eyes and takes in the scent of the gallery. As you might expect, the aroma of champagne sits at the top, seeping over everything. Underneath there's the smell of almost-dry paint (which she presumes is as much from the freshly painted walls as it is from the canvases) and then there are the myriad notes of all the people standing around: there's some sweat, of course, but most of them are wealthy and smell like it, so she's mainly getting a pot-pourri of colognes and perfumes. Nothing alarming here. Nothing to fear. The room feels safe. Without threat.

She opens her eyes and looks around the room, no sign of anyone she knows, and no Annick, so what else is there to do other than take in the art? She's not totally loving the idea of being here alone, so to help her out with this appreciating art act her right hand slips into her pocket and eases a 20mg diazepam from its blister packet with a gentle pop, and casually brings it up to her mouth with all the sleight-of-hand skill of a stage magician. Time to take in the paintings.

Here's the question though: how long is she supposed to look at one painting before moving on to the next? She's never been clear on this. She usually studies the other people in the room to see how long they're spending looking at the paintings so she can gauge an average, but no one's looking right now, everyone's talking, having a lovely sociable time, leaving her as the only person currently taking in the show. Still, appearances count, so she'll have to work this out on her own.

The canvases are six footers. Large. Each one is a mess of different colours, and each has the name of a woman as its title. A woman, Eldo presumes, who joined Fougére in the, let's say, creation of the artwork itself. There's *Monica*, *Isabelle*, *Asia*, *Christy*, *Abigail*, *Caroline*, *Zoe*, and on and on and on and on and on. The plaques have the names of the women written large, and then some much smaller writing underneath, probably explaining something profound, but just like with the digits on her watch, Eldo's having trouble making the fine print out at all, so all she's really got to go on is the name, although she makes sure to stare at the smaller illegible text for a few seconds, just so she looks sufficiently informed. As we know, it's all about appearances.

She reckons that after reading the name, staring at the

illegible, moving text, and then turning her attention to the six-foot canvas, she's looking at building up somewhere around 60-90 seconds on each artwork before moving on. And this is what she does – reads, stares, and silently counts in her head, over and over again. A model of culture. And then she comes to a grinding halt in front of one particular canvas which is covered in only three colours: cyan, yellow, and magenta, and all the hues they bring about when mixed together. But it's not the colours that stop her. And it's not the composition that removes all the sound from the room leaving her in isolated silence. No. It's the name of this piece: *Annick*.

As everyone knows, nothing has ever passed between Eldo and Annick. They've known each other for the longest time and have the kind of friendship that requires very little work. You know: the talk flows effortlessly, they like the same things, hate the same things, with very little variation, enjoy each other's company, have something to teach to and learn from each other, and everything's just so god damned easy between the two of them. But what Eldo wants more than anything else is to move things on with Annick. To take her from being a friend to being a special friend, or even significant other (even though Eldo hates that term). But Annick doesn't play that game. She has no significant other. Never has, never will. At least, that's what she says. And to make matters worse, she's completely unaware of how Eldo feels about her. Always has been, always will be. At least that's how Eldo thinks it will be. And while Eldo knows all these things, and is intellectually aware that the sickness at the pit of her stomach as she stands in front of the canvas that Annick and Fougére made love on is a complete waste of her energy, there it all is: a heaving wave of jealous nausea.

Eldo stands and stares at the canvas for as long as she can take it, punishing herself. Imagining whether they went through a number of different positions, whether Annick was pleasured or not, whether she did this because she liked Fougére (a likely impossibility, as Annick has no special feelings for anyone, not in that way), whether any of Fougére's semen was on the canvas, or any of Annick's sweat. She journeys down this multitude of byzantine conduits in her mind, but no direction leads her to any conclusion she is happy to reach, so the sudden interruption from a person standing next to her is the sweetest of reliefs. She jumps ever so slightly as the female voice next to her says.

He makes love to his subjects.

Eldo replies without looking at the speaker, keeping her eyes on the painting.

Yes, this is what I hear.

It's ingenious: a natural extension of the artist and his muse. The conclusion we've been waiting millennia to reach.

And yet so reminiscent of Pollock, don't you think? Is there anything more in line with abstract expressionism than sex itself? It appears to be chaos, random, but what we're looking at is the replication of patterns – the smallest area of any part of the canvas simply a microcosm of the composition and structure and execution of the painting as a whole.

Eldo can see from her peripheral vision that the speaker has turned slightly to look at the painting once more, then back at Eldo. The half octave rise in her voice tells her that Herman's top tip has struck a chord here. Ring one up for Herman.

The owner of the voice, now believing Eldo to be a monstrously clever fellow, starts talking again, and Eldo has to keep pretending to listen to her and being interested in what she has to say, so it is with epochal relief that the diazepam begins to bleed throughout her system. She makes the requisite number of *Uh-huhs* and *Hmms* to show that she's still listening and engaged and in the moment, when really all she's doing is taking in as much of the crowd as she can, looking out for Annick and wondering which one of these people, if any, is Fougére himself.

Everything's a hell of a lot easier with the sweet wave of benzodiazepine warmth washing the pink champagne up and onto the shores inside her body, caressing her behind the eyes, allowing her to become very aware of everything around her: of the cream hue to the lighting in the room (Is that from the light bulbs, or a reflection from the walls?), of the tall man at the far wall laughing at a joke and how you can just tell that it's deeply genuine, not fake at all, at a slender hand hovering over a plate of vol-au-vents, carefully selecting which to choose, at a very familiar looking fat man with bulging eyes making a gesture that just seems so friendly and authentic that Eldo simply can't bear it. And as all this is happening Eldo begins to feel that this is one of the nicest rooms she has ever been in (even though she knows full well that it's just the diazepam talking) when suddenly her reverie is interrupted by three distinct sounds that rise above everything and sweep her euphoria away:

1. A glass falls to the floor and smashes (most likely a long-stemmed glass)
2. A woman screams
3. Uh, okay… this third sound is something like a flock of birds flying past, but there are no birds, and as the sound happens there's also a wind that she can smell rather than feel, and that scent is so rich and seems so familiar and the combination of this aroma that she knows but can't place and the sound of birds in flight means that she's unclear of what this is at all

The speaker stops, the crowd goes silent, and it quickly emerges that something has happened in one of the other rooms of the gallery, and a rabble forms. Some are braver (or simply more curious) than others and get themselves closer to the action, whereas other, less bold attendants, hang back, looking on from afar. But despite the commotion, Eldo still loves how everyone is so engaged with what's going on, how alive everyone in the room has become in the face of something happening, of something breaking them out of their routine, out of the masks and facades they were wearing when the context was simply a social gallery event. And now that *Drama* has been thrust into the room everyone seems to glow, seems a little more here, a little more present, but all these insights turn to shit in Eldo's head when she discovers what has happened. Annick is dead.

It's difficult for her to take in the specifics here, everything feels staccato and bare, without much detail or feeling. This is all compounded by the fact that it's not until the police arrive that Eldo is actually allowed to see her, allowed to enter the scene of the crime. And this delay, combined with her current throat-clawing despair and a natural ability to process chemical stimulants swiftly and efficiently, means that she's pretty much completely straight by the time she sees the body. Well, straight by her standards anyway.

Here's the general shape of this in-between phase: after one of the gallery waitresses discovered the body the entire gallery was kept under total lockdown, no one allowed in, no one allowed out, and when the police arrived it just so happened that the leading officer was Francis. And Eldo and Francis? Well, they go all the way back. They met at university. And, like Eldo, Francis is not her first name, it's her last name, the name Eldo chose to call her by in the game that stuck forever. And before we continue with Eldo and Francis in the room of the art gallery with Annick's dead body lying on the floor, we should probably talk about Mona.

Mona was the third member of Eldo and Francis's group, a debauched, louche band of three. They didn't care a shit for their studies, and why the hell should they? Because Eldo and Francis knew Mona, and Mona knew them, and once she came into her inheritance everything was going to be just dandy for all of them, until the end of time. They all knew this. In the end it happened sooner than they had expected, a mere two years after graduating. Mona got her inheritance and moved straight into Big Pharma – which gave her control and production and pricing on medication around the world. And the 80s had been desperately kind to this industry, with more and more demand for pills and powders and research and innovation, and the subsequent enormous price hikes Mona was able to impose on the permanently in need members of western society, which, as it turned out, was most people. As promised, Mona kept her word and put together a master plan to take care of her band, an act of *ultimate synergy* as she called it and, well hell, Eldo and Francis just couldn't turn it down.

The pair of them accepted, let's say, ethically questionable roles which were loosely connected with Big Pharma: Eldo would move chemical ingredients around the globe, ingredients used in the production of pharmaceutical products, but which could, in the wrong hands, be used to bring those products to the regular man on the street. And it was Eldo's job to make sure that these ingredients did indeed fall into the wrong hands. But not to the little man. Oh no. She had to take everything to the big man. The man at the top who is never caught, but who everyone in the know knows. Oh man, the stories Eldo could tell you. And Francis? Despite having some pretty hefty disdain towards law enforcement, plus not knowing anything whatsoever about how it worked, Francis swanned into the police force as a Captain to aid Eldo, and people like Eldo, to carry out their business without any trouble. Sure, she had to learn the lingo, and quell a whole bunch of macho bullshit, but that didn't take long, and eventually Francis was respected and, to the untrained eye, indistinguishable from any other member of the police.

So Eldo kept the supply up to the big men, and Francis took down all the little men who worked for those big men, and Mona sat at the top of it all, selling her wares to the wealthy and respected members of society in one form, and the desperate and hopeless in another. The plan was a work of genius, like a symphony, a machine made of many moving parts. Francis and all the other Francises around the world were given just enough breadcrumbs in the form of the little men on the street who always get caught to make it look like the police's war against drugs was actually a thing that was real, and not something made up by Mona, and Eldo and all the other Eldos did the rest. As you might expect, most people would be terribly upset to find out exactly how this all worked, so the complete picture was known to very few. Even Eldo and Francis didn't have a clear understanding of what it all looked like. But then they also didn't care all that much.

Anyway, the point of all this is that Mona is the big boss, and Eldo supplies, and Francis maintains an appearance of keeping control, so as soon as Francis saw Eldo at the gallery she let her straight into the scene with her trademark

What the fuck do you think happened here?

Eldo usually knows what to say, but not here, not now. The room is big, white, well lit, but too austere, too echoey, too pristine and real, for what it contains to actually be happening. Annick (or rather her body) is lying on the floor. Dead. This is no dream, this is really happening. She's wearing a little black dress, but that's no surprise as she only had two outfits: the little black dress, and items which she was temporarily wearing (such as a towel, a blanket, etc) before getting into her little black dress. The material across her midriff is torn, exposing her stomach. Her bag still looped over one arm, like she slipped and is now lying down. And all Eldo wants is for her to cough, take a breath, sit up, and for all this nightmarish bullshit to come to an end. But that doesn't happen. She just lies there. Still and silent. Nightmarishly so. Like stone. Her skin so white, and her short hair, so dark, tousled over her face in a position that's pure repose, like she's sleeping. But there's a heavy weight to her face that makes it clear that this is not a sleep that she will wake from. Eldo had wanted to see her all night, but not like this. It wasn't supposed to be like this.

Eldo pushes her distress down deep, where it won't interfere with her ability to walk and talk, and approaches the body, taking in the hyper-real, yet simultaneously deeply artificial, surroundings: the room is like a movie set, filled with square plinths made of some kind of stone, and on each plinth is a crystal body – a representation (or so she presumes) of each woman who gave their body and time to Fougére – and each of these bodies is wrapped in a towel stained with a rainbow of paint. Presumably the actual towel that a given lady used to clean up with after the painting, and the artist, was brought to completion. If it wasn't for the towels the bodies would be hard to spot, that's how clear the crystal is. And standing around all of the plinths are people, so many people. Most of them dressed in police uniforms. The arrangement far from random, almost like they had individually been placed in a certain position for a reason, something like characters in a painting, or a play.

But these observations only filter through to Eldo later. On reflection. Right now all she's thinking is *shit* and *fuck*. And she moves her legs, which carry her body through the space separating her and Annick, crouches down next to her prone body and passes a hand across her face, before lowering it to touch her pallid, ice-cold skin. Francis speaks.

Well?

Eldo knows what Francis is doing. She doesn't want to give her the space to wallow in self-pity at the sight of the dead woman she loved more than anyone else she had ever met. Hell, ever would meet. And there's something here, there always is, Eldo just knows it, all she has to do is thrust out the last vestiges of pink champagne and diazepam. She'll find it.

Eldo leans forward, her head heavy, inches her body further, ever so slowly, so that her face is now hovering over Annick's body. And it's right here when it happens. Francis smiles as Eldo's eyebrows rise ever so slightly, suggesting she's getting something. There's a spark in her eyes, and she leans down, her face so close that the breath from Eldo's mouth stirs the fine hairs on Annick's body, and she moves back and forth, from her bare thighs, up and over her torso, along her arms, and then finally up to her neck. Breathing her in all the time. One of the officers on duty leans very close to Francis and mutters

What the fuck is up with this chick?

But Francis just waves it away, she likes the look of where this is going. Eldo gestures for her to come closer, and speaks quietly, almost a whisper.

Get a load of this.

Francis crouches down next to Eldo.

What is it?

Tell me what you can smell here.

Eldo points to Annick's neck, and Francis leans in, inhales.

I don't know what that is. Perfume?

Sure, but describe it to me.

I don't know. It smells rich, like gold, like luxury.

And here?

Eldo points to Annick's wrists and Francis follows, takes a

deep breath.

It's the same perfume, but it's weaker. Harder to pick out.

And here?

Eldo casts a hand over Annick's midriff. Francis pauses for a moment before moving her head over the bare body of a dead woman, then moves in, breathes deeply.

Oh. That's perfume, but it's not the same. It's different.

Eldo nods.

Right? That richness, that gold scent that you were getting at first, that's oud. She has the scent of oud, here (gesturing to her wrists/hands) *but most strongly here* (gesturing to her throat).

Oud?

It's a kind of agarwood, I think. A rich, wood resin smell in any case.

Francis points to Annick's midriff.

And what about here?

Eldo smiles.

Aldehydes, of course. My girl would never be caught dead wearing oud. Not in a million years. She thought it was only for rich assholes who want everyone to know that they're rich. Annick was aldehydes, all the way.

She was what?

Aldehydes. Chemical compounds. They're… lighter, fresher, metallic, artificial. I mean, whatever they are, you can smell the difference, right?

Oh yeah, sure.

So, what it tells us is that whoever attacked her was wearing oud. And not just a little, a lot. Buckets of the stuff. So much that they completely enveloped her in it where they grabbed her. So much that it rubbed off them and onto her hands and wrists when she tried to fight them off. So much that it's completely masked the Chanel she was wearing, like she's stained with it. And now we know that this cocksucker choked her to death.

Maybe she was trying out a new scent?

Impossible. She always sprayed it in three places, creature of habit: neck, wrists, navel – head, heart, base. It's still on her midriff because the killer never touched her there. Go through her bag, you'll find a bottle of Chanel in there. Guaranteed.

Francis nods to one of the officers, who crouches down and goes through the bag with gloved hands. The bag is small, and there's not much in it, so it doesn't take them long to produce the bottle. They hold it up so that Francis can read the label: No 5.

So, our killer wears oud?

Eldo nods.

A lot of it.

What does this tell us? What do we know about oud?

And just as Eldo's trying to think what the fuck any of this could mean she becomes aware of a sound that doesn't seem to come from anywhere that she can identify, and then she wakes up.

III
3rd April, 1994
10.20
The City

When she opens her eyes Eldo sees a burnt-out cigarette between her fingers. It's one beautiful column of smooth, unbroken ash.

Huh.

She thinks.

And then she closes her eyes again and there's a brief, hazy period where Eldo gets it all backwards and thinks that this waking life is some kind of dream, and that she has to get to sleep again in order to get back to the gallery. Back to Annick. But then the disappointing, yet slightly relieving, reality of it all slowly dawns on her: this is the real world, that was the dream. This is this. That is that.

The scents she's experiencing here are all too familiar, it's undeniably her home: cigarette ash, mildew, damp wood, coffee, and paper, and she opens her eyes and first of all there's the glare of too much light, and then it slowly balances out and she can see everything she expected to see. This tedious, brightly lit, sparsely decorated room that she exists in, with the constant hum of traffic from outside is the real world. Of course it is. How could she have been so dumb as to mistake the dream world for reality? Again?

The room is bare, largely cream coloured, with woodchip wallpaper and Georgian windows: no furniture or objects save for a bed, a rug, an ashtray, pile of clothes, and books and books and books and books. They're piled up against all four walls, creating something that looks like a diorama, like the landscape of a distant city. On top of the pile of books next to the bed is her mobile phone. Eldo reaches out, picks it up, and dials Annick's number. She listens to the dial tone on the other end, and then to the answering machine pick up. She knew it would be the machine because it's always the machine, but even so she's consoled to hear her ever so familiar voice intone the words:

Hi, I'm not here right now, but leave your name and number after the beep and I'll get straight back to you.

Eldo listens to the entire message, just to hear every syllable, every tiny snatch of Annick's breath, and then hangs up, just as the beep begins to sound.

The kitchen. Eldo flicks the coffee maker on and looks at the dishes in the sink. It would take her roughly ten to fifteen minutes to get those dishes done (she's not sure how one lady can dirty so many dishes, but there you go), so she drops a depth charge of an eighth of a gram of mdma and gets to work. By the time she's finished the minimal housework she takes a look at her left arm, at her wrist, at her vein. But everything is normal, and so she gets her coffee together (black, no sugar) and goes into the other room and begins organizing her books. Piling them up, alphabetically, for something like the 8th time in the last two months. She reaches 'M' and is holding a book by Maupassant and wondering whether she should put this somewhere more accessible than just in a pile because darn it if she doesn't feel like re-reading this one again soon, when she suddenly feels pretty happy for no reason at all and looks down at her wrist and sees the tell-tale vein there, pumping away rhythmically, a clear indicator that the mdma is working its magic on her system. This visual affirmation of her high gives her the confidence she needs to get back on the phone and call all the people she needs to call. First off is the person she usually calls first. Serge.

Hey Serge.

What's up, dude? What you want?

Serge never seems to use the word 'do' or 'did' or 'does,' something which the former English student Eldo finds difficult, but tolerates.

Can't I ever just call to say hello?

Sorry man, sure, hello, how's it going? What you get up to last night?

Eldo opens her mouth to reply, but nothing comes out. Wait a minute, what the hell did she get up to last night? There are flashes of someone, somewhere, sparkling wine, cigarettes, a scent that Eldo recognizes but can't place, no complete picture to be ascertained. Eldo scratches her neck. Draws a complete blank.

Hell. You know what, I can't remember.

Black spots. Never good my friend. That's God telling you to slow down a little. Hold on, I've got a fax coming in.

Look, I was just calling about the Berlin meet tomorrow…

What Berlin meet?

The one tomorrow. The 4th, right?

I no know what you're talking about. Hold on. Let me check out the fax.

For a moment Eldo doesn't realise why she's confused, and then she remembers:

Oh yeah, that was in the dream, there is no Berlin on the 4th

and she's about to apologise when Serge comes back on the line.

Eldo, this fax…

Shit yeah, sorry man. That was a dream. Geneva and Caracas. Kurt Cobain is still alive.

Okay, uhh… whatever. Yeah, the 4th. Today's Sunday the 3rd, and this fax says tomorrow you have a trip to Berlin. Berlin *on the 4th… how you know about this?*

What?

This is the first I'm hearing about this, so how you know? Who tell you?

Shit Serge, I dunno, maybe Mona swung me something about it that settled down in my subconscious and laid little eggs and now they're hatching. These details baby, do they matter?

What you mean they no matter? Of course they matter, man. Everything matters.

You worry too much Serge, it'll put you in the ground before your time. Like Cobain.

Cobain is fine man. What you talking about?

Oh yeah, shit, that's also the dream. Right. Right.

Eldo, serious, tell me how you know about the Berlin gig.

Eldo is walking around while she talks, like she usually does. She's back in the bedroom now and apart from the bed and the books and a pile of clothes and her half-finished cup of coffee, the only other object is a vintage bottle of Chanel No 5 that Annick left here one time, and now keeps here for whenever she's running past. She likes to keep a bottle here and there, because, well, you just never know. Anyway, Eldo can't think of a good answer to Serge's question, so she just says:

Lucky guess, maybe.

I feel like you fucking with me, man. I'll be honest, I'm still a little messed up from last night, but seeing into the future? That's some yage shit. And you no shaman.

Eldo pauses. She knew about the 4th. But that was just a dream? How can something in a dream bleed into the somethings of the waking world. With her phone held in the crook of her neck, she sprays a light touch of the No 5 onto the back of her hand and closes her eyes. Inhales. There's a vision of Annick: smiling, with that skin she always longs to touch, that hair she longs to bury her face into, but never dares. Still with her eyes closed, and thinking of Annick, Eldo says

Serge, man, let me call you back.

Sure thing.

Eldo hangs up and takes another hit of the No 5. Has another flash of Annick. Dials another number, Annick's agent. If she can't get hold of Annick she'll call Jasmine. She'll know where Annick is. Jasmine answers on the first ring, she always does.

What do you want, Eldo?

Woah. How did you know it was me?

Caller ID. What do you want?

You mean, my number comes up on your phone?

Eldo.

Like you have a screen on it?

Eldo.

What a world we live in.

Eldo! What do you want?

I'm just looking for Annick.

Of course, I should have guessed. She's in New York.

Oh right, yeah, I think I heard something about that. She lies. *Hey, do you happen to know where she's staying?*

There's an animal sound of frustration from Jasmine, which tells Eldo that she's nearing the end of her good will.

Obviously. But you know I'm not supposed to give out confidential information about clients.

Jasmine. Come on. This is me.

There's a pause and Eldo worries that Jasmine's not going to tell her, that somewhere along the line she moved from 'friend' to 'stalker' without meaning to or even noticing the transition. But then Jasmine sighs with a weariness beyond her years and says two words.

The Chelsea.

Jasmine you're the best. The best.

I did not say this. I was not here.

And like that, Jasmine hangs up, and Eldo gets dressed.

Normally Eldo gets dressed crouching underneath the window, because she has no curtains, and doesn't want to be seen naked. But there's no time for modesty now. And during the dressing process her mind wanders back to the dream. She'll do this several times over the next few days, and although other things will occur to her in the future, right now there's one element of the dream that's pushing itself to the forefront: her meeting with Naomi. The dream character looking for codeine. And as she's buckling her belt, she picks up her phone again and dials another number. She starts off with the area code for the city, then a 4, and then carefully presses the six remaining digits: her birth date. The phone rings. A woman's voice answers.

Hello?

Hi... this is gonna sound nuts, but... is Naomi there?

Lemme go get her.

The voice is insouciant, cold, uninterested. The receiver is placed down on something hard, a wooden table most likely, and Eldo listens to the distant sounds of one woman fetching another – voices, footsteps, all very far away. Finally, the sound of approach, a hand lifts the receiver, and another voice comes onto the phone.

Hello?

Is that Naomi?

Speaking.

Naomi with the throat piercing?

Uh huh...

There's trepidation to Naomi's voice here. Like she doesn't know where this is going, but it may well be somewhere she doesn't like.

Naomi with a penchant for codeine?

A what?

A penchant: a liking or fondness for something. You dig codeine, right?

Hell yeah, are you holding?

The trepidation in her voice completely disappears at the mention of codeine and is replaced with an open eagerness. A smile that you can hear. Knowing what Eldo knows about the version of Naomi she met in her dream, this transformation isn't that much of a surprise. All the same, the revelation is enough to make it clear enough that this person and the dream person are the same. And, unfortunately for Naomi and her love for codeine, Eldo never says another word to her.

Hello? Hello?

The phone falls from Eldo's hand as everything in the room is covered with a veil of darkness. Maybe it's the mdma for breakfast. Maybe it's the fact that she knew about the meet on the 4th, or got a woman's phone number from a dream. Maybe it's the fragments of conversation with a dream character in the real world. Maybe it's the fact that she hasn't eaten for… what is it now, three days? But as Eldo loses consciousness and falls to the floor, there's only one thing she knows for certain right now: Annick has 5 days to live, and Eldo is the only person who can save her.

Annick flash #1

Eldo's dreaming, but this time she knows it because she's going through something that's already happened. Flicking through a photo album of old memories. Moments she's already experienced. Watching a re-run.

She's in the room that she just 'left,' only it has fewer books in it, because this is back when she had only recently moved in. She's trying to read the back of one of these books, but the words are largely obscured by white powder, and the letters aren't staying still long enough for her to decipher which letters they might be, and Annick is here, and the pair of them have taken something that's made them both lethargic and giggly, and they're now trying to pull themselves together enough to go out by talking and making up tiny lines of cocaine, baby bumps, which they're both convinced will sober them up. Eldo and Annick are the kind of people who feel that more drugs of one kind is the answer when you think you have taken too much drugs of another kind.

Annick has been talking about getting dressed for the longest time, and every time she mentions it, she breaks down into a hysterical giggle. Her inability to perform this simplest of tasks after taking the purple pills is hilarious. She's also wearing nothing but white Sloggi underwear, and getting Eldo to smell the perfume on different parts of her body, a game that could be seen as flirtatious if Annick had any idea she had any impact on Eldo, which, apparently, she doesn't. Annick breathes deeply, conquers her laughter, and starts talking about the scent.

It has three aspects, head, heart, and base.

Eldo is chopping up lines on the back of a book, using a bank card to crush the larger clumps of powder into pieces and then a razor blade to cut the pieces into a fluffy white cloud of joy, and, like always, the excitement and seriousness and minutiae of the task brings out a sweat in her hands which makes the whole thing a bit trickier than she'd like. She also has no feeling in her gums above the space between her two front teeth, which is something she always gets when she's on coke. And this numbness and the sweats make it tricky for her to focus on both the task at hand and pay attention to Annick. All the same, she's doing a pretty good job of ignoring her corporeality and playing it cool and interacting with Annick like she's the king of it all, not even a little bit edgy.

Girl, you've run me through this three-part thing a whole

heap of times.

And now I'm doing it again because you never really listen to me.

I do!

Prove it. Explain them to me, one by one, what they are, and why they matter.

Annick's voice is croaky here, seductive. Eldo moves her face (specifically her breathing apparatus) away from the coke, careful not to blow it all away, brings her head closer to Annick and breathes her in. Closes her eyes.

The head is at the top, it's made of lighter notes. They evaporate first. But while they're around they're the sharper scents, more noticeable. And then below that you have the body, and the base underneath.

Annick swipes at her, Eldo cracks an eye open to make sure the gust didn't send the coke flying (it didn't) and then closes her eye again, listens to her sweet, sweet voice.

That's scent 101 you ass, everyone knows that stuff. Apply it to what I'm wearing.

Okay, I like a challenge.

She moves closer. Breathes in deeply. Takes it all in. Thinks for a moment, and then starts to break down what she's wearing.

So the head is... cold, metallic... but there's definitely citrus in there too. It's the clearest note, sharp, rising above everything else.

And then...?

And then lying underneath... but I'm not completely sure this is the heart – I'm getting flowers. All floral, I'm not sure what the flowers are though. Iris? Lily? I suck at identifying flowers. And lying underneath...

Her eyes are closed and Annick is making no sound at all, but Eldo can tell that she is achingly close to her. Then she speaks, three words

Tell me more.

Eldo leans in, even closer, trying to pick it out, but it's not easy. The purple pills and the coke and Annick so close - it's hard to think straight.

It's not easy, it's mixed in with your own scent.

And what would my own scent be? Tread carefully.

She smiles.

It's like an old chair, made of palo santo or some kind of scented wood. Mixed with a powder, like the smell you'd get from a fine lady's dressing table in an old house in France.

Eldo can't see Annick, but she can hear the smile in her voice as she speaks.

Tell me more about that base.

It's subtle, and it can't compete with you, but... it's sweet, and resinous, like an amber maybe.

There's the sound of Annick moving backwards. The fleeting scent of her hair catches on the air for a brief, wonderful moment.

I take it all back. You are one hell of a good listener.

Eldo opens her eyes to see Annick's face, her body, she shifts herself to be closer to the cocaine and she watches her, in her underwear, here with her right now, and how the late afternoon sunlight streams in through her curtain-less window, and drapes itself across her pale body, bathing her in gold light, and with the purple pills abating and the coke building and her sinuses clearer than they've been in a long time, it almost seems like there's a silent musical note ringing through the air, and Eldo feels more alive than she ever has before, and it's right there and right then that the vehicle judders and she opens her eyes and looks at her true surroundings.

She's sitting in the back of a black taxi. A cigarette burning in her hand. The taxi driver is talking to her with an accent that seems familiar but which she just can't place and, besides, Eldo's too distracted by both the surprise of being here, and the worrying fact that she can't read the digits on the meter. She wonders for a moment if this is real at all, but the hot leather scent of the interior is just too present and marks this out as a clear sign that she's back in the real world, and without thinking that this might strike the driver as unusual Eldo blurts out something dumb.

Where are we going?

The taxi driver stops talking, his eyes go straight to the rear-view mirror, and he studies Eldo's face before replying.

The airport. You said you had a flight to New York.

I did? I mean… shit. Yes. I did. Of course.

On the radio a song by Babes in Toyland is playing (is it *Dogg*?) and Eldo looks out the window of the taxi and if the driver is worried about the sanity of his passenger he sure doesn't act like it as he continues talking about whatever it was he was talking about before Eldo so rudely interrupted him, and although Eldo the passenger is making all the right 'active listening' noises the truth is that she's withdrawn inside and is listening to no word of it at all. Instead, she's talking to herself, in her head. Playing two roles.

Why are you going to New York?

Because that's where Annick is.

Sure, but why are you going there now? We know where and when she dies, and that's not New York.

You want to just sit around here? Maybe she's meeting the killer now.

The killer?

Yeah, whoever the guy was who slathered himself in oud and choked her to death at the gallery.

You're making a lot of assumptions here. A lot of guess work. You remember where you got your intel from? A fucking dream, guy.

Who wants to take any risks? Look, all I know is that Annick might not have much time left, and I'd rather be with her right now. If I'm proved wrong, and she ends up being alive, and everything's okay, then that's fine. I'll live with that.

Is that all this is? That you'd like to be with her?

Don't start that again.

Because aside from the fact that your obsession borders on being disrespectful not only to Annick but to women in general, it seems to me that the best thing to do would be to get to the gallery early, catch whoever it is in the act.

Disagree. Get on the trail now. I'm not sitting around for days just to see what happens at the end.

And what about the police?

Eldo, please. Just... please. Tell me you didn't suggest that.

Why not? Isn't that what people do in situations like this? Call the police?

Okay, A: You're an international drug dealer and you hate the police. B: what are you going to say? I had a dream? Where's that going to go?

We could call Francis.

We could... but I'm still saying no.

And what do we do if we find the killer?

Let's find Annick first and take it from there.

And just then the taxi drives past a betting store and, with a Nirvana song now playing on the radio, a voice that Eldo doesn't entirely recognize, but which comes from her mouth, says:

Stop.

Eldo jumps out and tells the taxi driver to keep the meter running, that she won't be a moment, and without another word she runs into the betting store.

It's bright inside, and bare. Thin carpet. Formica

furnishings. And as Eldo makes her way to the window she wonders whether there's something about this room that is not only revealing the stark exterior of everything (the dirty tattered clothing everyone's wearing, tea-stained carpet and walls, the damaged fittings, the ruddy complexions of the faces around her, all made bare by the bright lights that span the entirety of the ceiling), but is also revealing the hungry interior (the desperate souls, the needy eyes, the hollowness of it all, the constant need and desire for more and more only to be met time and time again with little more than frustration). And with this thought in her mind, she gets to the window, smiles, and says:

I can bet on anything, right?

The man behind the counter looks up with a start, eyes slightly confused, before replying.

I beg your pardon?

I mean, like I can bet on when I think it will next snow, or when aliens will land, or that kind of thing.

You certainly can.

So, I could bet on when I think someone's going to die?

Uhh... I suppose so. As long as they're famous. And you don't murder them. Anyone in particular?

Hell yeah. I want to bet on Kurt Cobain being announced dead on the 8th of April.

There's a moment here where the man behind the window, thin, moustache, glasses, swallows hard. And then he says:

The 8th of April?

Yes.

Which year?

This year.

The thin man looks at his watch.

You mean... in 5 days?

That is correct.

The thin man makes a surprised sound, pushes his glasses up his nose with one finger, leans forward.

Are you working with string theory here?

String theory?

The thin man nods.

A friend of mine's working on it. The idea that everything isn't an individual point, not like pins on a board, but more like beads on a necklace, the idea that there are strings connecting everything together.

Uhh… I don't think so.

The thin man makes another sound, one where Eldo can't really tell what feeling it's supposed to express, and he then turns to a computer and types something. He waits a moment, and the printer chugs out paper, he rips this off with a flourish, hands it to Eldo. It's the odds. Eldo reads, does some maths in her head and on her fingers, then nods, and her hand goes quickly to her pocket.

Okay then. Let's put 1,000 on that.

She brings out a rolled clip of 1,000 in 50s.

There's another pause. The thin man looks at the clip, then at Eldo, then back to the clip.

Very well, Miss. 1,000 on Kurt Cobain dying on the 8th of April.

Eldo interjects.

Announced dead on the 8th.

The thin man pauses again.

Announced dead?

Yes.

Therefore allowing for the possibility that he may have died before the 8th?

Yes.

The thin man pushes his glasses up his nose again, speaks quietly.

And you're absolutely certain that you're not working

with string theory here?

I promise you I'm not.

Hmm, okay. I'll recalculate the odds while I run this through.

The thin man makes a noise, turns, and walks far back behind the counter, through a door and into another room, scuttles over to a colleague who's little more than a whisper of a person, a suggestion of someone hidden away behind several obstacles, a few flashes of a hand, some clothing, movement, nothing more than this. The thin man converses with the hidden figure, unheard words to an unseen person, and on a different day Eldo would start to get paranoid about this whole setup, but not today.

Eldo looks out the window to see if the taxi is still there. It is. Of course it is. She hasn't paid yet. Why would it not be? Then she gets another burst of that weird feeling she had in the dream – the sensation that someone or something that has no shape is watching her and waiting. What the fuck is that? And it's while she's craning her neck and looking in every direction for this unformed person that she notices a row of payphones on the wall and, either out of habit or simply because she's forgotten that she owns a phone which is in her pocket, she steps over and drops a coin into one of the phones and dials Serge. He takes a while to answer, and when he does he sounds like ass.

Serge, buddy. How you doing?

Serge coughs and splutters several times before he responds. So Eldo fills the gap with more words.

That good, huh?

Eldo, that you, man?

Yeah, listen, I'm going to need you to go to Berlin for me.

What?

I'm on my way to New York right now, something big's

come up.

Bigger than Berlin? Get real guy.

Serge, this'll be fine, you're ready to step up to the bat.

Seriously, I can't.

Now look, I'll be staying at The Chelsea if you need to find me, okay?

Three short beeps sound out.

Okay man, that's my money going. Berlin'll be fine. You got this Serge.

Eldo, seriously man, you're not listening to me, I can't...

And then the line goes dead.

Eldo steps back over to the counter, pleased that she got that sorted. Serge'll be fine, he's one of those people who always likes to catastrophise, but as far as Eldo knows everything always turns out okay. She looks behind the counter and sees her thin friend is still in the back room talking to his phantasmagorical colleague. And after she gets bored of trying to work out whether this phantom is male or female Eldo looks at her watch, but the numbers are doing a jitterbug again. Whatever.

The flight to New York is, what? 8 hours? Something like that. If she's on her way to the airport now, then that's a... 2-hour wait for the flight? 3 at most. That's roughly 11 hours altogether, tops, but let's be conservative and say 12 hours to get into a taxi at JFK. Weighing all of these factors up Eldo decides that a windowpane of acid would just nicely carry her from this tedious moment right here to the point at which she's sitting in the back of that cab leaving JFK in the distance. She fumbles around in her pocket and finds just what she's looking for, swallows it as deftly as usual, and only then asks herself whether the acid was a 12-hour trip, or double dipped (which would give her a 24-hour trip and would definitely interfere with her investigations in New York). Oh well. Only time will tell. Eldo closes her eyes. There's a roaring sound in her ears which fades away to an eerie silence, like all the air was sucked out of the room.

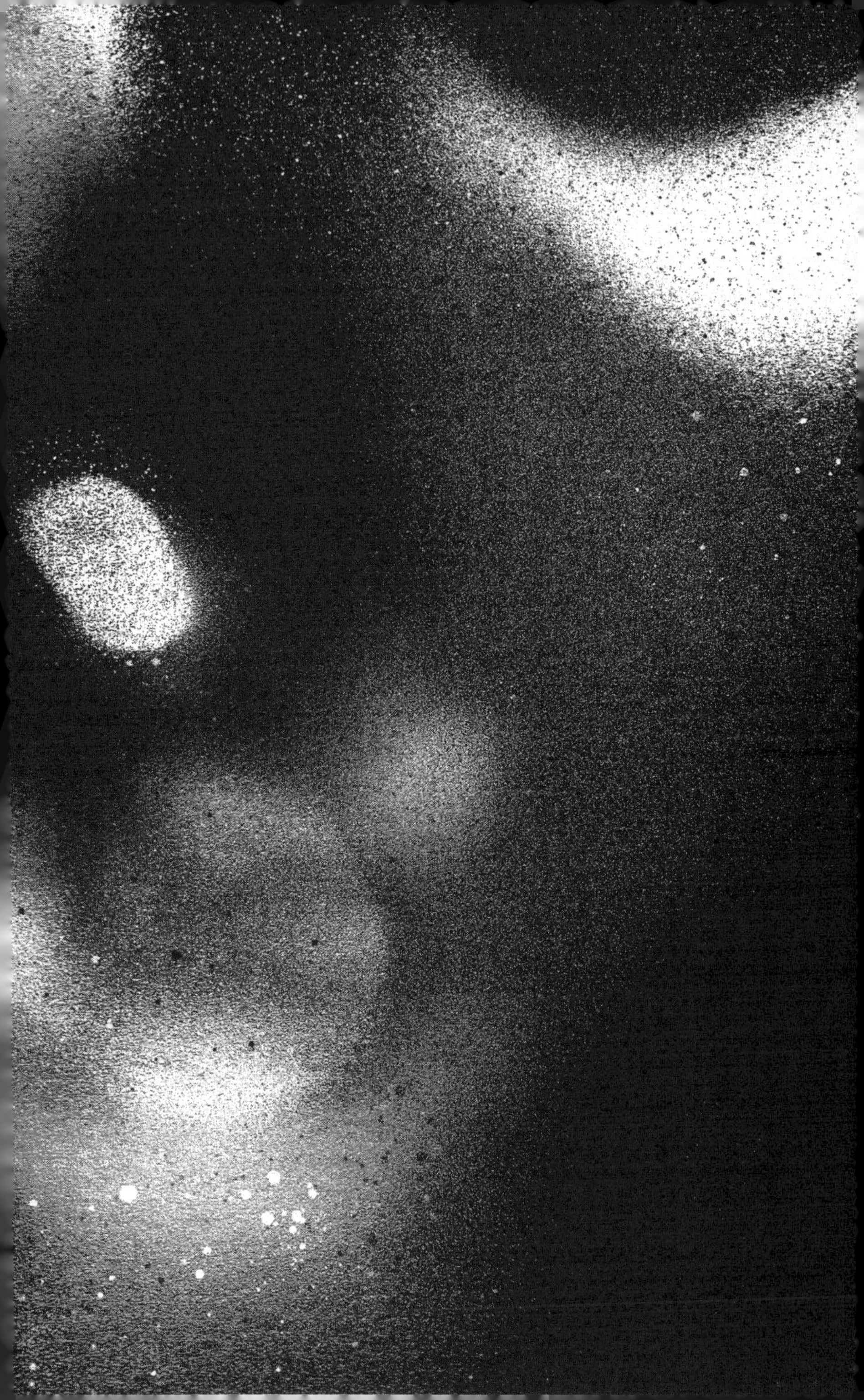

IV
3rd April, 1994
15.20
Above the ocean

And when she opens her eyes again, she's only slightly surprised to find herself staring at a voluminous bed of rose-coloured clouds stretching as far as the eye can see. Slowly, the complete silence she's encased in is replaced by the rising white noise of the airplane experience until Eldo attains complete awareness of being sat in a seat, on a plane, buckled up, flying through the air.

The first scent she gets here is the acrid aroma of airplane food. What is it that they use that always makes it smell the same? Something between some kind of meat and some kind of vegetable, but she'll be darned if she knows which. For a brief moment Eldo thinks she can smell Annick somewhere in the mix too, and then she realizes that she's still got traces of Chanel on her hands. She lifts her hands to her face and breathes in, and her surroundings disappear in a burst of pure white and she's taken to…

Annick Flash #2

…a park, bright sunshine, a gentle breeze running through the boughs of the trees, leaves rustling. You know the scene.

She's looking at Annick, sitting on a bench, holding a burning cigarette, and looking down at something between her feet. They're sitting near a studio of some kind, waiting for it to open. Eldo's thinking about how Annick smokes. She doesn't do it the way a lot of people do: brow furrowed, exhaling hard, face screwed up, as though the whole affair were distasteful. No, Annick smokes slowly, inhales deeply, and lets the smoke escape her lips in playful wisps which slowly thicken to resemble something not unlike time-lapse footage of plants growing, twisting, reaching for the Sun. And then Annick wakes Eldo from this reverie by asking her a question.

Do you think ants know we're here?

There's a beat as she realizes that this is now and she needs to say something in return, and quickly. Better make it good.

What?

Ants. These ants. Here. Do you think they know that I'm sitting on this bench, watching them? That when they walk against the sole of my shoe and then stop and go the other way that they've walked into the foot of something enormous? Or am I too big for them to understand?

Uh, I don't know. I guess they don't really know we're here?

Annick nods in agreement.

It's got to be, right?

Annick takes a drag, and then, as tendrils of smoke begin to drift out between her lips, a smile slowly spreads across her face.

So what if, like, there's someone or something watching us, big, or different, or something, and it's just too much for us to understand. Like, we just don't even know how to make out it's there?

Eldo pulls her jacket tight as the wind picks up, stronger, colder, biting all of a sudden. She looks down between her feet, at an ant. It's wandering this way and that, fast, so very fast. Ants live so fast, and their lives are so short. But maybe to them it feels really long? Like maybe the life of an ant feels comparable to how long our lives feel? We certainly move a lot slower. And trees. They move even slower but live even longer. What does time mean for them? And the planet Neptune, taking 165 years to orbit the Sun, what does time feel like for Neptune? Would it be so crazy for there to be something or someone above us? With a different experience of size and time? Watching us live out our lives, erratically running this way and that, at what probably looks to them like a comical speed? The ant between her feet reaches the tread of Eldo's shoe, rubs its feelers across the rubber, and then turns swiftly in the opposite direction. Eldo made the ant make a decision simply by existing. She didn't have to do one damn thing other than that. And then everything changes.

The scents and sounds and colours of the world of the plane come back. Eldo is still looking down between her feet, but instead of the gravel pathway, or the ant, she sees her hand luggage. That's right. She's flying to New York. She knew that.

The bag is in its habitual position, wedged between her feet, so that no one can lift it without her noticing. Of course, that's so her. Always too paranoid to leave it in the overhead compartment. She checks what she's brought with her, because lord knows she doesn't remember packing a god damn thing.

In the bag she finds:

money
passport
ticket
keys
two lighters
cigarettes
diazepam
amphetamines
tramadol

codeine
Benzedrine
cocaine
mints
Annick's vintage bottle of Chanel
a paperback copy of *Les Fleurs du Mal.*

She takes this last item out and places it on the small tray table in front of her. Then pockets the cigarettes and one of the lighters. What she doesn't notice is that her phone is missing, and it'll be some time before she spots that at all. Anyway, she puts the bag back down between her feet, safe and secure, and checks out the scene she's in.

Window seat, good, good, so far so Eldo. Even better, the seat next to her is unoccupied, things are looking up. She leans across the empty seat and scans the aisle, quickly works out that she's in approximately the centre of the plane, and then sees a Stewardess walking towards her. Eldo raises a hand, gets her attention, and beckons her over, although for the life of her she has no idea why. It just feels like the right thing to do in this situation. Before she knows it, she's standing right there, talking to her.

How can I help, Miss?

Eldo's pistons start pumping, her eyes searching her surroundings, desperately seeking something valid and totally not weird that she can talk to this woman about, until at last her gaze falls on the screen in front of her. The one she can't hear. The one she can't hear because... Eldo points at the screen.

Can I get headphones for this?

This is the first time Eldo's spoken for a while, and her voice sounds incredibly thick to her ears, as though she were suffering from a heavy cold. But if the Stewardess notices anything she sure as hell doesn't give it away.

Absolutely Miss, you'll be able to purchase a pair for $5.00.

$5.00? Eldo feels around in her pocket. Does she even have any dollars? She has no pictures to draw on of her arrival at the airport, or the check in, or the tedious waiting around in brightly lit spaces. There's nothing of the journey at all. It's just the betting store, the thin man with the moustache, something about a payphone, and now this.

Surprisingly, Eldo's hand pulls out a $10 bill. Gold. She hands it over and the Stewardess makes change and says:

Just one moment, Miss.

And walks off, and Eldo leans back in her seat and waits. A lot of people have been calling her *Miss* recently. Weird.

She flicks through the silent screen in front of her using a control that's buried in the armrest. She can select either the news, TV, movies, or cartoons. She settles on movies and is flicking through the options when there's a gust of a scent that sends a shiver down her spine: oud. And not just any oud. Eldo pushes through the fear and very, very slowly leans into the aisle again, cautiously looks around. She can make out some of her nearby fellow passengers. Regular looking folk. Nothing suspicious looking at all. But there that scent is, unmistakable: thick, strong, and very close.

Eldo gets out of her seat and the first thing she notices is how very fucked up she is. Shit.

Okay, pay this no mind. Rise above it.

She checks where the bathroom is, sees it, then turns, walks the opposite way. She knows that when she gets to the end of this aisle, she'll have a perfect opportunity to click her fingers and go *Gosh, darn it!* Or something like that, and then turn around and go the other way. The point of this walk has nothing to do with finding the bathroom, the point is to work out where that hit of oud is coming from.

The whole time Eldo keeps her focus on the scents she's

passing, tries to take in as many of the faces as possible. And as she walks and ignores the fact that the aisle seems to be stretching into infinity, and her legs seem to have been replaced with two sticks of rubber, making it a challenge to keep her inebriated ass from falling flat on the floor, she reflects on how this all makes sense now that she's here. On the plane. High above the world.

Annick is in New York right now. Not only that, but the killer is travelling there on this motherfucking plane. She was meant to do this. Eldo's doing the right thing. It is the plan. Okay, so it must be that this fucker meets Annick in New York. Accompanies or chases her back to the city. Then kills her at the gallery, for some reason yet to be ascertained. Everything is falling into place. Like she's lining up the colours on a Rubik's cube.

She keeps walking, but the smell maintains its strength. It doesn't dissipate, it doesn't swell, it remains constant. As though she were neither walking away from nor towards the source of it. And at the end of the aisle she's stopped by another Stewardess who asks her where she's going. Eldo explains that she's looking for the bathroom, so the Stewardess, with perhaps the gentlest suggestion of irritation, points out that the bathroom is at the opposite end of the aisle. Eldo plays it perfectly, turns, makes a noise of realization, makes her apologies very convincingly, and recalibrates.

The walk the other way reveals just as little. The strength of the scent of rich oud does not change. And Eldo keeps scanning the faces of everyone she passes, but there's not a flicker from anyone, and no one seems out of place. But what is 'out of place' anyway? And then she gets that feeling again – someone unformed is watching her. What the fuck is that? She looks around, as nonchalantly as she can, but there're no eyes on her at all.

Would an unformed face even have eyes?

She thinks. And then.

What the fuck does that even mean, guy?

She reaches the bathroom and, not knowing what else to do now that she's here, steps in, and locks the door behind her.

Eldo takes out a cigarette and lights it.

Fuck. Get it together girl. There's a killer on this plane and I can't find him.

And sure, maybe if she wasn't so fucked up she'd be able to deal with this better. How'd she get so fucked up anyway? She spots a groove in the wash basin, a nicotine-stained, melted incline in the plastic, created by legions of cigarettes being set down in the same position. She looks up at her face in the mirror. At her eyes. The light falling on her skin gives her the complexion of a corpse. And wait… is that even her face? And then it all comes flooding back to her – the windowpane. Of course. It's the acid. That's not how she really looks. She's just on acid. The windowpane is changing the way she perceives light falling on objects.

Yeah, yeah, that's all it is.

She rifles through her pockets, and as luck would have it, she finds two bennies loose in her inside jacket pocket. If there's one thing Eldo's learned over the years, it's that if you spend the majority of your life in an Oswald Boateng suit you rarely get searched by the authorities. She knocks back the bennies with water from the faucet and has three more drags of her cigarette, then puts it out with a hiss under the running water and drops it in the toilet bowl. Locks eyes with herself in the mirror again.

Sweet pupils, girl.

Back in her seat Eldo finds the headphones ready and waiting for her, no sign of the Stewardess. She plugs herself in and, not wishing to continue searching through options, she settles on pressing play on whatever movie she had reached when she decided to go for a walk. What the fuck does it matter what film it is?

It turns out to be a new version of Dracula, which Eldo is quite pleased with as she finds the plots of films difficult to keep up with, but she has a pre-existing understanding of the general shape of the story of Dracula, so this should require little to no concentration. And Eldo, who usually hates movies, finds this version far more enjoyable than she was expecting. It's colourful, stylized, and it doesn't hurt that the bennies kick in right as the young count Vlad (who will, eventually, Eldo presumes, turn into a more recognisable version of the ancient vampire) sticks a sword into a stone crucifix, and blood pours out, and Eldo feels the bennies rise up in her right then, flowing through her like the blood flowing out of the stone crucifix, casting waves of euphoria through her.

The film plays on, and although Eldo gets the general shape of everything, she has little to no idea of the specifics of what's happening, but it all looks beautiful, and the people are attractive, and everything is lit like a movie, which is always nice. And then there's a point in the film where everything changes.

One of the characters finds himself walking around an abandoned castle or something, and he goes into a room where a number of female voices are calling out to him, all layered over and on top of each other, and the door closes magically and he lies down on a bed and then, like, out of nowhere, these three women appear, and even though you can just tell that there's something dark going on with them (and being that it's a Dracula movie, it's pretty easy to guess what that might be) Eldo finds herself utterly enchanted by them.

And one, in particular.

She's the first to appear, her partially clad form rises up from the bed, between the legs of the man who's stumbled into this worst/best room of all time, and she crawls up his body, rips his shirt open. There's a crucifix there, and she draws back, arcing her body and hissing, demonically, and the crucifix melts away, like mercury.

Good God.

While all of this plays out on the screen Eldo's not sure whether all the air has disappeared from the plane, or if she's just forgotten how to breathe.

The scene goes on, and there are glimpses of this woman slowly becoming more and more vampiric, and all the while the image of her face is slowly being seared onto the back of Eldo's retina: her white headdress, arched eyebrows, alabaster skin, that divine mouth, and those eyes, Jesus, those eyes. And even as the scene grows more vicious, and as her predatory nature comes to the fore, there is no part of Eldo that wouldn't give itself over to her, body and soul. Particularly soul. Who is this creature?

A tremor goes through Eldo, the weirdest fucking sensation, and somehow she can feel something... taking form? Not inside herself, but somewhere in the world. Something unformed is taking shape, becoming real, while her eyes stay locked to the image of this un-fucking-believable woman. She can feel it happen.

The rest of the film plays out as films do, and Eldo keeps waiting for the return of this vampire, and although she does briefly appear again a handful of times, it becomes quite clear quite quickly that she is going to remain on the peripheries, so after about another hour or so Eldo is tiring of all this story shit and she's gently reminded of her body thanks to a sensation of tiredness, and an irritating, cloying dryness in her mouth, and decides that a bottle of sparkling water would deal with both of these problems pretty damn well.

She leans out and looks down the aisle to see if there's a Stewardess around, and indeed there is: a trolley of snacks and beverages slowly moving towards her, pilot out of sight. Well, okay, at the moment it isn't actually moving, because the Stewardess is leaning in to help one of Eldo's fellow passengers, something like seven rows down, or whatever. And then she catches that scent again: oud. Stronger this time. Much stronger than before. Suggesting, what? That the wearer is closer now? Has applied more of the scent? Whatever it is, it's time for action.

Eldo raises herself in her seat and looks all around for someone suspicious, but everyone just looks like a passenger: business types, tourist types, a few families, old people, like Basquiat would say: samo. No one who fits the profile of murderer that Eldo has created in her head. But then maybe the image she's working with is too stereotypical? Too TV? Is she expecting to see someone in a top hat stroking their moustache? A brutish thug with a shaved head and a leather jacket and a number of tattoos? Perhaps she should be ready to be surprised? She looks back over at the trolley to see if it's any closer, and although it isn't, she's looking in this direction at just the right moment to see the Stewardess stand back up again, and this is where her blood freezes and she suddenly feels a whole fucking load more awake.

The woman in the Stewardess outfit is the woman who was playing the vampire in the film.

Eldo swings back into her seat. Makes herself small. Takes a breath.

Okay, wait, reality check.

Maybe this isn't as surprising as she thinks? After all, it was what they call a bit part, right? Did she even have any dialogue? Eldo doesn't remember hearing her voice. But all that aside, this could actually be her, right? It could be that acting just isn't a regular gig for her. Or she didn't like it. Or she got sick of movie creeps. Or whatever. And sure, the windowpane has been playing a heady dance with the faces of everyone she looks at, keeping them moving and shifting, and difficult to identify, and the bennies have her breathing and thinking with a touch more difficulty than usual. But there's no doubt in Eldo's mind that she could be mistaken. That face, that perfect face that seems to have been created just for her: that's what she saw. It's the same face. That *is* the lady who was on the screen just a moment ago. And even though she's now wearing a Stewardess' outfit, everything else about her is identical: her hair, poise, and hell… even her make-up.

Eldo cautiously leans back out into the aisle, fixes her eyes on the Stewardess again, and she's dealing with a different passenger now, smiling politely, and then without skipping a beat she looks up and over, and straight into Eldo's eyes, and her smile grows a little wider, her eyes become just a little more seductive, and beneath her blood red lips protrude two bone white pointed incisors. Just like in the movie.

Eldo dives back into her seat. Fuck. What's she supposed to do now? Fake like she's asleep and hope she passes her (it would be nice if she could actually drift off, but the combo of the windowpane and the bennies is a tough one to snooze through) or interact with her when she gets to her seat and make out like she isn't some kind of vampire? She can hear the trolley drawing nearer and decides (probably more out of fear of what might happen if she's in her vicinity with her eyes closed) to go for the latter, and to greet her like a normal person would. Playing it cool.

Eldo keeps her eyes on the limited view of the aisle that she has from her seat, listening, and waiting for her to appear. No more gawping for her. And when, finally, she appears, she doesn't step into view, no, she fucking glides, as though she were on wheels, in a gondola, smiling that smile, and being the closest thing to perfection she's ever seen. The question she asks seems to be a knowing innuendo.

Anything you would like?

She speaks with an accent, maybe Eastern European. And even though Eldo totally can't remember her saying anything in the movie at all, this is *exactly* how she imagined she would sound in her head. She finds two words, they do the trick.

Coffee. Please.

Her smile widens, revealing those sharpened incisors again. Eldo looks away as quickly and inconspicuously as she can, playing like she doesn't see them.

Is this even happening? Is it just all in my head? Am I awake?

This feels like a nightmare. With her laid bare, vulnerable, and her just standing there. She gets a kick like she's not looking at her enough, behaving weirdly, not being normal, so she turns her gaze back, and stares straight into her eyes. Dear God, there's an enchanting hunger there, something that she can hear, which says the words:

Come with me, forget everyone you know and everything you want, you only want me, get out of your seat and follow me wherever I want you to go.

And just as Eldo's about to get to her feet and follow her to the ends of the earth, a hot cup of coffee is placed in front of her. And the scent of the coffee (strong, with beans that have been over-roasted, and made with water that was too hot and has scalded the brew) pierces the sensation that this is a dream, and she knows this is real. And even though that badly-made-coffee smell is overpowering, there's something that rises up above it: a thick cloud of oud.

The Stewardess is smiling, static, leaning across the empty seat, the opening in her shirt revealing just enough cleavage, and everything around her seems to turn russet-hued tones of gold, and just as Eldo's thinking that she could reach out, touch her, actually feel her skin with her hands, run her fingers through her hair… the Stewardess stands upright, smiles, and moves away from her, and out of sight. And now Eldo knows. It's her. The oud is coming from her. She is the source of it. This is Annick's killer. No fucking doubt at all.

As soon as she's out of sight the spell is broken, and Eldo is left with her proverbial dick in her hands, feeling like a big dumb lovesick puppy and wondering what the hell she should do now.

Okay, let's be realistic for a moment and go through our options.

Could it be that this is just a woman who happens to be wearing the same scent? A woman who has randomly chosen an oud perfume that smells remarkably similar to the one she smelled at the gallery?

In a fucking dream, guy.

Sure, some might say that was possible. But Eldo dismisses this possibility. We're not talking about any oud here, this is such a particular type: richer, thicker, darker than normal. Her mind tries to recall the specifics of it, to gauge how identical this is, and the match feels pretty damn identical. It's not just oud either, there are other notes to it: petitgrain, mandarin, leather, and cedar, for sure. But something else too. Something so familiar, something that feels important. Eldo isn't as good at picking apart a scent as Annick, even though she taught her so much about it in her time on Earth.

Wait, she's still on Earth. Remember?

Shit. Yeah. Gotta stop confusing dream with reality

Eldo cuts this internal dialogue off. She has a question to deal with in the now: what to do about the Stewardess? After a bunch of muddled, acid-tinged thoughts, Eldo makes the Herculean effort to get back out of her seat and walk down the aisle in the direction that the Stewardess went.

Yeah. Take action. Follow her. Fucking do something.

But as soon as she's on her feet she discovers that the Stewardess isn't where she thought she would be. She thought the vampire and the trolley would have moved about ten seats past her by now, max, but there's no sign of her at all. Okay, so presumably she's already reached the end of the aisle and now both trolley and vampiric, ridiculously attractive Stewardess are safely concealed behind that rippling red curtain at the end of the aisle. Yeah, that must be it.

Eldo takes a deep breath, and stumbles down the aisle, towards the red curtain, which sways just like a prop from the film she was watching. Everything shifts into slow motion, as though the chemical mix inside her has somehow created a magical third formula that's playing a tune that Eldo hasn't heard before, something new. She has to steady herself on the headrests of the seats she passes to stop from falling over, trying her utmost not to touch anyone's head as she does so, failing on a number of occasions as the whole walking-down-a-moving-plane thing has taken a dramatically wrong turn for her. And, after what feels like a motherfucking age, she reaches the foreboding curtain and the wall of white noise from her surroundings dies away completely and every sound the curtain makes as she pulls it back is heavily pronounced and all-encompassing. Amplified. The sound of a thousand pounds of fabric being dragged across the desert. It goes on forever.

Sitting behind the curtain is another Stewardess, a different one, not the seductress Eldo's looking for. She looks surprised, is smoking a cigarette, and quickly, and clumsily, dashes it away, stands up, straightens herself out.

How can I help, Miss?

Eldo's brain hurls words out of her mouth as fast as it can.

I was... just looking for your... colleague! The, uh... brunette. She didn't... give me... my change.

Great work, brain, totally normal stuff.

Anyway, a situation develops, and everything starts getting a little noisier and far more public than Eldo would like.

This Stewardess calls another Stewardess (the one who provided Eldo with her headphones) who in turn finds another Stewardess (the one who passive-aggressively pointed Eldo in the correct direction for the bathroom) and it quickly transpires that Eldo *was* given her change for the headphones.

She persists in the face of confusion.

No, not the change for the headphones, the change for my coffee. That other stewardess, the brunette, she's, uh, I don't know... Romanian or something. Czech maybe?

The three Stewardesses look at each other, and then back at Eldo in unison. Turns out there is no fourth Stewardess. These three are the only ones on the plane. Eldo laughs.

Don't be ridiculous, she just sold me a coffee.

The three women have nothing to say to this at first, and then they repeat their mantra: there are no other hospitality crewmembers on this flight apart from them.

Eldo continues, but with each word she can hear how increasingly unhinged she sounds, and the growing fear in the eyes of the stewardesses gets her to question herself so much that she finally comes to the conclusion that maybe this *is* all in her head, and that even if she is on this flight this particular moment is something she's going to have to let go of for now.

Eldo falls back into her seat. Frustrated and confused. Feeling like a failure. She lights another cigarette and switches the screen off in front of her and turns her attention to the window and the billowing clouds beneath. So still. So silent.

This planet is so unworried by all of this shit about dreams and killers and scents that's consuming her, and just as Eldo is beginning to wonder whether maybe there is less to this than meets the eye, and maybe she is losing her grip somewhat, a finger taps her on the shoulder.

Sitting in the previously empty seat next to her is a large man. A sweaty man. No, sweaty isn't the right word, greasy, that's better. A greasy man. Somewhat familiar somehow. He leans in close and speaks, he has an accent, his speech is classy, refined, his breath carries the scent of raw meat.

I saw her too.

Eldo doesn't really get it.

Her?

The Stewardess. The one who looks like the actress from the movie.

Eldo can't tell if this is all going to get weird and saying something might send the wrong message, so she just nods, and some kind of noise that signifies agreement crawls out of her

I heard the entire interaction. I mean, not eavesdropping, of course. But I believe I understand how you're feeling. Confused? Unsure of what's real and what's not?

Eldo nods, takes in the man's appearance as casually as she can: he's fat, with bulging eyes, too bulging to not be some kind of medical condition. And despite the grease and the weight and the eyes he's wearing a super dapper suit, just like Eldo, and it fits his form real damn well, even though there's so much of it. He's polite. Well spoken. A class act in many ways. And then Eldo gets to thinking

Wait a minute? Have I seen this guy before?

And then she starts rapidly flicking through the catalogue of faces in her memory, pretending to listen to what the man is saying, and then it hits her.

I've seen him before because he was in the art gallery, in

the dream. But that's not possible.

Eldo's eyes involuntarily grow a little wider, but she reels her surprise in, lets none of how she's feeling show at all. She does a great job of hiding this revelation, honestly, you wouldn't believe it. And then Eldo finds herself starting to listen to what the man is saying, because, actually, it's all kinds of interesting.

Here's what you need to understand: this kind of event has happened before. I'm no stranger to it. In fact, you might call me a specialist of sorts. No, those women back there were not lying to you. You and I are simply witness to something very rare indeed. Something difficult to understand.

The man reaches into his jacket pocket.

Here, give me a call when you get to New York. You're both investigating and, I believe, instigating something unique here, and I can help. Events like this don't just happen – they have triggers, people who make these things happen. Usually subconsciously. And that may well be your role in all this.

Eldo decides it's safe to converse, her voice sounds tired and croaky as she talks.

Are you saying I'm making all this shit happen?

Touché, perhaps that's a poor choice of vocabulary on my part. Not making. Facilitating might suit it better. Come see me. And oh, do take one of these. Trust me, the remaining duration of the flight will be far less eventful. And don't worry at all, you'll be quite safe. Of that I can assure you.

The fat man hands Eldo a triangular blue pill, which Eldo swallows without really thinking about what she's doing or what it might be, and she slips the man's business card into her front breast pocket.

Thank you.

Don't mention it. Just call me when you get to New York. I look forward to seeing you there.

And like that, the fat man is gone. Eldo doesn't recall

seeing him get to his feet, but he's not in the seat next to her anymore. And Eldo never notices him on the plane again, because the triangular blue pill is already holding a pillow down over the windowpane/bennies combo, smothering it, putting it out of its misery and replacing it with a deathly feeling of bliss and exhaustion.

And as she realizes that she can no longer move her arms, and her eyelids are failing her, and the world around her is becoming little more than a slit of grey light in a sea of darkness, the vampiric Stewardess silently glides back into view, around the edge of the seat in front of her, effervescent, smiling, everything she ever dreamed of. And she leans in towards Eldo, baring her fangs, and despite how close she is to oblivion she's hyper aware of how impeccable her skin is, and how her eyes build a complex dizzying desire in her, and how so very close her lips are to hers. But what she notices most, what rises up above all else, is that cloud of swirling oud, thick, and tangible and filled with ill portent. And then everything goes black.

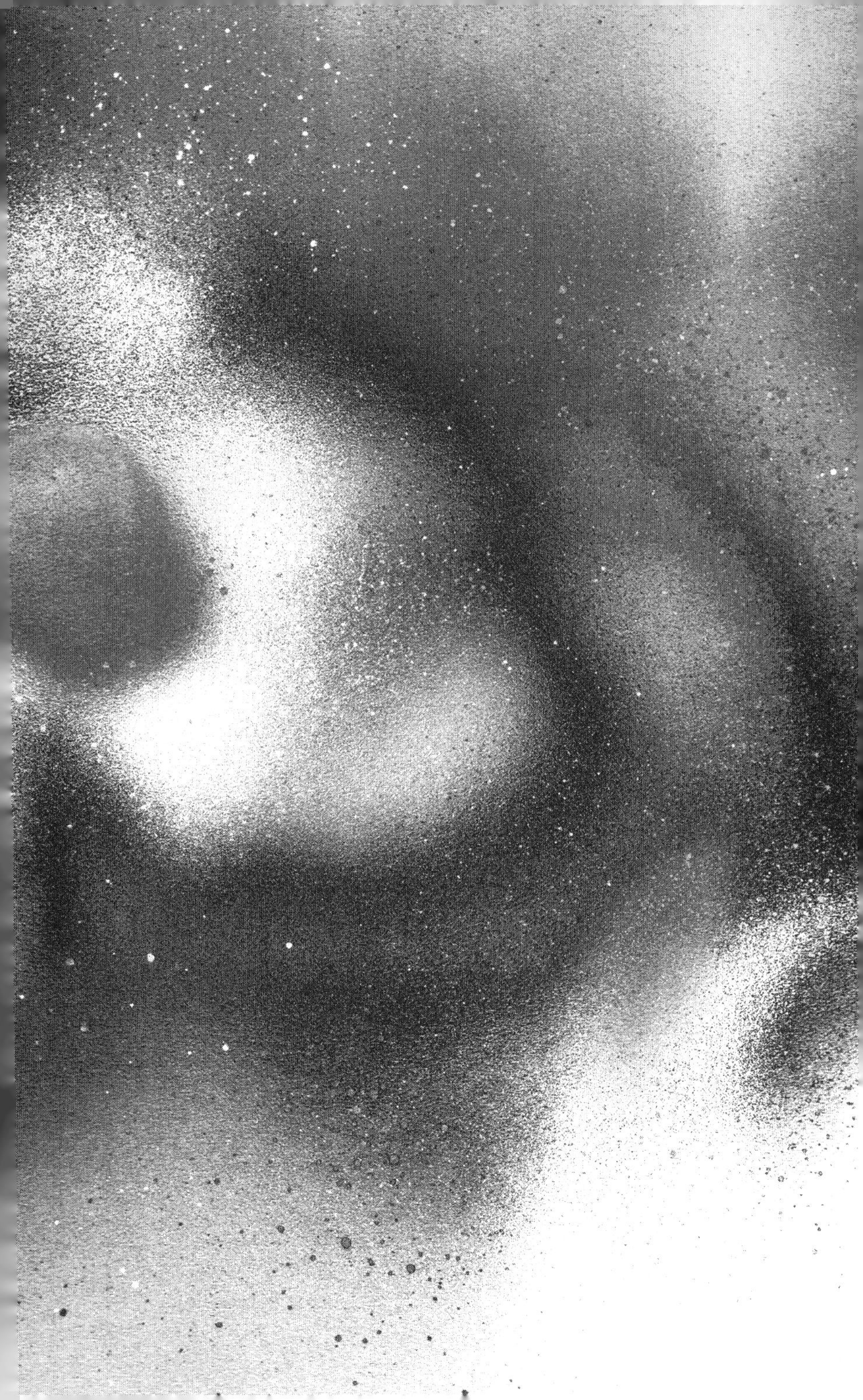

V
5th April, 1994
08.20
The Chelsea

Before she opens her eyes, Eldo can tell the room she's in is dark. And then her eyelids lift.

Yup, knew it.

Even though she's only freshly conscious, she's dimly aware that the reason it's dark in here is because the curtains are drawn, wherever the hell they are. Wherever the hell she is. Jesus, so tired.

Outside it's day. She can tell because there's a sharp line of sunlight cutting a swathe into the room, through a break in the shades, also the muffled sound of traffic outside is full, unrelenting. That's not a nighttime chorus. But this doesn't sound like The City to her, this sounds like somewhere else. And then a familiar siren starts up out there. Oh yeah, that's right. New York. She's in New York. And the knowledge that she's in a different place, with the day going about its business out there without her is enough to give Eldo the strength she needs to sit the fuck up.

Or at least to want to, to try to.

The actual doing of it is a little more complicated.

There's a spark of electricity in her brain, a message telling her arms and legs to move, but something must be going wrong with the receptors, because the message doesn't seem to be getting through.

God damn it.

Eventually the signal is received, and some semblance of life returns to her limbs. Kind of. Granted, she has a little less control than she'd like. Which might have something to do with that blue triangular pill she took on the plane (hazy memories of a greasy hand pressing it into her palm), but the body that picks up that message seems to have almost no muscle strength whatsoever, it's just withered, dried out, used up. Spent.

After a lot of gentle rocking back and forth her body begins to remember how this whole shitshow of movement is supposed to go, and slowly but surely she inches her feet towards and off the edge of the bed, keeps her body shuffling until the backs of her knees are bent by the bed and the soles of her feet land flat on the floor. The next stage requires Eldo to pull at the side of the bed, the bedside table, whatever the hell's within reach of her enfeebled arms to get her off her back and onto her feet. It's hard going, but she gets there, and there she is. Standing. On two feet. Unsteady as shit. What a rock star.

The next step is to walk across the room, over to the curtains, gracefully look outside at the splendor of the city she's in. But that's not how it goes. Instead, meaning to take a few tentative steps forwards, she ends up stumbling, careening across the room, her knees smashing into the wall and her head and shoulders thrust unceremoniously through the raggedy ass strip of curtain and out the open window. Her eyelids narrow as she goes from the inky gloom of the room to the blinding bright sunshine outside, and fear catches in her throat at how motherfucking high up she is, and how outside that window is New York, New York, in all its realness, all its glory, in every direction. The noise and commotion and vastness of it all.

Her breath comes back to her, rasping and desperate at first, but eventually slowing, easing, and after a series of ever-calming inhalations she's relieved to discover that she has the ability to move normally again, and slowly, ever so carefully, she pulls the top half of her body back inside, through the window, lets the curtain fall closed, turns, and examines the room she's woken up in: bed, TV, two doors, dresser with a mirror, her bag, mini bar. Yeah, this is a hotel. On top of that there's a stale cigarette smell to the room, which covers an unmistakable waxy aroma, probably from a harborage of cockroaches secreted somewhere behind the walls.

No doubt about it. This is a New York hotel.

Eldo's eyes flit around the room and she internally prioritises which parts of the room to go to, and in which order. Her parched throat tells her to start with the mini bar. She stumbles over. Opens it. From the array of options available Eldo chooses a miniature size bottle of soda. She cracks the top off, the size difference between her hands and the bottle making her feel like a giant, drinks half of it, and thinks.

God damn it, what the fuck am I doing in New York?

The oud, remember?

And one by one, the memories start falling like dominoes, each one activating a following one until Eldo's brought right up to speed (although the question of the order of events, or which memories come from dreams and which don't, will continue to wrap her in knots for the next few days) And then she starts speaking out loud, to herself...

Annick. She's here. Got to save Annick. But what happened on the plane? Fat man's hands, and the stewardess... what happened with the stewardess?

There's a hazy flash of the stewardess's face, leaning over her, fangs bared.

Eldo tentatively goes over to the dresser, to the mirror, and stands face to face with her reflection. Hesitant, she pulls at the collar of her shirt with one finger, checks her neck. For what? Vampire bite marks?

Jesus H.

She feels dumb even thinking this, and the feeling of

stupidity, of dumbness isn't alleviated by the fact that there are no marks whatsoever. Nothing. She even takes her shirt off to check as properly as she can, but there's not a mark on her.

Of course there aren't. Vampires? What are you thinking, Eldo?

All this stuff is getting to her, that's all it is. And it's with a weary sigh that her eyes find themselves resting on her bag, and she gets to wondering:

Did I pack any diazepam?

The next thing Eldo knows the pammy's kicked in and she's got an almighty calm going on, but is thirsty again, and, annoyingly, she's lying flat on her back on the bed once more. How much time has passed since she woke? It can't be night, because the noise from outside is pretty much the same as it was when she woke up. The only difference is that now there's a new sound in the room.

Where the hell is that coming from? The television?

It sounds like someone turned the TV off a while ago and now it's off, but making a sustained high-pitched whine which is slowly getting louder.

Is that a thing?

Since when did you start talking to yourself so much?

Eldo still has her eyes closed, so she can't investigate whether the TV is the source of the sound. But even if she did go through the exhausting effort of opening her eyes to see what it was, what would she be looking for? A TV that isn't switched on? Or possibly, she thinks, someone else standing in the room? A mystery person. With their hand near the TV switch. Yeah, that could be it. And a creeping sensation of dread ripples across the surface of her skin as Eldo considers this image, the mystery man looking at Eldo, smiling, fingers near the TV, and she now finds herself flicking through a variety of faces and forms and personas that this figure could have taken, and wonders whether it's possible to bring a being into existence simply by thinking about its image for long enough. Maybe?

And then the sound shifts, moves, changes pitch. And now she recognises it:

That's no television, that's a mosquito.

This revelation tells Eldo that it's safe to open her eyes without her gaze falling on the figure of the mystery person, probably, so she does. But she soon learns that this confidence was ill founded.

Yes, she's still in the same room, yes, still in what is presumably the Chelsea, yes, there's still daylight creeping in through the closed curtains. But there's no sign of this mosquito, even though she can hear it loud and clear. Eldo tries to get her ears to work in tandem with her eyes, to use both senses to track the sound, find the insect, but just as she's getting close the high-pitched whine stops abruptly. Silence. God damn it.

Now, sure, it could be the last dregs of windowpane that's keeping her from telling where the sound was coming from, but what with the vampire on the plane and the greasy fat man handing her a pill and then disappearing this is all feeling a little more ominous than it normally would, even if it is all in her head.

It's not in your head.

The sound of the mosquito picks up again, and she turns this way and that, trying to make as little noise as possible, to avoid drowning out that whine, masking where it's coming from. She tries to keep her breathing as shallow as possible, and this in turn builds a feeling of anxious desperation: her heart rate increases, fear mounts, and she twists her body to face what she hopes is the general direction of the source of the whine, and finally, there it is.

Little motherfucker.

The creature is on her upper left arm, with its proboscis buried deep in Eldo's flesh. The words...

First mosquito of the year

...run through Eldo's mind and then she remembers something about West Nile Disease, and Encephalitis, and decides that even if this *is* the first mosquito she's seen in 1994, the creature still has to die. But she doesn't really want to swat the thing while it's eating, because then she'd get dead bug on her, and that'd be kind of disgusting. And then a hazy memory starts forming, something that someone told her this one time... something about mosquitos not being able to retract mid-flow if you pull the skin tight around the entry point. And wasn't there something else about retraction being the point at which the creature injects you with its saliva or whatnot, and how that's what contains and/or spreads disease? Eldo goes through the dusty filing cabinets of her head trying to place where this memory came from. Was it Mona who told her this? Maybe. Could've been anyone really. People say a lot of things. But whoever said it, she decides to try this out. It's always fun to try new things. And, after all, what's the worst that could happen?

Let's find out.

It starts well. The mosquito makes no attempt to flee as Eldo's right hand moves closer, like a stealthy hunter, approaching the feeding animal. She carefully bunches her fingers around the creature, all without scaring it off, and pulls the skin taught with the bug at the centre. The idea here being that now the mosquito can't remove its... Nose? Feeding tube? Proboscis? Whatever that thing is called. Anyway, instead it's then forced to keep drinking, and drinking, and drinking, until it can take no more and explodes.

And the horror show begins.

How long do mosquitoes take to feed anyway? A minute? Less? More? At what point will it try to fly away? Not a clue.

But after a short while (perhaps 40 seconds?) with her fingers pulling the skin tight around the entry point, the insect is in a visible state of distress. Its legs buck, like it's trying to jump backwards, to take off, its wings come to life, making that characteristic high-pitched whine, lifting it a little, but not getting it away. The thing is stuck fast and is swelling larger and larger.

By this stage Eldo can make out the dark red hue of her blood through the ever-thinning skin of its abdomen. And although it's not really hot in this room, a build-up of sweat (or maybe grease?) has developed under her fingertips, and it's becoming difficult for her to keep her grip. So Eldo pushes harder to stop from slipping, so hard it hurts, both her fingertips and the flesh on her arm are throbbing now, but she's got to keep the skin as tight as she can, holding the parasite in place.

And so it continues.

The mosquito's body has swollen up to the size of her thumbnail now, its wings beating out a continuous hum of desperation, its legs raised off Eldo's skin completely as some primeval part of whatever it has for a brain realises that its very existence is on the line now and it tries harder than ever to get away. But it just can't. It's going nowhere. Stuck fast.

And the swelling accelerates.

Now its body is the size of a golf ball, and mere seconds later it's grown closer in size to a tennis ball. The build-up of slime, or whatever it is that's between Eldo's fingers and her skin, is thicker than ever, and has the stench of something rancid to it, and there's a gorge rising in her throat at the combination of the reek of the grease and the sight of this vast thing twisting and turning to get away, ballooning, its skin so thin now that it looks like nothing more than a softball of blood floating above her arm. And then Eldo gets flashes of lights in her eyes, followed by dark spots. And she knows all too well what this means. She's going. Losing consciousness. Bright flashes burst behind her eyes, quickly becoming incandescent, and then darkness takes her, and her head hits the pillow. And she thinks…

Fuck.

When she opens her eyes, the setting couldn't be more different. She appears to be in some kind of chalet, the sort of setup you might get in Switzerland, or Austria, or some such place where people of leisure can be found in the mountains.

Everything is made of wood, there's a fire crackling in the corner, and a familiar woman sitting at a long table with her. This incredible table. It's made of aged wood, rough-hewn, clearly once smooth and well varnished, but that's all changed now after years and years of human traffic has tattooed the surface with cups and glasses and arms and hands and whatnot. Still, both the table and the wood have some kind of nobility, a brand of rustic authenticity, alive with the scent of oak that's been frequented by an uncountable number of wealthy people eating and drinking and having the greatest of conversations over the span of many, many years. What a crime it would be not to notice the history of this table.

Eldo is sitting upright on a hard bench, and although her vision is blurry and indistinct, the scent which emanates from the woman at the far end of the table tells her exactly who she is.

There's a gauzy haze to everything, like she was looking through a filtered lens, and she blinks a few times, each blink bringing some degree of sharpness back to her surroundings, until she can make out that not only is it exactly who she thought it was, but also that she's no longer wearing her stewardess outfit. She's now in some kind of burnt umber coat, long, 20s style, with a thick, luxurious fur collar. There's a cup in front of her, which contains steaming hot chocolate (the air drenched with the scent of cocoa, sugar, nutmeg, and cinnamon) and two glasses: in one is champagne (scent clean, sharp, fresh), and in the other is glühwein (thick, boozy, infused with cloves). She's looking at her. Smiling. Her eyes like two impossible cosmic bodies, floating in the crispest white space. And then she speaks, emphasising the word *you*.

What are you doing here?

Eldo coughs, clears her throat. It feels like an age and a day since she last spoke.

Am I here?

She moves a hand across the surface of the table, feeling the grain of the wood. Yes. She appears to be here. She looks back up at her, blinks a few times, brings her into even crisper focus.

What happened on the plane?

She looks at the drinks in front of her, assesses her options, chooses the hot chocolate, takes a sip.

On the plane?

The Stewardess outfit? Flight to New York?

Oh! That wasn't me. I'm a shadow.

A shadow?

If you stand in the centre, with lights all around you, you will cast many shadows. That's what I am – part of something intangible, yet solid. Yes. Something larger. One of many. Our name is Legion.

And then she locks eyes with Eldo and gives her that ever-so seductive smile. The next time she speaks her lips part slowly, with a soft sound, and Eldo flushes as she wonders what it would be like to feel those lips against hers.

We're linked, you and I.

Truth be told, the blood was pumping too loudly through Eldo's ears for her to hear what she said. She swallows hard. Didn't hear her, but got to say something, so she goes with:

Where are we now? The Alps?

But the shadow just shrugs. And then she talks again, twisting her body this way and that as she speaks – Eldo does her best to listen to the words, and not to think about the body.

I don't know. A lot of this isn't anything I understand. I simply respond to what's happening, go along with it all. Existence in this realm is simple and reactive. Catch and release. All you have to do is smile and be attractive and say yes to everything you want and no to everything you don't. It's very simple. I like this place, wherever it is. The shadows are in many locations. We can see them all simultaneously. We have seen many things in our short time here, but this one place right now is my favourite. Everyone is friendly. It's warm inside, pretty outside, the air is sharp, and you can drink whatever you like.

She passes her hands over the three drinks in front of her, presumably to consolidate her point about being able to drink whatever she wants.

She? So this monster's a she now?

Thinks Eldo, hoping those words were just in her head.

Instead of continuing down this path and wondering whether the shadow is a monster or a person she decides to ask her a question about the drinks.

Which one's your favourite?

Why would I have a favourite? I like them all. They offer different flavours. Different moods. Different textures. Different feelings. There's a lot of that here: opportunities for different experiences.

That's new for you?

It didn't exist before.

What did exist before?

She tilts her head this way and that as she mulls the question over. One hand goes to her face, her fingers absent-mindedly tapping against her lips, and, as she watches her eyes slip to her skin, to her hair, to her downturned eyes, Eldo's once again reminded of how utterly perfect she is, how sculpted, and how very much tailor-made she is for her own tastes.

God damn it, when did I become such a mother fucking lech?

She gives up searching and answers with...

Not this.

And just as Eldo starts considering whether maybe she's being given an opportunity to find answers here, to collect breadcrumbs that will lead her to Annick, and that maybe she should ask questions related to her quest, she realises that her eyes are in fact closed.

When she opens them again Eldo finds herself lying flat on her back in the hotel room in New York and decides to stay right the fuck there for a bit, looking at the ceiling, listening to the world outside, thinking her thoughts.

How long was she gone for? Did that meeting with the shadow actually happen? What was it? Did she in fact waste an opportunity there? It sure feels like it. And then, the memory of the mosquito rises up, above all others. She jolts, twists round to look at her left arm. She's expecting a mess of blood and an open gaping wound, but there's nothing save for a small red, raised dot. She goes completely still, listening for the tell-tale sound the mosquito makes. Silence. Nothing but the sound of the world beyond her window.

What the actual fuck?

Eldo is up and in the bathroom now, splashing water on her face. Not because her skin needs cleaning. Not because it's greasy. But just because she wants to feel the water on her face. To feel something. To feel anything.

She leans into the basin, listening to the water running,

feeling the cold ceramic under her hands. Pushing her fingertips against it, and then shifting slightly and tapping her fingernails on the basin. Listening to the sound. For some reason her feet hurt. And this sensation reminds her of how much Herman's feet had been hurting when he was standing outside the gallery.

Wait... Herman's feet?

Eldo thinks back, just in case she's made a mistake here. No... it's not a mistake, that was a dream, but she directly experienced Herman's thoughts and feelings as though they were her own. She could feel the sensations of Herman's body: that ache in his feet, the breath in his lungs, his specific physicality. Those sensations felt exactly the same as how she experiences the weight and presence of her own body. Is it possible that she can enter other people? See things from their perspective? Feel things that they feel? Surely not. But maybe? Perhaps? And this possibility, combined with the memory of the mosquito, begins to get under her skin (no pun intended) because now she has to sit with the uncomfortable fact that she can no longer cleanly tell the difference between what's real and what's not. And that's an awfully sharp stone to have in your shoe when travelling.

Fuck this.

She needs to talk to someone. Someone real. As solid as this basin that her hands are both resting on and cooling themselves with. Not some phantom from the dream realm. And as she steps out of the bathroom, face and hair wet, she spies the phone.

His fingers go to her front breast pocket, almost without knowing why, but it all becomes clear as she takes a business card out – the text too hard to make out in the dark of the room, so she goes over to the window and pushes the curtain back, and although it's not super easy for her to focus on the tiny font on the card, the extra light enables her to make out the words *Cuir Absolue*. If this is a name then it doesn't exactly tally with the fat, greasy man Eldo spoke to on the plane. Underneath these words there are two phone numbers: a landline and a mobile number. Eldo doesn't recognize the area code for the landline as being in the States, so she settles on the mobile. Damn, she's going to rack up a hell of a bill here.

The phone rings with a very unusual tone: distant, with a pitch and rhythm unlike any she's ever heard. The ringing goes on forever, and just as Eldo's starting to think that maybe she should ring off, someone picks up.

Hello?

Hi, someone gave me this card yesterday, on a plane.

For the longest time there's no sound other than the rasping breath of the person on the other end of the phone, and then this breathing transforms into a soft chuckle that has more than a touch of emphysema to it.

Ah yes, Miss Eldo. I do trust New York finds you well.

It's just Eldo actually, and...

Eldo pauses for a second. First of all, she doesn't remember ever telling the guy her name. Secondly, when people say things like this do they actually want the full, honest story, or are they being polite? Does the fat man want to hear Eldo talk about how her experience in New York is offering certain challenges? Does he want the details, or does he want something else? Something glib? Something conversational? Erring on the side of caution, Eldo gives the voice:

Yeah, great, thanks.

And I presume that you're calling to continue the discussion that we began on the plane last night.

Exactly.

Are you free today? Right now?

Yes, where are you?

Get a pen, I'll give you the address.

Eldo scrambles for a pen and doesn't ask how the voice on the other end knew she wasn't holding one. She finds a ballpoint pen that gives intermittent ink in a frustratingly scratchy, spidery scrawl and writes down the address of somewhere on the upper east side, and then with no real memory of hanging up, or getting ready to go out, Eldo finds herself dressed, shoes on, and walking down the echoing stairwell of the building.

One hand goes to her right-hand jacket pocket: there's a key there with an abnormally large piece of plastic attached to it with what feels to be her room number embossed in it. Okay. Good. She was worried she'd left it behind. From looking around she can see that this is definitely The Chelsea. And although the journey from the plane to the hotel is completely missing, Eldo's consoled to know that she seems to be heading in the right direction, even when on autopilot in the throes of oblivion. Jasmine told her Annick was at The Chelsea, she's on target. Everything's fine. Well, fine-ish.

She stumbles down what seems like way too many flights of stairs, and eventually arrives at the reception desk. Behind the counter stands a man who looks for all the world like the thin, mustachioed man at the betting shop back in the city. Eldo steps up, sweating somewhat, a little out of breath from the stairs. The hotel foyer smells of meat, stale bread, some kind of lemon scented cleaning product, combined with the ever-present addition of that ashtray-stale-cigarette odour, and an undertone of that unmistakable waxy aroma belonging to a hidden abundance of cockroaches, just like in her room. Very New York. The clerk doesn't seem to notice her enter the foyer, so Eldo speaks.

Hello.

The thin man looks up, an initial look of irritation on his face melts away and is quickly replaced with a very American service-worker smile.

Ah, Miss Eldo. How can I help?

Eldo ignores this second use of 'Miss Eldo,' and gets straight to it.

I'm looking for a woman named Annick, she's also staying here.

The clerk makes an inquisitive sound and brings out a large registry book from under the counter. He flips it open, the heft of the book making a thud as it falls open to the most recent page of entries, and he runs his index finger down a column of names, stops, and inhales deeply before speaking.

Ah yes. She's staying on the third floor. A friend of yours?

Yeah… listen, this might sound weird, but do you have a brother? Maybe works in the gambling industry? Abroad?

The clerk doesn't flinch. Just smiles.

No Miss, I can't say I do. Are you by any chance telling me that I have a doppelganger out there?

I guess.

I get that a lot. A friend of mine, he's working on something called string theory, tells me that there's a huge number of people out there who look just like us, but that we're extremely unlikely to ever meet them.

Did you say string theory?

Either the thin man pretends not to hear this, or he misses it completely. Either way, he moves on.

Now let's see if your friend is in her room.

He turns to the wall behind him, a vast collection of identical wooden boxes, each one is either empty, or contains a key or a slip of paper. And then Eldo notices the calendar and that it's… wait… the 5th? What the fuck happened to the 4th? Did she sleep through an entire day? Eldo falls into a brief reverie trying to work out how this could have happened, when she's suddenly brought back to the now by the desk clerk speaking again.

I'm afraid her key is checked at the moment.

He turns back to Eldo.

Which means she's not in her room right now.

Eldo doesn't say what she's thinking, which is...

Is today the 4th or the 5th?

...and instead goes with:

Any idea when she'll be back?

I'm afraid not Miss.

Okay then.

Eldo hands her key over to the clerk.

I'm heading out for a while, but I'll be back. If you could ask whoever's here later to leave a note in my box when Annick comes back...

The thin man smiles again. Pushes his glasses up with one finger. Jesus, that similarity to the guy in the betting store chills Eldo to the bone.

But of course, Miss.

And the next thing Eldo knows, she's sitting in the back seat of a yellow taxi. The world tearing past, a flurry of images, almost like the view outside is a train and she's at a complete standstill, but that just can't be the case, right?

The Driver is babbling away, and has an accent that Eldo can't place for the life of her. Is that Russian? Irish? South American? Whatever. What Eldo does know is that where this man comes from isn't what matters, what matters is how by this point Eldo's become almost too accustomed to these time skips. And even though she may well be losing her grip on the normal patterns of reality, because she's increasingly subscribing to a philosophy of rolling with what's happening instead of fighting it, she has no qualms whatsoever about leaning forward, both into this moment that she finds herself in, and towards the seat that the driver is in, and saying:

Hey man, where are we going?

In a loud voice.

There's the requisite pause of confusion before the taxi driver says:

Cuir Absolue, upper east side.

Eldo eases back into her seat.

Right. Right. Yeah, that's what I thought.

The Taxi Driver fixes Eldo with a look, not by turning round, but by finding her eyes in the reflection in the rear-view mirror. What's behind that gaze? Concern? Fear? Hard to say.

You alright, man?

Alright. Alright. Well that all depends. What would you classify 'alright' to be?

I'm no Doctor, but, do you feel like… you know where you are? That you know where you're going?

Eldo's hands feel the leather of the seat, she brings her left hand up to the window and lets it fall against the cool smooth glass. Takes a breath of the air in the taxi, which is part car scent (a combination of upholstery and petrol) and part artificial pine scent (which must be coming from the green tree hanging from the rear-view mirror). She keeps talking, and while she does her right hand goes to her jacket pocket and finds two loose Benzedrine tablets in there. Her hands think all by themselves and come to the conclusion that Eldo could do with a little pick me up. Some people have coffee. Eldo has amphetamines.

Yeah, I think I'm doing okay.

Not really knowing where they came from, Eldo notices that she's now wearing shades, and lowers them to peer at the meter ticking away in front. It's a series of digital numbers, and just like several times before with small print and led displays, she can't get a fix on them at all.

I don't seem to be able to read the meter though.

The Taxi Driver's eyes find Eldo's in the mirror again.

Maybe you in a dream.

In a dream?

Yeah. In dreams you can't make out small details. Like, if you try to read the fine print on a packet of food, or read the numbers on a calculator, or a digital watch. The words and numbers don't stick, they move around, like water. That's one of the ways how you know you're in a dream.

If this is a dream, are you just a dream character?

The Taxi Driver laughs.

I guess I would be. Man, I don't know how I feel about that.

Hey, this guy we're going to, Cuir Absolue, do you know who he is?

I don't think he's a who, my friend, more of a what.

How do you mean?

Cuir Absolue just means leather. Sounds like the name of a store or something if you ask me.

You sure that's what it means?

Hell yeah. I'm Algerian. French is my first language.

Eldo clicks her fingers. Algerian. Of course, it seems so obvious now.

I was wondering where you were from.

Algiers man. My Grandmother knew Camus.

Straight up? No shit?

Straight up. No shit.

Turns out that not only is Cuir Absolue a place, but it's a scent bar, which Eldo didn't even realize was a thing. After she's paid the taxi driver, and walked in through the ornate wooden doors (more like a 19th century pharmacy in Northern Europe than a store in New York in 1994) she's asked to wait in the foyer on a cushioned ottoman, and she's waiting because in order to meet the voice on the phone apparently she needs someone to appear at this small reception desk, but it's been a few minutes now and there's still no sign of anyone. Why must everything take so damn long?

There's a packet of perforated Armenian papers on a small table next to the ottoman, and because Eldo can never resist an Armenian paper she tears one off, carefully folds it down the centre, lengthwise, and then stands it up on one end in an ashtray. Her fingers are ever so slightly tacky (sweating out the last of the windowpane maybe? Or the first swell of the bennies?) so every time she takes her hand away her skin adheres to the paper ever so slightly, just enough to make it fall over. She rubs her hands together and goes through her pockets to see if she's got anything that might take away the inevitable benny edge she's about to get. As luck would have it, she's got a small blister pack of 32mg codeine pills. Pops both, dry swallows, and then turns back to the paper.

After a few failed attempts she eventually gets the folded Armenian paper to stand on its own. She then lights a match and puts the flame to the very top of the paper, then uses the same flame to light a cigarette that's magically appeared in her mouth. She waits, puffs, and watches as the flame on the Armenian paper gently goes out, and a bright orange ripple slowly runs down the paper, turning everything it touches to ash, and Eldo watches, as enchanted as she could possibly be, as the smoke from the Armenian paper drifts into the sunlight that strays through the art deco windows and blends its grey hue with the blue smoke from the end of her cigarette, a swirling, ever-changing sculpture of smoke and photons. God damn, things can get so fucking beautiful sometimes.

Eldo takes in her surroundings, checks out the place. It's made up like a bar, only instead of spirits, they have scents. And people are sat at barstools, sampling them, the way you might order a selection of drinks. You know, if you were into that kind of thing. And although Eldo knows that she's supposed to wait here, there's still no one at the reception desk, and she's itching with curiosity, so she decides to approach the bar and see what the rumpus is. She stubs her cigarette out before doing so though. After all, people here are on something of a scent journey, and she's not *that* much of a dick.

When she gets just a few paces away from the bar Eldo picks up a strong scent of something she can only describe as pink leather suede. She picks up a lot of scents in a day, some of them good, some of them bad, but this one is different, special, it's the kind of scent that needs you to stop what you're doing so you can pay attention. The kind of scent that begs to be identified and catalogued for future reference. Put simply, this scent rocks Eldo's world, but she's not sure where it's coming from.

She walks back and forth along the bar, pretending to look at the array of bottles in different shapes and colours and sizes, but in actual fact simply trying to track down the source of this pink suede scent. Eventually, she nails it: it's coming from the woman behind the bar – short, jet-black hair, pale skin, dark red lipstick. Once Eldo works out that she's the source she can't seem to take her eyes off her, as though something about her image is connected to the scent she's emitting. Visual and olfactory symbiosis. Finally Eldo happens to catch her gaze, holds it, smiles back, and sashays over, and although Eldo is fairly sure she's awake and that this is really happening, there's no doubt that this woman has clearly been plucked from one of her better dreams.

The first thing she says is that her name is Miss Barberry, the second is to ask how she can help. Eldo has to fight the allure of her scent and eyes to focus on the conversation.

This is going to sound a little odd, but what is that scent that you're wearing?

Oh, you like it? It's a new one, Tout va Bien.

What are the notes?

It's incense, rose, leather, oakmoss, patchouli, aldehydes… a few others.

Miss Barberry extends her wrist and Eldo lowers her head and breathes it in. It's the warm comfort of childhood confusion mixed with an angelic, buxom, naked woman easing herself onto her body as she hides behind a pew in an old French church. Yes. She likes it. Yes. She wants to buy a bottle. 100ml. She has it shipped to her place in The City.

You don't want to take it with you?

I'm travelling pretty light at the moment.

Of course. Is there anything else I can help with?

Eldo thinks for a moment. Really she's just killing time, but she's enjoying being in Miss Barberry's presence, breathing in the scent of Tout va Bien, listening to her voice, looking into her eyes, so she finds a question.

What can you tell me about oud?

Is this for yourself, or a gift, Miss?

Miss. There's that word again. Maybe it's just become fashionable to use this word and she didn't notice it segue into common parlance.

Oh just, you know, a general interest. You know, like what is it exactly?

A light goes on behind Miss Barberry's eyes as a wave of understanding washes over her, and she speaks.

Oh, okay then. Well, it's from agarwood. The oud itself forms when the tree is infected by a parasite.

Although Eldo has kind of heard this story before (not well enough to recount it mind) she plays dumb. Maybe there's something in this that she missed.

A parasite?

Yes. The oud itself is a protective oil that crystalises into a resin. It's created by the parasite, by the infection.

So, the parasite infects the tree and then oud is created as... an antibody?

Yeah, pretty much. It appears as a resin that forms as... I don't know, something that looks like a dark, knotty part of the tree. But most of what you get these days is synthetic. Real oud is expensive.

Synthetic oud?

Oh yeah. Most perfumes use synthetic ingredients. A chain of chemicals which, when blended together in the correct proportions, will be indistinguishable from the original.

Could you tell the difference?

Between a synthetic and a natural scent?

Yeah.

She thinks for a moment, a finger goes to the corner of her mouth.

I don't know. I don't think so though. Why all the questions?

I'm, I don't know, travelling, learning.

Miss Barberry leans closer, adopts a conspiratorial tone.

Are you, by any chance, a friend of Mona's?

Eldo stops breathing for a second.

How did you know?

You have that vibe. Hey, if you know Mona then you should go see Oriza next time you're in Paris.

Miss Barberry hands over a book of matches.

Oriza?

She's a friend of Mona's too, the oldest person you'll ever meet. But she's great, knows a lot. Her address is written in there.

Eldo flicks the match book open, there's writing inside it but, as we all might have expected by this stage, she finds that she can't read the letters and instead of dwelling on this she just says *Thank you* and puts it straight into her pocket.

Eldo stubs her cigarette out in the ashtray, alongside the ashes from the Armenian paper. She freezes, looks around. Why is she sat on the ottoman again? Wasn't she just at the bar? She looks over at the scent bar and sure enough, there's Miss Barberry, flicking through a magazine, paying her no attention whatsoever. Did she just imagine the entire exchange, or did that really happen? She goes through their conversation and asks herself whether there was anything in there that she learned that she would have no way of knowing if she hadn't 'spoken' to her (other than her name), but it's hard to extrapolate details like that at a time like this. And as Eldo wrestles with the urge to get to her feet and make the long walk over there and put an end to this line of self-questioning by just asking…

Hey, Miss Barberry, was I just talking to you a second ago?

…someone arrives at the front desk: female, devastating (naturally), and smiles.

How can I help you, Miss?

Eldo rises, places her hands on the desk. As her fingers spread across the oak, scented by a thousand different samples, she completely forgets about Miss Barberry, about the time skips, about the oud, and instead focuses solely on this new character.

I met someone yesterday. An, uh, large gentleman, well spoken. He invited me here.

The lady smiles. She speaks with another accent that's difficult to place.

Ah yes, you must be the lady from the plane. Frederic's waiting for you upstairs. I'll let him know you're here.

There's no hit of pink leather suede from this lady, instead she smells of lilies, and something underneath which could almost be corpses, something rotten for sure, but surprisingly pleasant with it. She picks up a phone and confuses Eldo by speaking in a language that she's not even sure she knows.

What is that? Dutch? What does Dutch even sound like?

She moves the phone away from her mouth ever so slightly and covers the mouthpiece with one hand and husks the words...

He'll see you now.

...while gesturing to the wall behind her.

Eldo turns, and sees an elevator in the wall, a wall with a vast fresco of something that looks like celtic knots or mandalas or scientific diagrams all painted in blues and golds. She'd noticed neither the elevator nor even the wall until now, how is that possible when they're so eye-catching, so present? Accompanied by an unseen singing chorus, the brushed bronze doors of the elevator open to reveal an all-red interior, like a mechanical body opening up the deepest part of itself. She turns back to look at the woman at the desk in case she's going to say anything else. For a moment it doesn't look like she will, but then there's a movement, and Eldo leans closer, quietly elated that she gets to spend another moment in her presence.

Can I ask you a question?

She asks. And Eldo, not wanting to point out that she just has, replies with...

But of course.

She pauses. Demures. Breaks eye contact and looks like she's having difficulty finding a way to put this, like she's about to explain something that could be considered rude, and finally says...

Why do you think it is that all of your encounters with women recently have been with an array where each is more beautiful than the last, and all are quite distinct – whereas all of the men you have met are either repugnant, or blurred into one indistinct miasma?

Eldo doesn't reply, and so she punctuates her silence with...

You don't have to answer it now, but maybe it's worth considering.

And Eldo blinks and that face, that perfectly wonderful face, doesn't change position at all, but is now much farther away because Eldo is no longer standing right in front of her, by the desk, but is now inside the red interior of the machine womb. The elevator doors close. And she ascends. Leaving her, and Miss Barberry, and all memories of both of them, behind.

There's a single chime from a surprisingly melodious bell as the elevator glides to a halt, the doors slide open, and two things hit Eldo immediately: the first is the sound of many voices, indicating that she's about to face a swell of people, the second is a thick aroma of hashish hanging in the air in palpable, pungent clouds. So thick she feels she could tear it out of the air and chew it, so overpoweringly strong that she has to narrow her eyes. Like someone somewhere was cutting onions.

Anyway, she moves towards the source of all the noise and resinous aroma, and discovers a second bar up here, serving scents, just like the one below. The big difference being that while the bar on the ground floor was as quiet as a church, this place is more like a bordello. And a particularly rowdy one at that. Everyone here also appears to be on something. I mean, hashish, for sure, that's a given, but there's other stuff going on. You can just tell.

People are holding drinks, but no one seems to be drinking much, and Eldo doesn't see any food anywhere. These two datums of information are always a bit of a sign. She goes up to the bar and orders a lime and soda and it costs her $8, and although the money doesn't really mean anything to her, it raises a red flag that says she's somewhere where what should be a $1 drink at most costs $8, and that tells her even more about where she is. The clientele tell her the rest.

They're all dressed up in the same 1920s or 30s theme, and the women are all beautiful, and the men all look like they're cut out of vintage copies of Vogue, and Eldo is beginning to feel like she's sticking out like a sore thumb because she didn't get the memo about how to dress and she had always thought that a suit is a suit is a suit, but now that she's standing amongst suits tailored to an older time period she realises how very contemporary her look is and just as it's all starting to feel a bit overwhelming a familiar face appears through the crowd, and none of her worries about this upstairs bar matter anymore because everything moves on.

The first thing that Eldo notices about Frederic is how different he appears here compared to how he looked on the plane. Instead of 'fat' Frederic now fills his suit with the appearance of someone who spends a fair amount of time exercising. Oh, thick set, for sure, but that's definitely muscle under there, not flab. And there's no hint of grease to him at all now. In fact, he looks not only clean, but exfoliated, and exceedingly well-shaved. He almost looks like he's been airbrushed.

Huh.

Thinks Eldo.

Maybe he's just not a good traveller.

Frederic places a hand on Eldo and is saying words, but the noise of this room is too loud for her to hear any of what Frederic says, and so it is with epic relief that the fat man ushers Eldo through to another room, a silent tomb of a room, far quieter than you'd expect an adjoining room to this bacchanalian excess could possibly be. And as the door is closed it's almost as though the gathering in the next room simply disappears, or ceases to exist.

Eldo checks out this new location. It's made up like a 19th century library or study, with red-bound books on all the walls, and large, leather armchairs. The scent of leather and paper and wood is heavy in here. The curtains are thick, dark green, and knotted with short lengths of ochre-hued rope that end in decorative tassels. The whole room has the feel of a museum, like one of those rooms that someone well-known used to live in, and now everything is kept just as it always was, like a shrine to permanence in the face of the relentless march of time. This sensation is so strong that Eldo feels wrong as she slowly eases herself into one of the armchairs at Frederic's invitation, like she shouldn't be touching anything.

She leans forward and takes a cigarette from a metal case that Frederic is offering her. Her eyes find a large cube of polished marble on the table in front of her, which she recognises as a lighter. It looks heavy, and is. Her arm buckles a little until she readjusts her position and grip to counter the weight, presses the button down. There's a very pronounced 'click' and the flame that rises up from the marble cube is orange and thick and heavy.

Chanel No 5, am I right?

Asks Frederic.

What?

You're wearing No 5.

Eldo lifts her wrist to her face and inhales, oh yeah, she's fairly drenched in it.

Yes.

An unusual choice for someone like you.

Someone like me? Hey, it's 1994, baby. Rigid concepts are for the birds.

Frederic leans over and picks up a small glass bottle with practiced, delicate fingers. moves like a far nimbler, smaller, more agile man. Frederic presents the bottle to Eldo with a flourish.

Might I suggest this instead? It's an oriental. Been out of production for a long time. Quite valuable. And far more fitting for you and your work.

My work? What is it that you think I do?

Eldo takes the perfume. It doesn't have a spray cap, it's a splash bottle, so she removes the lid and passes the bottle under her nose. The scent hits Eldo fast: aldehydes, again, but much colder than the Chanel, with hints of incense and... is that pine? Whatever – cool, calm, and collected. Apt. Damn, this is a good match. But then Frederic interrupts the moment by speaking again, so Eldo puts the bottle down.

No need to be coy, Miss, I'm quite well versed in what it is that you do.

Oh yeah? And what is that exactly?

You get large quantities of product to the right person.

How the hell do you...?

Let's just say that we have a mutual friend.

Francis?

Frederic waves the suggested name away.

All you need to know right now is what I have to offer. Knowledge that I feel will be vital.

I'll go along with that, yeah.

This is one meeting of three, Miss Eldo, not including our brief talk on the plane last night, and eventually all will become clear.

Just Eldo, please. Now when you say 'all'...?

Principally the issue of the woman on the plane. That's where you'll begin, I'd imagine. The Stewardess. The Vampiress. Or perhaps you'll begin with the friend you're looking for. It's hard for me to predict where you'll go. But by the end, by the time you've reached three of three, I feel fairly confident that you'll be focusing on the confluence of it all.

The matter of how all the aspects you're concerned with tie together and coalesce. I should mention that I am outlining all of this here because in the dizzying confusion of the present, it is sometimes difficult to identify what matters and what doesn't.

Greatly appreciated, Frederic. Can I ask you a question about dreams?

Frederic smiles, extends a hand which seems to suggest *No more words* and says:

Well, I don't know the specificity of what has happened inside your mind, but it is my understanding that you had a dream that started all of this, correct? Subsequently, you may have found yourself concerned with how reality and dream are blending to become one. Don't worry, Miss Eldo, this is all quite…

Frederic waves his hand in a circular shape in the air

… normal. As far as we believe.

Nothing I love more than a mysterious we. Does that include the shit that went down in the chalet? With the shadow? A shadow is…

Frederic interrupts with that hand again.

I'm quite familiar with the concept of a shadow. Purely intellectually, of course. I've never actually experienced one in the flesh, if that's the right word. Anyway, I can assure you that yes, that topic will become clear too.

Cool, so lay it on me, Frederic. Tell me what you've got.

There is nothing for me to say. The answer you're looking for lies in the filter of the cigarette you're smoking.

Eldo is taking a drag, but these words still her inhalation. Tendrils of smoke spill out from her mouth. She holds her breath and eye contact with Frederic, who goes on.

In the filter you'll be able to feel a small ball, a pellet. All you need do is crush this between your fingers and a liquid will be released. You inhale, and your journey to find answers begins.

Really? You can't just tell me?

Frederic smiles, shakes his head, repositions himself in his seat, then leans in, places a hand to Eldo's knee (something Eldo isn't all that crazy about) and speaks a little lower, presumably an attempt to curry an environment of trust.

If I wished to explain heat to you, the words I used to describe it would be as nothing in the face of me providing you with a flame. That way you could experience the warmth it provides when close, the pain of its bite when touched, and how the heat grows colder the further you move it from yourself. What you're undergoing is not something one can always explain with words. This is something that you need to experience.

Intriguing.

Frederic nods. The smile on his face could be read as either friendly or threatening, it's hard to tell.

Crush the filter, Miss Eldo.

Eldo's forefinger and thumb run around the cotton filter tip, searching. Yes, there it is, a ball at the centre. Now that she's found it, she's kind of surprised that she hadn't noticed before. It seems so obvious now.

How do I know I can trust you?

Eldo asks.

I'm afraid I don't follow?

You want me to smoke some unknown substance in your presence – how do I know I can trust you?

Frederic laughs.

Oh, my dear lady, the simple answer is that you don't. The real question might be, what do you have to lose?

What indeed? May as well play the fucking creepy game and see what happens. So Eldo crushes the ball in the filter, which bursts with a soft, wet pop, and takes a deep inhale from the cigarette. Ooh, that seems alien and familiar at the same time. There's a metallic quality to the taste, but also something green. Frederic gets to his feet, smiles, moves an ashtray within Eldo's reach, gestures at the cigarette.

You're going to want to put that in here.

Eldo's brain tells her arm to put the cigarette in the glass dish, but as her arm begins its descent she realizes that she may not make it. She's already going. A dark cloud is building behind her eyes and her entire muscular system is mere seconds away from shutting down. She takes a gamble and decides to just let go of the cigarette and allow gravity to do the work for her, and as luck would have it the cigarette hits its target; the sound of the ashen tip hitting the glass is amplified, like an ocean liner colliding with an iceberg,

Eldo is vaguely aware of Frederic buttoning his jacket, and quietly gliding towards the door, the sounds echoing, the movements hazy. Everything is too quick and too slow at the same time. One thing's for sure, Frederic's voice reaches her ears with the words:

You'll want to close your eyes for the next part.

VI
5th April, 1994
16.20
One of Three

What follows is something that Eldo often finds herself recounting in the future to interested parties, those who have passed a silent assessment test and seem open to listening to and believing what she has to say. After all, this isn't the kind of thing that you can just tell anyone. These hushed revelatory moments usually happen in quiet corners, after stories have been swapped of things seen or experiences had while under the influence, and Eldo will lean closer to those she thinks are ready for it and say, in a hushed voice:

You want to hear something really crazy?

And even though the audiences are always carefully curated she still makes sure to preface the story with the heads up that she can only explain this by using language, which is a woefully inefficient tool for the job.

Words are dead, inert symbols, and this was… something different.

Is how she couches it when she has to explain the experience using nothing but language and hand gestures.

Anyway, back to the present.

This is what happens.

It all starts off in recognisable territory with a queasy wave of sound: a hazy suggestion of the reverie from the party next door, there's a shift in pitch as the door opens and closes and Frederic makes his escape, with the soft metallic click of the door mechanism falling back into place signalling his complete departure, and leaving the room shrouded in silence.

Eldo has half a mind to ignore Frederic's advice and keep

her eyes open, but she can't fight the heaviness of her eyelids, and they slide down like heavy steel shutters. The immediate surprise here is that instead of being met with darkness, or a haze of one colour or another, the kind of thing that normally happens when your eyes are closed, all Eldo can see is the very room she's sitting in.

Surely if my eyes are closed, I shouldn't be able to see the room.

Well maybe you're not seeing it, maybe you're just…

Wait… are you talking to yourself? Narrating this experience instead of simply experiencing it?

Uh…

Eldo pauses, unsure as to whether she's thinking these voices or saying them, sitting in the leather armchair and talking to herself. Either way, after what seems like both an eternity and a nanosecond of silence her internal voice concludes with

…yes?

Again, not clear whether that was spoken or thought.

She decides to concern herself less with the source of the voices and focus instead on how she could be seeing the room through closed eyelids, so she forgets about one issue (the words) and focuses on the other (the pictures); she opens her eyes for the briefest of moments, just a sliver, just to check, and then she lets them fall closed again. Okay. So, it's the same.

It's the same room, same view. Eyes open or closed.

But wait, that that's not quite the case, because now that she's easing into this experience, she notices that everything in this room (in the eyes-closed view of the room) is not exactly the same. Everything in here, the objects, but also the room itself, is covered in a very fine layer of hair, which flows as though there were a breeze rippling over it from somewhere, as though it were a meadow of hair.

And then she realises that that's not what it is at all.

Oh wow.

She needs to take a step back, so she takes a conscious deep breath, it's a tried and trusted first step to recalibrate, something she likes to do every time she takes a new substance for the first time. New things can be alarming, like riding a horse you've never sat on before. You need to get used to the rhythms and temperament of the horse, and sometimes these things can feel weird when you're encountering them for the first time, hence this one, deep, breath.

It's a reset button, a way of re-familiarising herself with the physicality of her body, with the weight of it, with the sensation that comes as she breathes. Put simply, it reminds you that you have a body. It's a great system and can really ground you at those points where you're somewhere new and starting to feel like you've grabbed hold of a balloon filled with helium which is lifting you up and up and up, taking your feet away from the safety of the ground you know so well. The only problem being that this time it doesn't work, because all sense of her own physical form has gone, there's nothing of her left, no body to take the breath, no sensation whatsoever.

Fucking typical.

So Eldo gives up on attaining any sense of the palpable, and focuses instead on the visual. To the room that she sees with her eyes closed. To the hair that covers everything.

Now in those yet-to-come future moments when Eldo is trying to explain this whole… situation… to an audience, she will refer to the hair not as hair to begin with, but as something closer to blades of grass. And while that's a better reference point to start with, she has to immediately interject, to interrupt herself, and explain that saying that it looks like blades of grass makes it sound larger than it is, when in fact these blades-of-grass-that-are-not-blades-of-grass are closer to the size and appearance of hairs. And then, in the face of the utter confusion that her audience are in at the motherfucking beginning of her damn story, she'll continue by saying:

Or… no, perhaps it's smaller even than hairs. And there's no wind running over them at all, even though they're gently swaying, even though it looks like there is a wind. Are you with me so far?

She'll ask the future crowds of people who are totally not with her.

So yes, there is no wind. No, the reason they're moving, gently swaying like miniscule hula dancers is because they're alive. And not alive in the way that a plant is alive. No, these are worms. Some kind of… nematode perhaps. But not in the way we know nematodes.

And then, to make it more complicated, she'll go on to point out that this is not many worms. This is one worm. One worm that runs through not only everything in the room, but also everything outside the room. Everything in existence. Hell, you'll even find the worm in the spaces where there are no objects. This is one worm with an infinite number of nodes that runs throughout the cosmos. Kind of like that forest which is all made of one tree.

What's that tree called, a panda? Poanda? Something like that.

Eldo knows that she knows what that one-tree-forest is called, but the facts and figures of the real world are distant and difficult. The whole eyes-open reality she knows and loves has become hard for her to recall or understand right now. It feels artificial to her, in the same way that a dream feels real when you're having it, but is so obviously a dream once you're awake. That's how she feels about the eyes-open world.

Instead, it's the eyes-closed realm that makes total sense to her. This is one worm that runs through everything. And everything ripples. And everything shimmers. It's just that simple. And yes, when she's back in the eyes-open world she knows how dumb that sounds, and yes language does a shitty job of explaining it all, but that's how it is.

And then she notices something else interesting – with her eyes closed everything is one colour. It only *appears* to have the same range of colours she can see with her eyes open because… what… her brain is being informed by the colours everything has when she sees them with her eyes open?

In those future moments when she's speaking to an audience she'll often slow down at this point and say:

Is that too… abstract?

If they need more then she'll elaborate by saying that it's like one of those optical illusions where you think everything is normal, but then you realise that it's all shades of red, or black and white, or something like that, and it's just your brain tricking you into thinking that a full range of colours is present. And once she removes the memory of the colours of the eyes-open world she understands that this eyes-closed world is a colour that Eldo's never seen before, which is, not to put it too mildly, something of a surprise. If people press her on this one colour that everything is she'll fall back on saying purple, even though it's not. But that's the closest our language and our understanding of colours can get.

And then, she momentarily forgets about all of this stuff with colours and finds herself focusing on the marble cigarette lighter on the table in front of her because she's suddenly able to move closer to the thing without actually moving any closer.

I must be zooming in

She thinks.

And hell, maybe that's not what's happening, maybe she's just sitting in the armchair and leaning closer and not realising it, but for all the world it really feels like her vision is zooming closer and closer and closer in on the lighter.

Not only that, but she's able to zoom far closer in than is normally possible. With the magnification and definition of something greater than any electron microscope.

She's able to zoom in so close that she can see that the worms that make up the physical body of the lighter are in turn made up of triangles, trillions of minuscule triangles that interconnect to make a whole. And with a movement which is more machine-like than human, she zooms out, and then in to other objects in the room. It's the same story everywhere, with everything she looks at: everything is made of worms, and when she zooms in, she can see that all of those worms are made of triangles, and everything tessellates beautifully. And then she notices something utterly enchanting.

The triangles are vibrating. And different materials vibrate at different rates or speeds, and the rate of vibration creates an audible sound, a sublime musical note.

To wit:

The triangles in the ashtray, which is made of marble, vibrate fast, but with little movement, as though they were in a room where a washing machine was on its spin cycle. The vibrations are so small that they're hard to notice. And the accompanying sound is high-pitched, falsetto, never-ending.

She zooms out, then pans left, and zooms in on the glass ashtray next to the lighter. The triangles inside the worms that make up the glass material vibrate too, but with a calmness, a serenity that is entirely lacking in the triangles that make up the lighter. And marble doesn't sound like glass. The sound that accompanies this vibration pattern is lower, more tranquil.

And then she zooms out, tilts up, and zooms in on the cigarette burning in the lighter, the tobacco and paper have a far more visible movement to them, as though the triangles were less densely packed together than in either the lighter (marble) or the ashtray (glass), and that movement is echoed in the sound it produces – a wavering, nauseating off-kilter atonal chorus.

And then she readjusts her view, finds the tip of the cigarette, and these burning triangles move and vibrate so much that they seem closer to a fluid, a liquid made of tiny intersecting shapes. The sound that accompanies them is a dizzying, carnivalesque nightmare.

And then she zooms out and finds the smoke that comes from the tip of the cigarette, and these are the freest, and most beautiful of all. Solid as liquid. Liquid as gas. The sound as the tessellating pieces vibrate against each other reminding her of the gentle chorus at the denouement of a Tchaikovsky opera she saw once. And if she had eyes at this moment, she would weep at the beauty of it all.

This makes so much sense. Everything is made of the same material. But it behaves differently depending on what it needs to be.

And then another voice inside her says

Everything in here, anyway.

And then she wonders if these triangles and vibrations and colours and worms are true for everything outside the room, so she moves.

Like a wind.

Through the walls.

And now she's out and over and above New York, and even though she's high above the streets there's no sensation of unease in the pit of her stomach, like there would be if she were looking out of a window from this height. Instead, there's nothing inside her but a burning curiosity to see, to see more, to see everything. With her eyes closed.

When she's zoomed out the scene looks like it always does, but when she zooms in, she can see that it's all worms, and then she learns that she can zoom in or out instantaneously – with a blink. What an experience this is.

And so she blinks, and the Mondrian-esque New York streets below become a vast field of interlocking, living shapes, moving in a non-existent breeze. All semblance of similarity to the familiar has been destroyed. She's seeing the city as a whole, but also simultaneously in the microscopic. Near and far are one. The small has become everything. Or maybe there simply is no difference between the large and the small. She's seeing a level of existence, of matter that no one has ever witnessed before.

And then she sees something completely different.

At first it looks like it might be smoke. But it's not. It's something else. And it's neither 'purple' nor 'made of worms.' It's something unlike anything else that she has seen so far.

The smoke is moving not-like-smoke, it's moving like-person. And she zooms in as close as she can to ascertain a better understanding, but it's indistinct, it's just smoke all the way down. A hazy labyrinth. No matter how close she goes, no matter how far she zooms in, the smoke remains smoke. Even the vibrations are unlike anything else she has looked at so far: not fluid, not intense, they seem to be moving to another pattern altogether. Creating a sound that is unlike any other that she has heard so far. And everything that she's picking out tells her one thing: that the like-smoke-person is not made of anything from this world.

What the fuck are you, buddy?

And at that point it looks up, straight at Eldo, straight into her closed eyes. And then it smiles that wickedly seductive smile it has (even though it has no recognisable facial features in this eyes-closed world) and that is when Eldo does not feel fear exactly, but is reminded of the existence of fear.

This is the vampire.

Here in New York.

Walking the streets like a person.

Made of something that does not exist in our world.

Mother. Fucker.

And it's here that Eldo notices that the smoke has… lights (?) aimed at it from every direction. Or perhaps it's drawing light to it from everywhere, focusing it, like it's some kind of… light magnet? Either way, this light is casting shadows of the thing, but these shadows aren't normal, oh no, they are unrestricted by boundaries, they pass through everything, stretch far further than they should. Without clearly realising what she's doing or how she's doing it, Eldo follows the shadow trails, taking epochal steps across the planet, travelling unimaginable distances in the blink of an eye, faster even. But because she's so fascinated by this, because she wants so much to understand what she's seeing, the enormity of what's happening to her right now, the vastness of what she's doing, evades her completely.

Information is hurtling around her head at a supersonic speed, but for one reason or another she can process all of it with ease. It's almost as though she has the ability to inspect each datum as it passes, as though it were falling in slow-motion, and she can reach out, grab it with her hands, turn it this way and that to understand all the truths it has to reveal, and then release it to continue its journey.

The only problem is that each piece of information seems just as important as every other. She can't remember what the Eldo in the eyes-open world is looking for.

What am I looking for?

What is she looking for? Or, more to the point, why has Frederic sent her here?

Presumably this all has something to do with her quest to find… fuck.

What am I doing in…?

But the name of the city she's in is information that she can't access right now.

Think you fucker, think!

And Eldo flies all over the world, with this question at the front of her mind – what is she looking for? What is important to her? Where, the cock, is she?

And then, as she flies over a particularly hectic area, she sees something glimmer, like a jewel catching the light, and she descends, and what she discovers is almost too beautiful to understand.

The jewel moves through space and, when she zooms in, has a vibration pattern in its tessellated triangles that is like a symphony and a requiem at once. And although there's no physical sensation in this realm, no feeling, no texture, despite the fact that her body has no presence whatsoever, she just *knows* that if she could reach out and touch this jewel it would feel wonderful. And then something glitters inside the jewel, she reaches out, takes hold of it, and it's a word, and she reads it, and everything comes flooding back to her because the word is:

Annick.

This jewel is Annick. She's in this place because she's looking for her, and here she is. And, sure, she's unable to make out any of the recognisable features of her face or hair or body, but the jewel has the unmistakeable feel of Annick, through and through.

And then she sees something inside her that she hasn't seen before (is she learning to navigate this place better?), she sees intention. And although the jewel is not yet moving, she can see where it intends to move. The location is far away for the jewel, but just a mere few paces for Eldo.

She takes those paces, goes to the location where the jewel is going to go, where it intends to go. She looks around, triangulates her position, burns that place into her mind so that she's able to access it later, and then journeys back to see the beautiful jewel one more time. One more time before…

… wait… what's that scent… lavender?

VII
5th April, 1994
16.21
Cuir Absolue

Eldo gets the briefest flash of the leather and book clad room before her eyes close again and she gets the sensation that she's falling backwards.

There's the sound of water moving, and she finds herself wondering why it echoes so, why it sounds as though she were in a completely uncarpeted room, and then she opens her eyes and realizes that that's exactly where she is. She's in a bathroom.

Everything here is fitted out in light colours, rose, pastels, etc, with a mixture of a soft overhead electric light, and hazy sunlight coming from a window she can't see or locate. She turns her head in the direction of the sounds of the water and sees a familiar figure in the bath. Of course it's her. Who else could it be?

She appears to be naked, but the surface of the bathwater is covered in so many bubbles that she can't be sure of this. What she is sure about is that every part of her that's above the water, the hair, the eyes, the lips, is all so perfect that she could cry.

What happened to the chalet?

She asks.

She cocks her head, not like she's looking for an answer to Eldo's question, more like she heard a noise and is now wondering where it came from, and what it was. Although, hell, what does she know? Maybe she's just thinking. Either way a confused look clouds up those beautiful eyes.

A chalet? I don't know that word.

Sorry, you must be another shadow. A different shadow.

The look of confusion melts away as understanding flows through her and a transformation occurs, like a snowflake coming to rest on warm skin, and slowly but surely her more usual confidence and surety comes back.

No. None of the shadows are different. We all stem from the same source. We cannot be different.

Poor choice of words on my behalf. So, where are we anyway?

She narrows her eyes at Eldo, assessing something.

I'm here, but you... you're not here, you're somewhere else. Somewhere... urban, I think you say.

So, this is just a vision?

Oh no, you're where you are, and I'm where I am, you're just seeing across distances, big distances, vast distances.

She narrows her eyes even more, as though this was helping her to see the truth of Eldo, and she goes on:

I don't know how you're doing this, but you've ingested something. Something blue.

So, what you're saying is that I'm not here, but I'm seeing here? We're far apart?

She shifts ever so slightly in the water. The sound of the water lapping against the sides of the bath, against her body, and the curiously audible sound of her mouth opening as her lips part is almost too much.

Yes, in terms of distance, and time, and understanding.

How can we be far apart in time?

How can you find yourself watching someone who is no longer here?

You can't.

I take it you're not a fan of photography then?

She finishes her sentence and takes a glass of champagne from the side of the bath, sips from it.

So you're, what, like, a photograph, a recording?

No, we're shadows, all of us. You know this already. All I'm doing is pointing out that there are ways of seeing someone or something that is no longer here. Keep an open mind and you'll go far.

She shifts her position in the water, playing a game of hide and reveal with Eldo, choosing which parts of her body to conceal under the bubbles, and which to show.

She starts by lifting her torso just enough so that the merest suggestion of her breasts is given as her body moves through the water. The pool is heart shaped. The walls of the bathroom are tiled in red and white. She raises her head and drains her champagne glass, one leg lifts, some of her thigh is revealed. Suddenly Eldo's convinced that the temperature in the room must have risen, and a fine sweat breaks out on her forehead and upper lip. The smell of rose oil is everywhere. She tastes salt in her mouth. Scent, taste. Oh, how she missed details like this in the eyes-closed world.

Eldo rests her arms on the side of the bathtub, and then her forehead against her arms. The ceramic of the bathtub is cooling, but the flesh of her arms is almost unbearably hot. It's hard for her to think, to discuss the topic of space and time with this woman, so she brings her head up and takes the topic down to a simpler level.

How did you end up in this place?

Men put me here. All you have to do is look like this, and men put you in all kinds of places. In all kinds of positions.

She smiles, and the softest laugh escapes her.

Eldo changes the subject by saying:

What do you want from me?

From you? Nothing. Nothing but your complete attention.

Eldo blinks slowly, her feelings towards this creature deeply ambiguous, and a sound builds up inside her which is released as a sigh. The sigh builds, rattles her teeth, becomes an echoing vibration that creates a rising sensation in her gut, a lifting, as though she were in an elevator. Moving upwards.

The echo inside her body slowly dissipates and Eldo opens her eyes. For once, she's not somewhere new. She's still in the room that looks and feels like a library at Cuir Absolue. The room she was in just a moment ago.

The rising vibration that carried her out of the scene with the shadow has moved into the room now, into the objects around her, so that everything seems to be vibrating as though it was one interlinked crystal glass. It takes a moment for all the elements of the room (walls, windows, floor, ceiling, objects, etc) to separate, retain their unity, for the resonance to die away. And once the room is still again, she inhales deeply and is overwhelmingly relieved to realise that she has control of her body again.

And as she pushes herself up from the leather seat, she finds herself… interested in the feel of the leather. Maybe not interested exactly, perhaps it's more that the texture surprises her. Not just the tactility, but the sensation of being able to feel again.

The eyes-closed realm had no touch, no taste, no scent. Man, it's been too long. Although she got a taste of the physical world in the bathroom with the shadow, what she's experiencing here is far fuller, far more affecting. She could feel the objects in this room for hours. But a responsible, trustworthy, reliable part of her knows she has to race back to the Chelsea (because now that she's back in the here and now of New York, or how it appears to be, at least, she needs to focus on the quest that is slowly coming back to her, piece by piece) and it's on auto-pilot that she finds herself picking up a pencil from the table in front of her and writing down a series of numbers and letters and symbols that are going round and round in her mind:

48.8600° N, 2.3266° E.

She has no idea what this means, but she knows that it needs to be recorded while it's fresh because it will be important to a future version of herself. And anyway, this present version of Eldo is enrapt by the solid feel of the wood of the pencil, the gentle brush of graphite against paper, the sound it makes, the trace it leaves behind. The sound of two physical objects interacting and resulting in a third object, a trail. A trace. Something entirely new. And as she's writing out the long string of numbers she remembers something about how two objects never actually touch each other – they repel each other – the molecules never meet, and yet here she is, writing legible numbers with one object on another. What a world this is.

She gets to her feet, her legs move heavily at first, but eventually get her to the door. When she lifts a hand to open it, she realizes that her sleeve is slightly damp, lifts her arm even further up to her face, inhales, and gets a hit of the lavender water that the shadow was bathing in.

Jesus. How is this possible?

She pulls the large heavy door open, the silence is broken by the swell of the sound of voices and the smell of cannabis resin. Oh yeah, that's right, the party. It's still in full swing. As she steps out amongst them and closes the door behind her she's relieved to see that no one seems to pay any attention to her whatsoever. Almost as though she were still in the dream, invisible, on another plane. Observing, rather than participating.

The first thing of note that happens in this party room is that Eldo is brought to a halt by a finger that stabs her in the chest. The owner of the finger is a young woman, aged about 22 or 23, who is wearing a silver backless dress, has a short bob haircut that Eldo finds very familiar, and speaks with what can only be a Kansas accent that's trying to hide under a phony (but fairly well assembled) east coast twang.

Do you have the time?

Eldo pulls her sleeve down to look at her watch, but then remembers that she doesn't wear a watch, so instead she just says:

Afraid not.

Don't be afraid of anything. Here, I have something for you.

She brings out a pocket watch on a chain and hands it over to Eldo. She takes it, says thank you, and inspects it: It's a silver casing with a button on the top where (presumably) you press it, and the cover mechanism flips open to reveal the watch inside.

So... what time is it?

Asks the bobbed Kansas woman, and Eldo presses the button and the hinge operates and the thing flips open elegantly. But inside there's no timepiece, instead the entire thing is filled with hashish. It's packed so tightly that there's an impression of the shape of the lid on the top. Like you might see in the contents of a tin of shoe polish, or a plug of chewing tobacco, if that's a better reference.

Well I'll be. This is for me?

The bobbed Kansan pulls herself closer and nods insistently, no words, as though this were a matter of great urgency, or perhaps simply because she now lives a silent existence. And then she moves back into the crowd, maintaining eye contact with Eldo with every step, until she loses sight of her, and she's swallowed by the throng.

Eldo keeps moving, wondering where the hell she's seen that woman before (Berlin?), and as she's walking through the crowd she hears the word 'Fougére' from somewhere and she turns and says:

Did you say Fougére?

To no one in particular, but as luck would have it the person who said it is standing right in front of her and nods and says:

Yeah, the Artist. He's over there.

The speaker points and Eldo identifies the figure – a man, holding a drink and cigar in one hand, his head thrown back with a bark of a laugh that just tells you beyond a shadow of a doubt that the man is a monumental asshole.

And suddenly Eldo finds herself consumed by a desire to make her way across the room to stand in front of the artist. Even though she has far more important things to do and doesn't really understand why this diversion is necessary. She pushes her way through the crowd, nobody moves without her having to make a concerted effort to physically move them out of the way. Someone passes Eldo a thick joint, the paper stained and dripping with brown oil. She takes a drag, and the first puff (as always) tickles her throat considerably, but she manages to keep the cough down, and the second inhale is much easier, and the third even easier than that, and Eldo's already feeling the benefit.

When Eldo reaches Fougére the artist is holding court, speaking to a small group who are in rapt silence, hanging on his every word. Eldo pays no attention to the words that are coming from the artist's mouth, because she couldn't give a shit about them. Instead, she just studies the man's face, lets her eyes travel from mouth to eyes to hair to nose, dissecting him, feature by feature, as though she could get a sense of who the whole person is by breaking him down into the constituent parts. She takes another drag on the joint she was passed, inhales a billowing cloud of dense, swirling smoke, and looks at the people on either side of her. To her left is a man in a well-fitting suit, wearing a monocle, a thin pencil moustache. To her right is a blonde woman in a long, blue, shimmering backless dress. She passes the joint to the blonde. Natch. And then she turns her attention back to the artist, this grotesque lumbering prick, who either has recently, or will soon, create an artwork with Annick.

Her Annick.

Eldo's Annick.

Fuck this guy.

And the next thing Eldo knows her right hand is bleeding and there's a throng of concerned vintage partygoers clamouring around Fougére, making sure he's alright, and his nose is pouring crimson, and there are two large men holding Eldo firmly by the shoulders and escorting her back to the elevator. And although Eldo has no memory of what must have just happened, a smirk sets up residence on her face and she thinks four words:

Motherfucker had it coming.

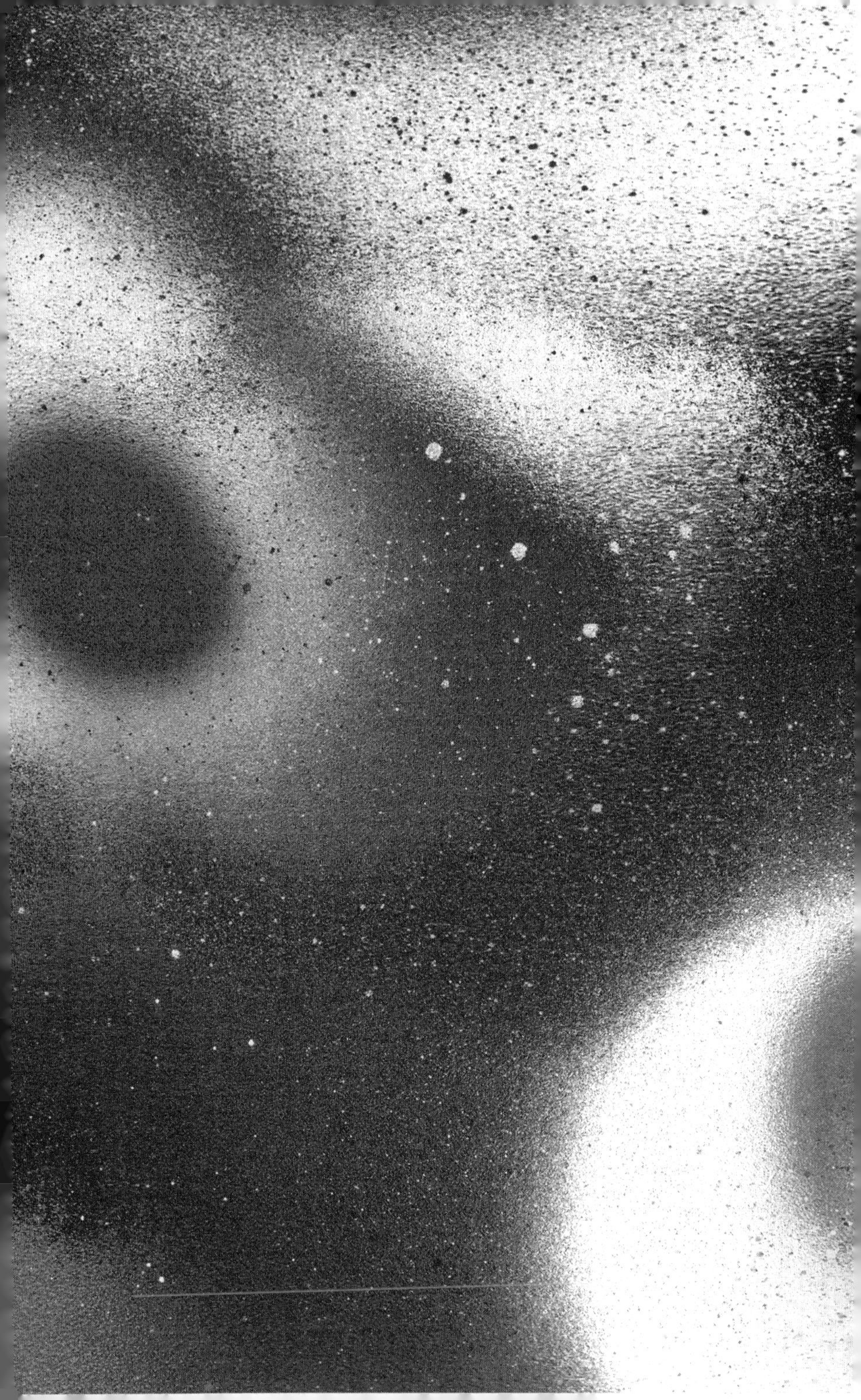

VIII
5th April, 1994
17.05
The Chelsea

Back at the Chelsea. And Eldo's through the door and makes straight for the reception desk, which is manned now by a woman in a black dress, white collar, tattoo creeping up one side of her neck. What is that? Some kind of snake? Octopus? Anyway…

Can I help you, Miss?

Hi, yeah, I'm looking for Annick.

Annick?

She's a guest here. I am too.

Oh, you must be the woman who left the note.

That's me.

The lady behind the counter makes a face like she just tasted something unpleasant, and then goes on to say:

I'm afraid she just left, Miss.

Serious?

Serious.

Eldo lets her head fall against the counter, not meaning it to come across as an aggressive gesture, more one of frustration, but the woman clearly doesn't take it this way as she stops talking entirely and her eyes flick first to Eldo's crudely bandaged hand (after cutting it on Fougére's teeth) and then down to the floor. And even though Eldo's not looking at her she can hear the tattooed lady's cogs whirring and can make out the basic shape of the narrative she's putting together from the visual cues Eldo's giving her, and it is with the sensation of an ass that she stands tall, apologises, reigns it all in.

Maybe it's just that her hand hurts more than she was anticipating. Maybe she needs another diazepam. Maybe this whole fucking quest with its monsters and time skips and inter-dimensional doorways leading from one realm to another is just getting a bit much for her. Whatever. She takes a deep breath and reacquaints herself with the way she needs to behave in the eyes-open place (if that is where she is).

She smiles and asks the lady if she knows where Annick went, but she doesn't. All she knows is that she checked out. Handed her key in. Totally gone. Okay then, so it's definitely time for some diazepam.

She gives the lady her room number and she turns to get her key, brings it back to her accompanied by 14 slips of paper. 13 of which have the same message on:

Serge called.

With the 14th being a slight variation of this:

Tell that Eldo fucker to call Serge.

This is the point at which Eldo realises she doesn't have her mobile phone anymore, as she pats herself down and discovers that it's not in her pockets, and she has no memory of seeing it anywhere in the room upstairs. No memory of seeing it at all since she was in the city.

Fuck.

She thanks the lady at the desk in as sincere a manner as she can muster right now, is briefly reminded of the impact she had on that ant that ran into her shoe and how she could impact the world simply by existing, and makes her way back upstairs.

Her first step is to stand in front of the elevator and press the button, but then she has a flash of the elevator at Cuir Absolue and a shiver runs through her and she decides that it's probably a better idea to take the stairs. She arrives at her floor with a not insignificant amount of breathlessness, but at least she was in charge, moving at her own pace, not under control from some machine. She unlocks the door fast and bursts into her room like she's robbing the place, starts looking everywhere for her phone, but comes up with nothing, and just as she's beginning to panic and gets to wondering why mobile phones don't have alarms on them that make a noise when you whistle or clap your hands or something, and is running through all the possible means at her disposal for how the hell she's going to get in touch with Serge, there's a knock at her door, and she opens it without checking who it is through the spyhole, and is monumentally overwhelmed with relief to see that it's Serge.

He's a mess: clothes disheveled, eyes sunken, and a thin layer of grease all over his skin, which looks a lot more pale than usual. His skin, not the grease. Eldo is so surprised to see Serge standing there that at first she doesn't even invite him in.

Serge. Man. What the hell?

Berlin went bad.

The correct social procedure finally comes to Eldo, and Serge is invited inside and starts to look a lot more comfortable now that he's ensconced away from the world of 'well anything can happen here' that we all suffer when we're not safely locked away in a hotel room with Eldo.

With Serge in the room there's a brief back and forth as Eldo confirms that today is indeed the 5th of April, which means she either slept through or blacked out the 4th completely, because she thought that was today. Then she gets a bit frantic because she's lost a whole day and every second counts and all that, but then she takes a deep breath again and says:

Spilt milk, spilt milk, spilt milk...

And then she apologises for all of this, because the person to focus on right now is Serge.

Serge sits down, takes out a cigarette and tries to light it, but his hand is shaking so much that the flame can't find the tip, so Eldo takes hold of his hands, and guides the fire to the end of the trembling cigarette that's dangling from his lips. Eldo fills the moment in which Serge is silent, but clearly preparing himself to speak, by sitting down on the bed and taking out the pocket watch that the lady at Cuir Absolue gave her and pinching off a healthy amount of resin and rolling herself a joint and when Serge does finally speak his voice doesn't sound entirely like his voice and he's frantic and making way more mistakes with his English than he normally does. But Eldo doesn't correct him, what is she anyway, a jerk?

Okay.

Says Serge.

Here's what happened:

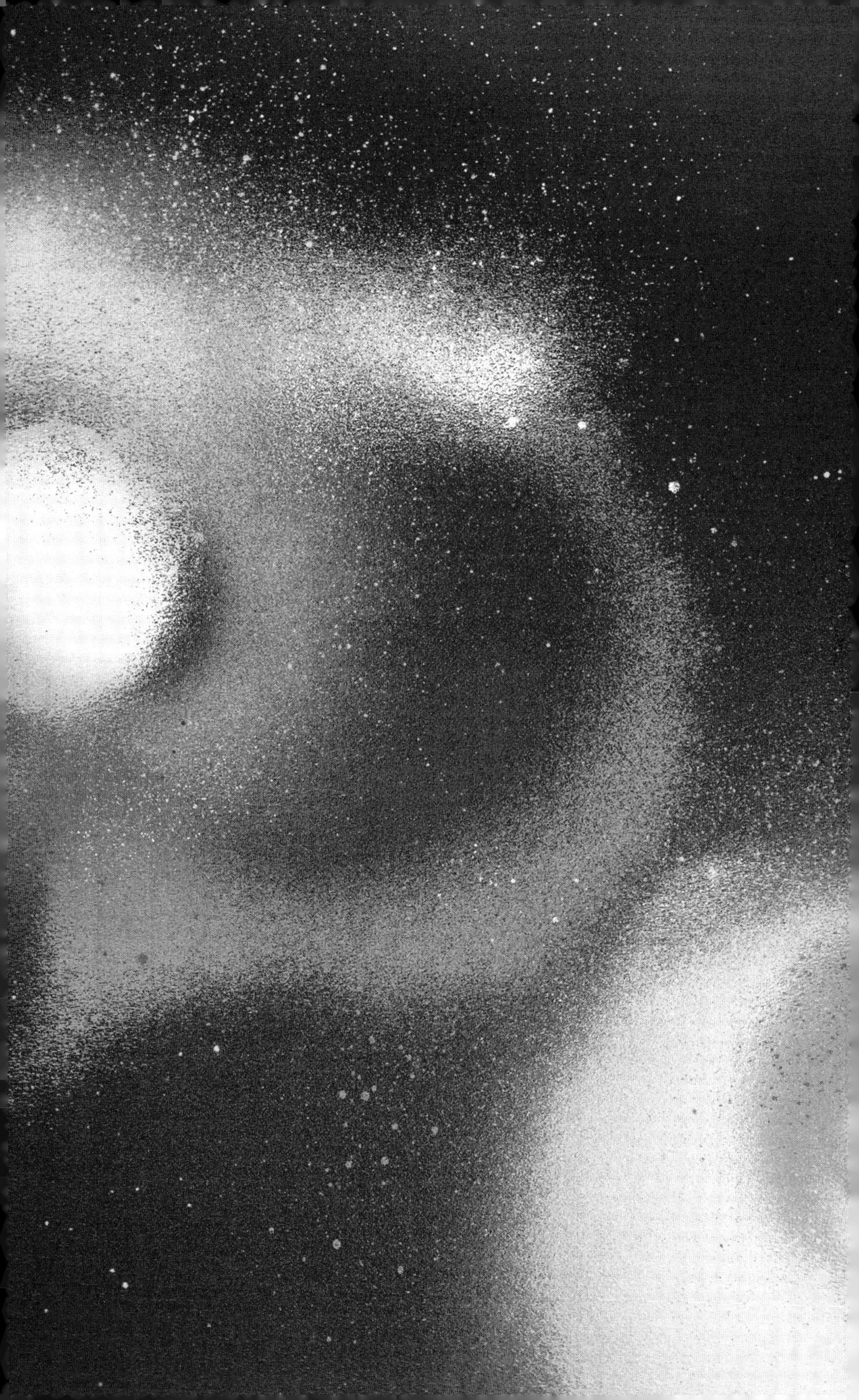

IX

4th April, 1994

19.12

(Serge's experience of) Berlin

So I never been to Berlin before. Hell, never been to Germany before, so first of all there's all that stuff to deal with: The language, the system, the signs, it was all so confusing man, I can't tell you. I kept thinking:

Well hell, people come to Germany for the first time every day, so I'm bound to get the hang of this

But shit no. I just couldn't find my feet over there.

And anyway, then there was the meet. That fucking meet.

The whole shitshow was set up to start at a café, and then we go over to a cinema in Berlin-Mitte or something. Some old crumbling, falling apart kind of place. Showing old movies. Enough people there that we no look like anything untoward is going on, but not enough people to really 'see' you, you dig? That's the whole plan, anyway.

So there's three of them, the guys I'm meeting: one old, and the other two are kind of young. I don't know, about our age maybe? More or less.

We meet at the café, and it's late in the day, but for some reason it's both really quiet and really bright, and I'm just not digging the vibe at all. And they no serve tea, just coffee. And I no like coffee. And I have to eat something called Maultaschen, yeah, I have no idea either, and the guys have not too much English, and my German is just nicht existent, you know? So the whole thing is really hard and... hey, is that hash? Could you roll me one of those? Thanks.

So anyway, we split the café scene and make for the

cinema. And the whole thing is starting to feel a little okay for, like, the first time since I arrived. Not great, just a little okay. And sure, it's grey, and cold as all hell, but I'm getting that:

I'm in another country

feeling in a good way for the first time. You know, different air, different scenery, general good vibes. And we get to the cinema and the chick behind the counter is just… too much. There's no other way I can put it. She's nice, with these killer eyes, and even though I've only just met her, hell, only just seen her, there's a feeling there of something… more, you know? I can't explain it, but it's there.

Thanks man.

You got a light?

Okay.

Anyway, everything's going well all of a sudden. And then we go inside to see the movie, and that, my friend, is where it all goes to shit.

Now the place is a rep cinema, and they're showing Francis Ford Coppola's Bram Stoker's Dracula, which is weird, because that's not rep, and if you're going to show a Coppola film then why not show one of his famous ones?

Ugh. That's not true, man. You know who Coppola is. He made, like, The Conversation, and Apocalypse Now, and… seriously? Okay, The Godfather, you heard of that? Okay, good, well that's Coppola. But showing this Dracula film he made is just…

Huh?

Really?

On the plane?

Was it the same one?

Well what was it like?

Yeah, I know it was Dracula, but was it all, like, baroque and ostentatious – huge costumes, lots of colours, cheesy acting and… yeah? Okay cool, so you know the film I'm talking about.

So anyway, we go in and get to talking business. And these guys want to shift two metric tons of heroin, so I'm thinking, like:

Cha-ching!

And we're talking about all the ins and outs of it, and then the film gets to this point where Keanu Reeves goes into this room… Keanu Reeves. He's an actor. No, I think that's his real name. He's American, from, like, Hawaii or something.

He was in that Bill and Ted film.

I no know, Bill or Ted I guess.

Anyway, so he goes into this room and these three vampire chicks appear from nowhere and start like seducing him and…

Oh yeah?

You remember that bit?

Okay, so you'll get this.

Hey… this is rolled this way too tight, man. Is not drawing properly.

Nah, I tried that.

Okay, well you try it then.

Yeah, thanks, that's pulling now.

Shit man, this is good shit, where you get it?

For free? Damn.

So anyway, it's this grand seduction blood-letting scene filling the screen, and the talk has died down a bit as one by one all of us has started giving the film our undivided attention, you know, taking it all in.

And that's when I see her.

Down at the front. Turning to look at us.

I'm already on the alert anyway, looking out for anyone who might be listening to us. And although this chick is probably too far away to be listening, she's clearly watching us because she's like, turned around in her seat and watching us. She pay no attention to the screen.

But here's the fucking thing, man:

She's the chick from the movie we're watching. I mean, same hair, clothes, make-up, everything. And I know you get people who go to shit like Rocky Horror Picture Show all dressed up and...

Aw man, really?

No?

It's one of those weird things, everyone dressing up in suspenders and... no?

Okay, well take my word for it. It happens.

Anyway, this film isn't like that, I mean, as far as I know. It's not the kind of thing that people dress up to go and see. But there she is, man. Large as life. And it's not even like she's in costume. It's more like she's just been cut straight from the screen and placed there. This isn't someone dressing like the character, this is the chick from the film. No doubt. And just as I was thinking all this stuff, and that it's all too crazy for words, that's when she stands up and comes towards us.

Now, she no walk over, it's more like she glides, like she's on wheels or roller skates or one of those round-and-round things at the airport, or something. And she goes right past us, eyes somehow on all of us at the same time, and God damn if we aren't all just eyes on her and looking nowhere else, and anyway... she go right past and reach this doorway which, I guess, goes to the bathroom. And it's got this heavy, dusty, old red curtain hanging down in front of it, and she pulls the curtain back and moves through the doorway, and the curtain stay hanging like she holding it even after she let go, and she pivots, faces us, but keep moving in the same direction, away, through the door, and she still fixes us all with this look, and sure, not gonna lie, I was a little messed up at the time (what can I say, meets get me nervous, so a little something to fight the nerves always helps), but I swear to you that this next part was real:

So she locks eyes with me and these words go through my head, like, I can hear her voice but her lips don't move, and the voice goes:

Come with me, get out of your seat and follow me wherever I want you to go.

And before I know what's going on, I'm getting to my feet, and following her, and the Germans are yelling something at me in German, which I guess is probably something like:

What are you doing, where the fuck are you going?

We've got business to discuss here!

And so on.

But I pay them no mind, because I know exactly what it is I want, and where I'm going. And that's with her, anywhere she goes, for ever.

The next minute, I'm standing in the bathroom. And I don't know if it's the ladies or the men's or what. All I know is that she is standing in front of me, against a row of sink basins. And behind her there's a whole wall of mirror, and in the reflection I can see me, and what's behind me (two rows of cubicles, facing each other), and everything in here is dark red. And the only thing I can't see (but I don't notice at the time, somehow) is that she has no reflection in the mirror.

Oh, and I forgot to say, this bathroom's got a whole Shining vibe going on.

Really?

What you even talk to people about?

Okay, it's a creepy hotel style bathroom, you can dig that?

A lot of red.

Like, a lot.

Anyway, there was a sound in the air, like a music track was playing, like a cold wind was blowing, all at the same time. But none of that was going on, the whole scene just had this mood that you could feel with your hands. And that was all pretty freaky to start with.

So. Anyway. Bathroom.

There's no one else in there apart from me and her. And then suddenly there's actual music playing in there, but I can't see the speakers anywhere. And although I'm no expert, I could swear that it's the music that was playing in my head just a moment before. And she's just staring at me with this... look. I can't describe it, because no words provide justice to her face, to her eyes. It was just something so... knowing and personal and sexual, like all together. And she says one word, I mean, I say said, but she no say it, I just heard it in my head, but loud, echoing, reverberating around the stalls. She said:

Eldo.

No, I swear man, that's exactly what she said. And then this stench hit me. This real big smell. Like, it had been going on the whole time, but all of a sudden it multiplied by a factor of, I no know, like a thousand. And it not necessarily a bad smell, but it just so strong, and I can feel this pressure on my throat, like my collar too tight, and all the time she's just standing there, like, ten feet away from me, smiling. And the smell is growing, thick and heavy and sweet, and some thing is restricting my throat real bad now, like it's actually getting difficult for me to breathe, so I get to panicking.

Now, I just had this sensation that something was choking me, so I let fly with a punch. And even though she's standing all the way over there, far away man, and there's no way in hell I could reach her, my fist collides with something soft and fleshy, and before I really know how this happened, she's suddenly much closer to me, reeling, blood pouring from her nose and the corner of her mouth.

I have no idea, dude, no idea.

I wasn't punching at her, I was just trying to get rid of whatever it was that was gripping my throat. I thought it was just the smell, man. So anyway, she's stumbling back now, and I'm wondering if I should step up and apologise or run the hell out of there, and then she fixes me with this look, those eyes, that gaze. And I just know that shit's about to go down, get bad…

and

I

run.

Through the red curtain, and away from the images of that face running through my mind:

Her smile, her eyes, her skin.

I run straight past the Germans, who, again, were yelling something in German, and I'm figuring at this point I've soured the deal kind of bad, no doubt, but I need to get out of there and away from her before she comes for me again, fixes me with those eyes, so I just keep going.

And I just run, run and run, out of the cinema, and past the girl at the counter. And even though I'm terrified, I still take the time to check out the girl one last time because just damn. I only looked at her for a second, but it's like her face make me feel clearer and more positive, and like yeah I can get away from all this. But the whole meet went to shit man, all fucked up. So I come here.

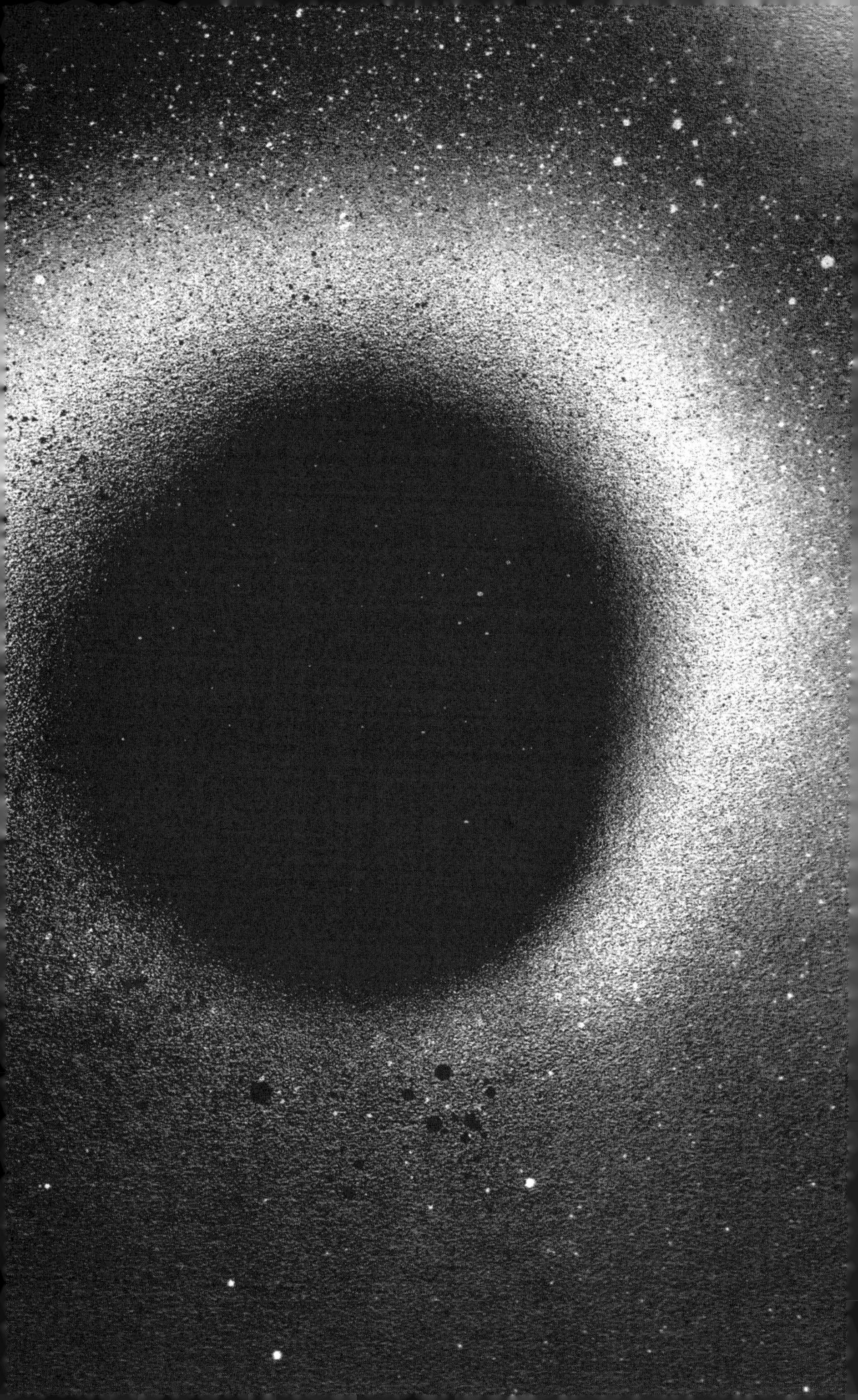

X

5th April, 1994

17.37

The Chelsea

Eldo finds all this stuff Serge is saying kind of crazy. Not crazy like it's unbelievable, more like crazy in the way that it bears a lot of similarities to what she's been experiencing. So she tells Serge about what happened on the plane, and, of course, about the woman from the movie. They spend a lot of time cross-referencing their memories of her face, her eyes, her hair, they even try drawing her at one point, but neither of them can draw for shit. And then Eldo asks Serge to describe that smell in the cinema. In detail.

I no know, man. Something. I no know how to describe it.

That's not really good enough. Did it smell like something else?

Like I say, I no know man, you're the smell dude. What you think it is?

Eldo has a pretty good idea what that smell is, but she really wants to hear Serge say what it is without giving him too much information. The best way would be for Serge to identify the scent from a selection, without guidance. And even though none of this has anything to do with the quest to save Annick, Eldo figures that there's got to be a reason that all this stuff is coming up now, and so, at Eldo's request, they both end up heading on out to find a perfume store, where Eldo will get Serge to smell a few things, and one of these things will be oud (although Serge doesn't know this yet), and then they'll see.

Yes, perfect.

A quick aside – to Eldo's mind what she's doing here is being flexible, responding to a situation. Now that Serge has sledge-hammered his way into New York it seems to her that this is the right thing to do. And sure, there are some who might say that Eldo takes her eye off the prize for a bit here – forgetting about Annick and where she might be and her quest to save her – and those people may be right, but Eldo is Eldo.

So anyway, before they go outside, and because Serge is still feeling pretty broken up by the whole Berlin thing, they decide to smoke a few more joints, you know, for the stress of it all. Then they shoot the breeze for a bit, drink a glass of water each, and head on out.

As Eldo closes the door to the hotel room she asks herself:

Am I in a dream right now, or is this really happening?

The fact that Serge turned up at the door of her hotel room in New York out of the blue feels weird.

How did he know where I was? Did I even tell him?

Eldo just can't fucking remember.

And without really paying attention to any of their journey from the hotel to the station, Eldo and Serge find themselves on a subway train, wearing sunglasses, hurtling through a dark tunnel underneath New York City. Surrounded by the stench of limestone and ammonia and bile and plastic. And because there's barely anyone else on the train, Eldo gets out a glass pipe that seems to have magically materialized in her pocket, and she and Serge take a few hits of the Cuir hashish. And god damn if the stuff isn't great, not getting either of them too tired or hungry (which is good, because Eldo has little to no time for food or sleep most of the time) but just nicely relaxed and talkative and in tune with each other, if, perhaps, slightly more paranoid than usual.

There's one guy down the other end of the car who gives them a few looks every now and then (maybe it's only a few looks, but Eldo's resin-soaked brain gives unprecedented meaning to every glance thrown her way), but otherwise everything's cool and they're just moving on to a random new topic in the free association conversation they're having when the train pulls into a stop and some other God damn people get on.

Now this new crowd just look like trouble from the get-go, and are clearly wise to what the smell is, for sure. They immediately make Eldo and Serge as being the sources of it too, not that that was ever going to be a challenge. Neither Eldo nor Serge are really trying to hide the pipe, and who on earth wears sunglasses on the subway at night anyway? That can only ever mean one thing. And that one thing is that the person wearing sunglasses is wearing them because they have eyes with a red raw story to tell. The final straw comes when Eldo takes a packet of Benzedrine out of her pocket, pops two, takes one, and hands Serge the other. At the sight of this the whole group shambles over. Eyes hungry.

You guys holding?

Eldo looks at Serge, then at the group, then back at Serge.

Shit.

Fuck.

Shit fuck.

Eldo's got no real interest in helping this crowd. First of all, she seems to have instantly taken against them for some reason she can't put her finger on. Something innate, subconscious: about the way they dress, or talk, or hold themselves. Hard to say. But a second, and more decisive factor is that Eldo's not holding enough to be sharing. Or she just doesn't want to share. Either way it gives her an easy out.

Eyes back to the group.

Sorry guys, Fresh out.

But the crowd aren't really buying Eldo's story, which is understandable because she didn't really put much conviction into her inflection at all. And the subsequent argumentative response of theirs just adds fuel to Eldo's belief-fire that these people are a bad crowd and not worth the time. But then they start getting loud, and from here everything gets a little bit, well, hectic.

There are threats and raised voices and everyone standing way too close to each other and whatnot, and the guy at the other end of the car quietly gets to his feet and nonchalantly makes his way over to the door connecting this car to the next, and gets the fuck away from this potential conflict, and just as Eldo reads this action as a great big fucking bell ringing out that something is about to go south in quite an astonishing way something terrible and beautiful happens.

Everyone's on their feet, Eldo and Serge slowly moving backwards, the group moving ever closer, and everything is lit from these spotlights that seem to have suddenly been turned on in the ceiling of the train, and all of them are right in front of the doors which will open as soon as the train stops. And as the brakes howl and the train nears a halt Eldo turns and looks through the glass and standing on the other side of the door are three cops. Boys in blue. New York's finest. They're already giving Eldo and the crowd some looks that suggest that they've identified the lot of them as troublemakers, and that shit's about to get real, heads are about to get busted. It doesn't even make much of a difference at this stage that the unmistakable scent of hashish permeates the train.

Two words fly through Eldo's mind:

Think fast.

The doors open and the cops flow in straight away, like water, and they make a beeline for the two foreigners, which isn't all that much of a surprise, because both Eldo and Serge are mumbling and sweaty and now everyone is talking and there are a number of hands grabbing and pushing at Eldo and a memory from deep deep down in her addled mind comes bubbling up to the surface like methane in stagnant water and Eldo cracks her neck as she twists her head to one side, and she folds her thumb over her little finger, leaving three fingers extended on her right hand and places them on the left hand side of her neck, and makes sure to hold this gesture until the cops see it.

One of them does and a light goes on behind his eyes, and he taps one of the others and gestures at Eldo and this second guy looks and there's a light behind his eyes too, and these two cops silently communicate to the third through glances and gestures and all of a sudden the cops seem to have developed an interest in the other group, and now there are no hands on Eldo or Serge and the two foreigners look at each other with an awesome relief and then step off the train. Unworried, and unhassled.

They make their way down the platform and Serge looks back, over his shoulder at the drama taking place on the carriage, at the faces of the indignant crowd members who are baying for the police to go after Eldo instead, and Serge just laughs at it all as he feels the bennies and the hashish tumbling around inside him, numbing all the sharp edges.

What the hell was that?

Gave them the signal.

The signal?

Yeah, Mona supplies us with signals to throw out when you meet the police. Different countries, different cities, different symbols.

How the fuck you remember that?

Nearly didn't.

God bless Mona.

Damn straight. Here's to Mona.

And Eldo takes a hit from the hash pipe and hands it to Serge, who does the same. Then both of them knock back a benny and a tramadol. Comme ci, comme ca.

And now they're in a perfume store, both feeling super chill, but thanks to the bennies neither of them is falling into a pit of silent paranoia, and thanks to the tramadol neither of them have any hard or sharp edges, instead everything is soft and round and they're both pleasant, relaxed, interested, and chatty. However, Eldo is suffering from a debilitating case of dry mouth, which makes her self-conscious every time she speaks. So, when one of the assistants, young, sparkly, blonde, very well-dressed, comes over to them and says:

Can I help you, Miss?

Eldo finds herself asking her for a glass of water without the usual embarrassment that comes with her making an unusual request, and although the blonde assistant seems a bit surprised by this, she goes and gets her a glass, which Eldo finds is surprisingly heavy once she's holding it in her hands. And she takes a sip and gets to thinking that the glass is probably so heavy because it's expensive, and then she starts thinking about what it is that makes an object feel like it's high quality, expensive; is it the material that you use, or the amount of that material? Or is it just the way that material is structured into an object? And then she remembers the triangles inside everything, and she wonders what this glass of water would sound like if she were in the eyes-closed space. And then the water hits her mouth and Jesus Christ, that's better, and she finds everything all so very much easier from this point.

Thank you. Can we get a few testers? I just want to see if any of them spark anything with my friend here.

Certainly, do you know which scents you had in mind?

Eldo names five scents, one of which is heavy with a particular agarwood that Eldo thinks is going to get Serge's memory banks kicking in, and then the lady disappears. Serge asks Eldo for a sip of her water, so she hands the glass over, and then Serge asks Eldo a question.

Hey man, why are we here?

Uh... it's a hunch I have. I want to see if we can find something that'll take you back to Berlin.

Oh no, let's forget this. Go back to Berlin? Bad idea, man.

Not like... go back back. I mean go back in your memories.

I no want that either.

Chill, chill. Trust me.

You no see the Berlin scene. You no feel it. It was fucked up.

Hey, we've all been going through some fucked up shit recently.

Oh yeah, like what else, man?

And then the scent assistant (or whatever she's called) comes back over, with five pieces of long white card with the logo of the store embossed on one end. The hit of scent on the other end.

Eldo thanks her and turns to Serge.

Okay, close your eyes, I'm going to pass these under your nose. Just tell me what you smell, and whether or not you get that Berlin cinema vibe going on.

Gotcha.

One by one, Eldo runs the cards by Serge's face, except that she's holding back the one she hopes will click with him. Instead, she's just rotating the other four, and Serge is saying stuff like:

I no know, flowers?

Smells kind of like animals or something.

Tea? Is that tea in there?

Okay, some kind of fruit. Like maybe from Thailand or something.

Talcum powder? Totally smells like talcum powder to me.

And so on.

Once Eldo feels the rotations have reached a ludicrously extended point she runs the oud under Serge's nose. Eldo is excited, because this is the moment that Serge is going to raise his voice, jump backwards, scream, whatever. He's going to recognize the smell and the whole thing's going to be big.

Except, that isn't what happens. Eldo passes the oud scented paper past Serge's nose time and time again, but no fireworks go off.

What's taking him so long?

Eldo thinks.

She doesn't want to lead Serge to make a decision that isn't 100% his own, but this is getting frustrating, so she decides to say something.

No? Nothing sparking anything for you?

Serge just shrugs.

Not really. That last one, like, it's kind of like it, but not exactly.

For real? No shit?

For real. No shit. I ain't never going to forget that scent.

What an utter failure.

Eldo drops the five pieces of card into a wastepaper basket and calls a halt to the whole dumb venture. What are they doing here anyway? Time to get back on the Annick trail. But just as they're making their way to the door another woman steps in front of them.

Would you care to try a sample of our new product, Miss?

Now Eldo's not particularly in the mood right now, because, well damn it all if her cool plan didn't just go shits up. But then she does a double take because the lady standing in front of her is Miss Barberry. Except that can't be possible, because she's back in Cuir Absolue. Isn't she?

But maybe, thinks Eldo, she got herself a job in more than one smell arena. It's in no way an impossibility. So just in case this is indeed Miss Barberry, Eldo smiles and takes a small splash sample bottle from her, because she feels it would be rude not to.

Thank you.

She says.

Tout va bien.

She replies.

Serge gets the door and the two of them step out onto the streets of New York and both of them slip their sunglasses back on because their eyes are suffering in the glare from the passing headlights and without really thinking about what she's doing Eldo prizes the lid from the sample and splashes some of the scent onto her wrist. Pops the lid back in. Rubs her wrists together. And takes a hit.

Fuck me.

Both of them stop. Eldo can barely get the words out.

This. Smell this one.

Eldo hands the sample over and Serge applies a little, sniffs his wrist. Eldo's face is pure, unadulterated joy because *this* is going to be the moment that Serge's eyes grow wide. This is the part where a fanfare of trumpets goes out and the crowds in the street all cheer.

Except it isn't.

Because Serge makes the same face of non-committal. And Eldo is crestfallen.

It wasn't anything like that.

What the fuck?

Eldo grabs Serge's wrist and breathes it in, surely it's the same. But no. It's an aqua, blue, fresh. No doubt about it, it could not possibly be any further from oud. Then she takes a breath of her own wrist: pure vampiric stewardess.

This doesn't make any sense.

Is okay, maybe it smell like her to you, but no to me.

Serge takes another hit from his wrist.

This kind of smells like, I no know, the ocean or something.

Eldo brings her own arm up and places her wrist in front of Serge, who has two options here: he can either smell it, or he can hold his breath. Not really having any leaning toward the second option, he performs the first.

His eyes grow wide.

Holy fuck.

And Eldo gets the reaction she's been looking for.

That's her, man! That's the smell!

Without missing a beat, Eldo turns on a dime and is straight back into the store. She goes over to the Miss-Barberry-who-can't-possibly-be-Miss-Barberry, who's facing away, and taps her on the shoulder.

Excuse me Miss...

She turns...

Yes?

Only when she turns around Eldo sees that it's not Miss Barberry at all. It doesn't look anything like her. How could she have made such a mistake?

What's that sample you're giving out?

Not-Miss-Barberry looks at the perfume samples on the tray she's holding as though she had no idea what they were, and then her face changes, and she speaks without looking at Eldo.

It's a variation on Iso E Super. Really really interesting stuff.

Eldo doesn't need to ask the question:

What the hell is Iso E Super?

Because she's heard of it before. It's some sort of synthetic super note that was discovered a few years back. Annick took her to this event where they were launching a new fragrance that she said:

Is basically 25% Iso E

And that was the night Eldo said:

What the hell is Iso E?

So being that she knows already she gets the space to merely nod sagely and say:

What are the other notes?

And now not-Miss-Barberry looks back at Eldo (wait, have her eyes changed colour?):

Oh, nothing else – there's only one note in there, one molecule.

Which is?

Like I said – a variation on Iso E Super.

I mean, what's the note, what does it smell like? What's the difference between this and regular Iso?

Nothing. Well, some trace elements of what you'd expect from Iso E – woody without being green, a quality that's almost like pencil shavings. But the real magic, what people are going crazy for, is that it brings out your own scent.

Your own scent? What do you mean?

You apply it to your skin, and it disappears, but it amplifies your own natural odour, taking something that normally you can't smell at all, something you and everyone around you is completely unaware of, and amplifies it by a thousand. No two people smell the same.

As Eldo is opening her mouth to say the next thing she's going to say her body shudders as though someone had just walked over her grave, and an incomprehensible number of thoughts go through her mind in the milliseconds before she makes another sound with her mouth. They go something like this:

No two people smell the same?

So that's why Serge is pure aqua while I'm drenched in the stench of the oud.

Sure, I get that. But it's not just any oud, it's that oud, her oud. It's that unmistakable, piquant variation of that sickly, opulent shit.

But what...?

It's coming from me?

It's something innate in me?

What the hell is that shit?

How could I produce something so patently un-me?

What does that say about who I really am, or who the stewardess is, the vampire?

Is there a connection between us?

Is that why she didn't kill me on the plane?

But if that's the case then why does she end up killing Annick?

Unless she doesn't. Unless I'm getting this all wrong somehow.

Hell, maybe she was trying to save Annick.

After all, the oud that you smelled on her body was in a dream.

This whole god damn quest is based off something that happened to you in a dream.

Can you really say what the oud in the dream smelled like?

Well... yeah, I'm almost certain it was the same as this one here.

Although I can't be sure what all the other notes are that keep this from smelling like regular oud.

Fuck, man, if Annick were here she'd be able to tell me what the other notes are.

Annick.

Where is she now?

Gone from the Chelsea, going somewhere else.

Where?

You wrote it down, man.

And Eldo's hand goes to her pocket and her fingers feel paper there and the internal monologue dies away and her throat kicks into gear and words come out and Eldo says:

Thank you very much.

And turns to Serge.

At first Serge just stares at Eldo, because both of them are wearing shades, so Serge can't see the signal that Eldo is trying to send him by opening her eyes wide and looking to the side, signifying that she wants to move away from not-Miss-Barberry to talk privately. And then Eldo realizes why this room lacks the usual range of colours and she lowers her shades somewhat, repeats the gesture, and Serge is totally up to speed now, and they both step to one side.

What you think?

I think I forgot about this.

Eldo pulls out the scrap of paper that she wrote the numbers on.

What is that?

Asks Serge.

Eldo shakes her head and says:

I just don't know, man.

And then Serge lifts his shades, revealing deeply red, vein-rich eyeballs, leans closer, squints, and says:

Those are coordinates, bro.

XI

5th April, 1994

21.12

Barnes & Noble

Back at the Chelsea, surrounded by the fug of twice-used coffee grounds and stale cigarette smoke, Eldo and Serge learned that the guy behind the counter doesn't know how to read coordinates, and seemed a bit confused by their supposition that he would be able to. Truth be told, Eldo didn't really get what was to be confused about. He's behind a desk, seems to have all the answers, no? And besides, surely it's flattering if someone thinks you can do something you can't?

Eh, whatever.

The whole Chelsea scene was starting to drag anyway, so she asked the guy behind the counter if he knew of anyone who might be able to help them and all the guy could say was that maybe they should go and see a cartographer, but Eldo and Serge don't know any NY based cartographers (or, in fact, any cartographers anywhere), so they made for the second-best thing. Which is why they're now standing at the counter in a Barnes & Noble. But there's no one at the desk, so, not knowing what else to do, Eldo raps on the hard wood counter she's standing in front of with her knuckles.

And then Eldo realizes that the wood is far flimsier than she thought it would be. And the air around her is hot, and suffused with something that could be bergamot, with an undercurrent of olives, or olive oil, and some other scent that she can't put her finger on. A flower? Yes. Possibly some kind of rose, because it's thick and sinewy, yet fragile at the same time. And the light around her seems to swell, to grow brighter, so much so that all she can see is the light, and as the brightness lowers and everything around her becomes visible again, Eldo realizes that she's in a village, sitting outside a café or something, the sound of mopeds coming from somewhere, and the light all around her is golden, and drapes itself across the form of a very familiar woman who is sitting at the next table across from her. Another shadow.

The shadow looks at her curiously, as though she were an insect which has been flitting around her for some time, moving too much to be cleanly identified, but now that she's come to a stop, she's able to peer at her in detail. Eldo knows the score and decides to make the most of this situation before it ends.

Have we met before?

She shakes her head.

But you are a shadow, right?

She nods her head, lowers her sunglasses.

And you're Eldo.

Instead of falling into a regular back-and-forth Eldo decides to get something more useful out of this, so she says:

Why are you here?

But she doesn't seem to want to play this game, and instead comes out with…

You think you're on a quest as a saviour, but you're a scout. You lead us there.

Okay, interesting, let's pursue this.

Lead you where?

To the gallery. To someone called Annick.

The shadow takes a cigarette out from a packet on the table in front of her and lights it. She doesn't offer one to Eldo. After waiting a beat or two Eldo reaches out, grabs the packet, takes a cigarette, and lights it. She does nothing to stop her, and they sit there in silence, smoking.

One reason Eldo doesn't say anything is because she's

lost in contemplation of the shadow: her dark eyes, the hair that frames her face, her legs crossed, one foot up high, tapping, her shoe free from the heel, dangling from her toes.

This isn't a person, this is an idea, a concept of beauty that someone dreamed up one day and which crawled into the world, perfectly formed.

The other reason that Eldo doesn't say anything right away is because she thought she was looking for Annick because she had to save her, because she was the hero, and she doesn't like this twist on the idea, this proposition that she is in fact playing an unknowing part in Annick's destruction. And although she doesn't say anything, she can feel the unspoken words her mind is generating bouncing around her body, only to finally knot themselves into a ball in her stomach. It's a thoroughly unpleasant sensation. Eventually, the shadow breaks the silence.

Cat got your tongue?

The shadow smiles, not only with her mouth but with her eyes too, there's such promise in that look.

Do you like that? It's something I hear them say. You say it when someone says nothing. I like it. I like cats. They make sense.

The shadows ashes her cigarette. The sound of it hitting the thin tin ashtray is much louder than she would have expected. Her tongue finds her lips and moistens them before she places the cigarette back in her mouth, making the softest sigh of pleasure as she does so.

Jesus. This woman.

Eldo bites her lower lip and closes her eyes and somehow finds the strength inside her to ignore the slideshow of images she's presenting and to summon up words. She goes with:

Why Annick?

Again, she smiles. The combination of this and the heavy scent makes Eldo stupid and for a moment everything goes dark, and she nearly falls off her chair, but her hands grasp the table, and she steadies herself, hides her discombobulation with an expertise that few could muster, listens to the oud's sardonic reply.

Because she occupies a space that we need to fill.

What?

We need to be your only obsession, and the road to this involves removing that which preoccupies you so much.

Seriously? That's why you want to kill Annick?

Not want to. We do. Every time.

Why are you telling me all this, why are you helping me?

Her smile drops, the look in her eyes shifts, something not altogether pure washes over her, something dark.

I do not see how any of this helps you in any way.

Eldo's hand on the edge of the table forms a fist as the darkness comes to her again. Instead of holding on to the table to keep herself from falling, she raps her knuckles against it, but this time it's not the rickety wood of the table that she expected, but something much firmer, stronger. The sound is deep, resonant.

And the lady behind the counter at Barnes & Noble says:

How can I help you Miss?

Eldo looks around: bright lights, dark windows, shelves and shelves of books, a number of customers that you can count on two hands standing around in silence, Serge to her immediate right. This is a bookstore.

How did she get here? Are they here? Is this real? She takes a quick look at the counter, it's different: the wood here is lighter in colour, less old than the weathered, threadbare thing at the café, and far thicker and stronger. It's not much, but Eldo takes this as enough evidence that she's not, in fact, still sitting outside a café. She thought she was getting used to this, but it's jarring, difficult, and she has to keep playing it like she's completely cool with this kind of thing happening all the time, which, of course, she's not. Who would be?

Eldo's fingers feel paper and her eyes flick to her hand: she's holding the paper with the coordinates on, and it all comes back to her. The quest to find out what these numbers mean. Eldo's gaze lurches gracelessly from the wooden counter and then comes to an elegant balletic stop right on the eyes of the lady standing behind it, and although she's dizzy with the weight of it all she remembers exactly how to play this so that she thinks Eldo and Serge are normal people. Normal people standing in a Barnes & Noble at some late hour of the evening, and asking an assistant to help them read coordinates written on a scrap of paper.

Yeah. Normal.

Hi Ma'am. (Eldo feels like kind of a dick for using the word 'ma'am,' but you know, when in Rome…) *A buddy of mine, I mean, ours, is really into sailing, and she gave us these coordinates to meet her at, but we're, you know, land lubbers. Not a clue what they mean. Could you help us out here?*

Eldo has no idea where this voice came from, what that vocabulary was about, but hey, this woman's never met her before so she'll have no clue how out of character all of that was. The lady behind the counter silently takes the slip of paper and peers at it. Eldo looks over at Serge who mouths the words:

Land lubbers

to her, his brow knotted in confusion. Eldo makes a face and a small gesture that's intended to communicate the word:

What?

to Serge, but she's not 100% sure Serge picked up on that, and without meaning to move in tandem, both of them look back at the lady as she looks up from the paper and says:

Yeah, these are coordinates alright. Just wait here a moment.

And she walks off.

Serge fixes Eldo with a look.

We have a buddy who's into sailing? That the best you got?

I didn't know what else to say. Who the fuck walks around with coordinates other than a sailor?

Making us sound like we from a cartoon, man.

Look, it worked, right? She's gone to get… the big book of whatever.

Yeah, yeah. Shit, I flagging man. You got any more bennies?

Eldo feels around in her pocket and passes one over. Serge asks another question as she does so.

Hey, Eldo, how we get to that smell place?

I don't know man, I really don't. I'm making it up as I go along.

No, I mean, like, how we went to there? I no remember any of it. Like one minute we were at the hotel, and then ***pow*** *that place. No in between.*

Eldo gives Serge an *are you fucking with me?* look.

The subway. You don't remember?

Huh?

The group on the subway, the cops? There was a whole thing.

Now it's Serge's turn to throw a blank look. His eyebrows rise, just a little, no recognition behind the eyes.

Eldo, man, what the hell are you talking about?

The subway we got over to the perfume place, you don't remember that tension party? The cops? The sign?

Eldo re-creates the sign for Serge's benefit, to jog his memory, but her friend just shakes his head. Eldo opens her mouth to say something else, but the words don't come, so her gaze veers away from Serge and round the bookstore.

So they didn't get the subway there? So, what, Eldo just dreamt that stuff on the subway? She wants to just ask Serge:

How the hell did we get there then?

But maybe it'd be best if at least one of them pretended they knew what the hell was going on.

Jesus, man.

And then with a gust of Iris the assistant is back, with a large black book that she places down on the counter with a slam.

Okay then, let's take a look at those numbers.

Eldo passes the paper over and looks at the top of the assistant's head as she ploughs into the book. Her eyes go to the nametag where she reads the word: *Iris.* Eldo makes a *huh* sound without meaning to, and then follows this up with a murmured:

Iris for Iris.

and when she realizes that yes, she did say these words out loud. She tries to play it cool by turning and nonchalantly looking around the store, at a shelf right by her. Normal behavior that normal people would engage in. Yeah, staring at books on the shelf, this'll do. And now that she's looking, she notices a copy of Baudelaire's *Artificial Paradises,* and she forgets her anxiety about subconscious words and made-up memories and black spots covering up her journeys from place to place because she's genuinely blown away by the sight of this book. She's never seen a real-life copy of it before, only heard about it, and although this is a critical point in her journey, she moves closer to the shelf to pick up the book (or does it move closer to her?), and that's when Mona appears.

Eldo doesn't notice Mona straight away. Let alone the fact that everyone else in the store is neither moving, nor talking, they're simply frozen, stock still, like statues. And after she's been standing next to Eldo for some time Mona speaks.

It took you a while to pick that up.

Eldo keeps her face pointed at the book in her hands, but her eyes flit to her, grow wide, surprised.

Mona?

Why are you in New York, Eldo? Aren't you supposed to be in Europe?

Isn't a girl entitled to a holiday every now and then?

Oh, so that's what this is? A holiday? Tell me, what have you been up to in your time in the city as a tourist? Have you been up the Empire State building? Visited MOMA? Had a pretzel?

Eldo tries to smile her way through this, but breaks. She can't lie to Mona.

Okay, I'll level with you. I'm here on business. Personal business.

Mona smiles and the following words are unnecessary, but she says them anyway.

I know this.

And it's at this point that Eldo suddenly realizes that no one else in the bookstore is moving. She doesn't need to ask the question, Mona can read it from her eyes as they glance from statue to statue.

I'll level with you too – I'm not here. Well, not exactly.

Your idea of leveling with people needs work.

Mona smiles.

I'm everywhere and not everywhere at the same moment – it's the only way this works – and in order for you to see me and hear me, for us to have this fantastic conversation, I need you to experience time far slower than you normally do.

Eldo mulls this over as quickly as she can, and then replies.

Everywhere?

Mona nods.

Turn around, you'll see me there. Go downstairs, I'm there as well. Head three blocks west, I'm there. Try the Taj Mahal, you'll find me there too. On the surface of Europa? Yup. I'm there.

Eldo turns around and sees what she means. Myriad of Mona. All over the store. Everywhere. She turns back.

Okay. Cool. Thanks for that. Let's discuss it further some time. When you're not being the wings of a hummingbird?

Mona laughs.

Oh, that's truer than you know. Bring me up to speed, Eldo. Tell me everything. Why you're in New York, standing in this bookstore, giving the clerk numbers written on paper. Tell me all about that dream you had.

Eldo doesn't ask how she already knows so much, and just lays the whole story bare: the dream, Annick, the trip to NY, meeting Frederic, one of three, the vision, the worms, the oud, the shadows, and ends with the coordinates. She knows that she doesn't have to take Mona's interpretations into account. This isn't like talking to just anyone. This is Mona, and Mona's cool. As expected, she takes it all in, with no audible sounds of disbelief, and nothing behind her eyes that would suggest she thinks this is anything other than gospel truth. She nods, then gestures to the book in Eldo's hands and says:

Consider this: That book is made of paper.

She lets the words hang there for so long that Eldo finally says...

Yes?

Paper that can be torn, or burnt.

Again, there's a lengthy pause, but this time Eldo decides not to fill the silence. She just waits, and eventually Mona starts again.

Any object can be destroyed. From the hardest to the most fragile. So, I'd like you to entertain an idea.

Okay, sure. What?

Imagine that time and space were objects, just like the book. Objects that you could hold in your hand. Own. Master. Tear asunder, if you so wished. This concept is important, Eldo.

Okay. Everything is matter. Everything can be broken apart. Even time and space. But I still don't get it.

Don't get what, Miss?

It's the face of the clerk in the store looking at her. Without really noticing, the bookstore has sprung to life again, everyone moving, everything making noise, and Mona isn't there anymore. Eldo looks down at the book in her hand, brings it up to her face, sniffs it, and gets a scent like garlic.

Garlic? Wait... could that be... DMSO? Some trippy substance mixed with DMSO which the book was covered with and was then absorbed through her skin to get Eldo into the hummingbird space? Could be. Or it could just be something that smells like garlic in any case. Like garlic, maybe.

And it's at this point that she realizes the clerk is waiting for her to speak, while she's just standing there smelling a book, and there's a possibility that this might make her look strange, so she lowers the book and says:

Nothing, sorry. My bad.

And the assistant's attention is taken by another customer who has a question, and the relief that rushes through Eldo as she realizes that the awkward exchange is at an end is blissful.

Eldo casts a sideways glance at Serge, who's looking at her like she's tripping balls at a children's party. Serge mouths something to Eldo, and although she doesn't pick up what this is she can presume that it's nothing glowing, so she just smiles, blushes, and nods her head, as though she were agreeing to whatever it was Serge was suggesting, and then Serge speaks louder.

She said it's in Paris, man.

What?

Paris! You no listen to a word she said? It's the coordinates for the Musée d'Orsay. It used to be a hotel, but it was turned into an art gallery a while back. She said a whole bunch of shit about it. Apparently, her Grandparents stayed in it when it was a hotel.

Eldo knows full well what the Musée d'Orsay is, because she's fairly cultured, and she's been there before. But she doesn't mention this to Serge because she feels like she probably did just miss a whole bunch of everything, and she wants Serge to have faith in her. Eldo wouldn't mind having faith in Eldo right now for that matter either. In a quest to regain some kind of respect in Serge's eyes Eldo comes up with three words which work towards getting across her apology for dropping the ball, ensure it's clear that she understands what's happening now, and also show Serge her appreciation. Those words are:

Shit. Cool. Thanks.

And then she feels like something of a jerk for not engaging with the clerk more, but by this stage she's pretty tired and the hash is really starting to hit her behind the eyes, and as soon as she heard the word *Paris* a part of her went through the entirety of the journey: airports, sitting, waiting, flying, everything. And the sound of a plane flying overhead causes her to look up...

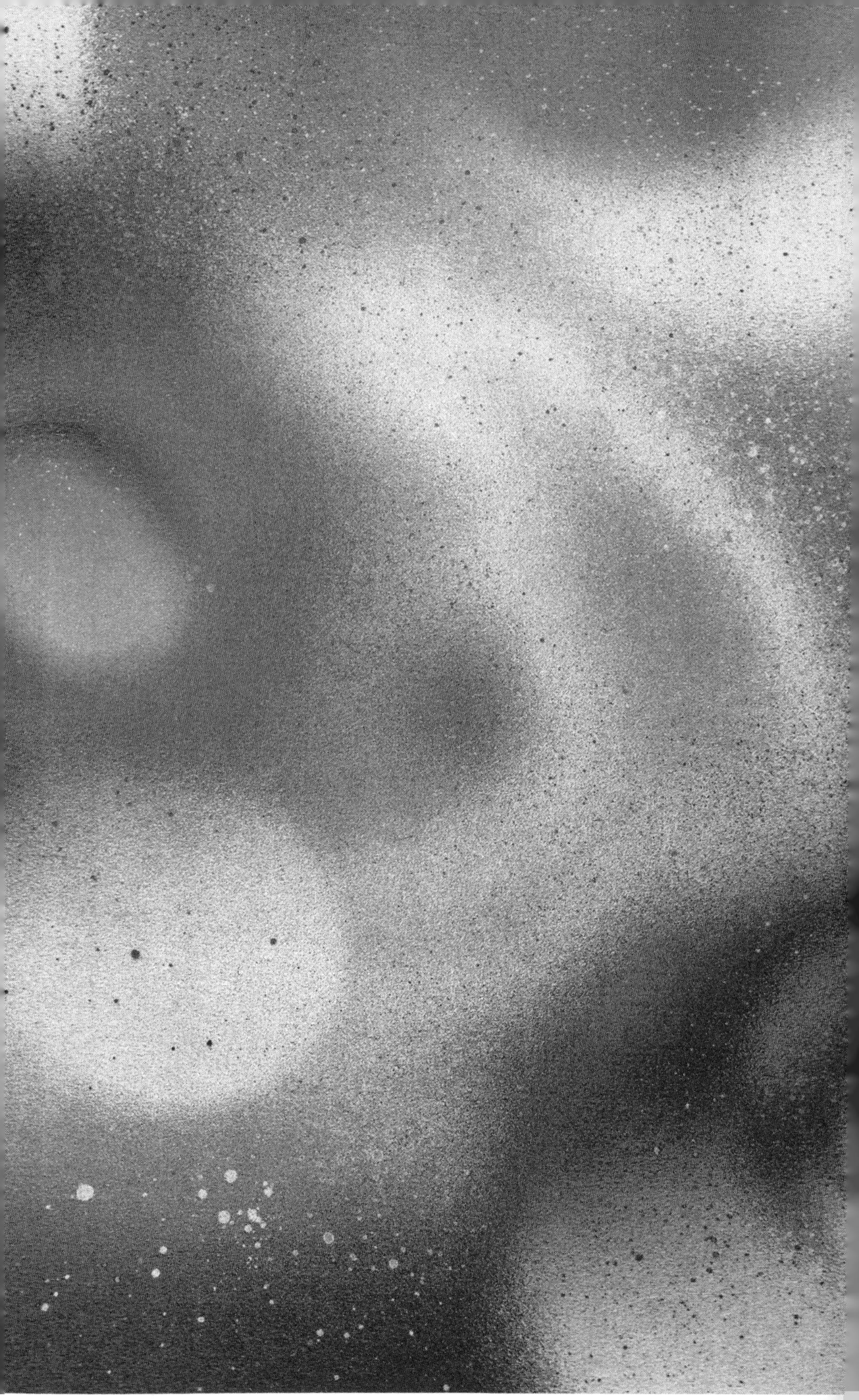

XII

6th April, 1994

02.46

JFK

And just like that, she's standing outside JFK airport, smoking a cigarette. Serge is standing next to her, looking at their tickets.

We only get standard seating. That means no meal and no movie.

Sucks to be us. I'm not hungry anyway and I should get some, uh... sleep.

Eldo looks around – where are they? Near the taxi rank? The bus station? How did they get here? She knows that Serge is making her for the old-confused-man act she's got going on, so she decides to say something to cover all this looking around shit.

Just love the views you get out here.

What? Flat and concrete?

Oh yeah. You know it. Brutal.

And Eldo flicks her cigarette away and they stroll into the terminal.

Then there's check in, and standing in lines, and getting coffee, much needed coffee, and a long stint in the bathroom where they organise their pockets and luggage to make sure that nothing would be found easily if they were frisked, but also so that if they absolutely need something while they're on the flight they have it to hand.

And finally it's time to board, and on the way onto the plane Serge and Eldo knock back a fistful of tramadol each, with some refreshing mints, the result being that neither of them are able to recollect much of the flight other than the scent of airline food and a whirring white noise that neither of them are sure comes from inside or outside the plane, but God damn it if they don't both have the freshest breath.

And then there is Paris.

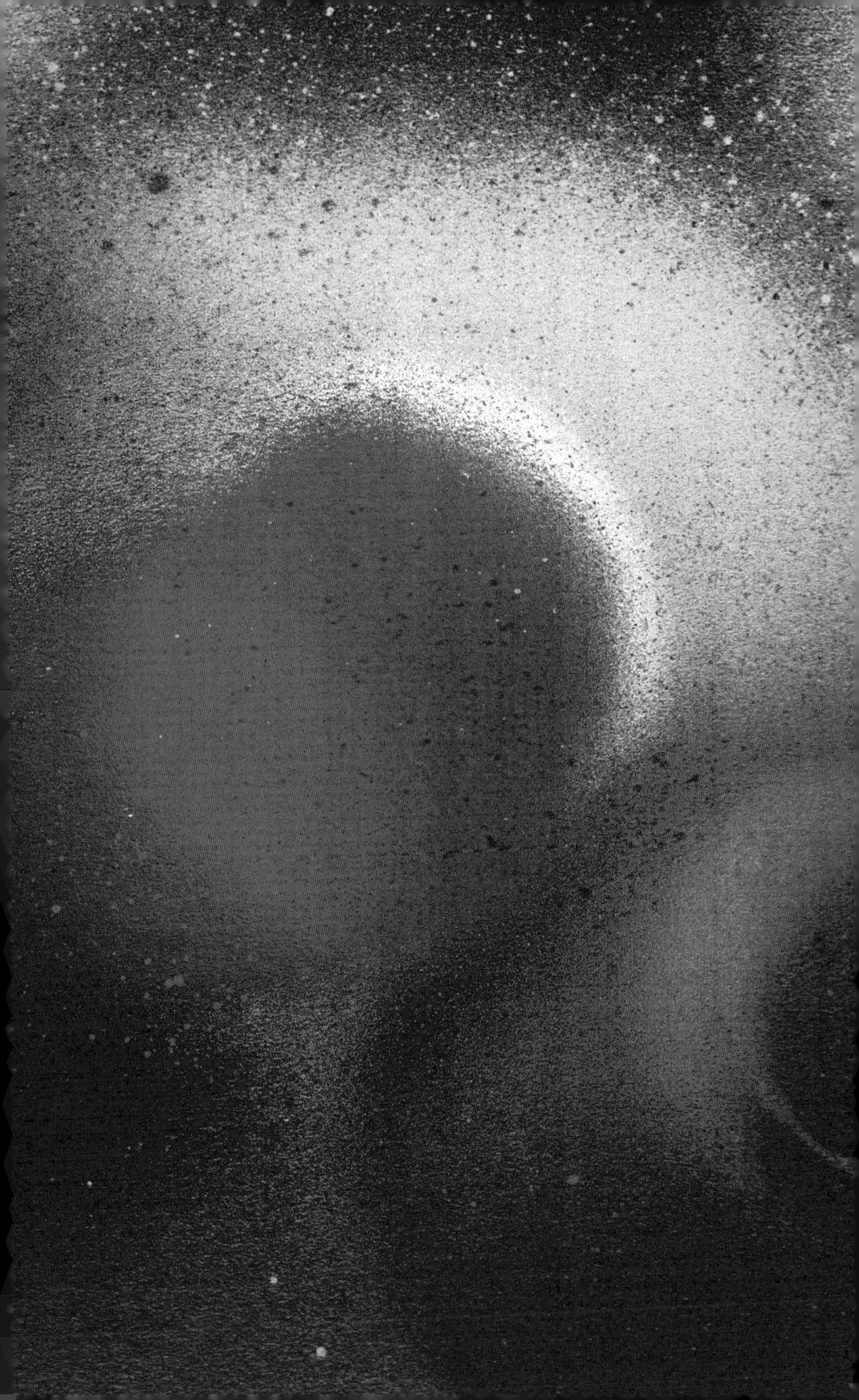

XIII
6th April, 1994
09.39
Gare Saint-Lazare

Eldo has been waiting outside the station for Serge for only a few minutes, but in this time she has managed to smoke half of one cigarette and give away four others to a parade of bedraggled Parisians, shambling up to her armed with no English other than the word *cigarette*, and Eldo's not entirely sure that's an English word to begin with. Maybe it's French.

She starts smoking faster, longer drags, taken more frequently, eager to get rid of the thing before anyone else walks up to her and says *cigarette*. She needs to get to the Musée d'Orsay as quickly as possible, we all know this. So when Serge suddenly got a vicious case of diarrhea before they landed something inside her died a little because she knew full well that it was going to lead to something like this: her killing time and hanging around waiting for Serge to finish shitting, instead of moving forwards.

It's a grey day, and Paris smells like Paris always does: wet concrete, tobacco, exhaust fumes, good food, wet carpet, excrement, and dogs. On paper it doesn't sound like a good combination, but, like a master perfumer, Paris always manages to turn this into something more than the sum of its parts, something better.

The shape of Serge stumbles out of the station and through the crowd, he's pale, gaunt, shaking. Even though Eldo could almost pull her face off because of the overwhelming desire she's got to just move, to find Annick as quickly as possible, she knows that getting Serge to a pharmacist is necessary. The guy needs fluids, meds, and probably sleep. Serge speaks fluent French, which is considerably more than Eldo's *rien*, but he's finding walking and seeing difficult. Hmm, how to navigate this section of the journey? The answer they reach is to form a two-person singularity and make their way, first, to a pharmacy, then to a hotel: arms linked, with Eldo playing the body, and Serge (with some assistance) playing the voice.

Jesus wept.

And as their human push-me-pull-you steps out onto the streets of the city, a face appears in front of Eldo and says one word: *cigarette?*

God knows how many minutes that walk took, but they're getting to a pharmacy now, so thank the Lord. Once Eldo has Serge propped up at the counter, and she feels sure that he's going to be able to deal with the conversational part of this by himself, she wanders off and looks at the shelves. I mean, what else is she going to do? She briefed the shit out of what Serge should say, repeatedly having to remind Serge that they were in Paris and that he was about to be spoken to in French, because Eldo sure as shit can't help with the conversation once it starts.

Eldo loves foreign stores, and walks past shelves stacked with items which are both extremely familiar and very foreign at the same time. Delicious. She's seen the faces on these packages before, but they were different somehow, less French. And then she finds herself looking at a box of face pads, infused with apricot. Eldo is familiar with another brand that makes these pads, you can buy them in the city, so she picks up the sample, lifts it to her face and inhales, and has one hell of an unexpected, if brief, Annick flash:

Annick Flash #3

Eldo is dressed, lying in a bathtub. She's wearing a

shabby tuxedo, the bow tie undone and loose around her neck. She has no idea whose house she's in, either now or when this first happened. Annick is sitting on the toilet, with the lid down, treating it like a chair. In the wash basin she's placed a bunch of items she's acquired (her word for *stolen, lifted*) from a cabinet. Amongst these items is a box of apricot infused cleansing pads.

What do you think the cleaning benefits of apricot are?

What?

The cleaning benefits of apricot. Do you think it has any inherent advantages over any other fruit, or do you think it's something to do with marketability?

Uh... the second?

Yeah, me too. Something to do with the way they feel: smooth, yet textured. Not like the smoothness of a nectarine, or the thick texture of a peach. Somewhere in between. Somewhere much closer to human skin.

Annick tears the packet open.

Eldo remembers this conversation word for word, but there's excitement here for her. Not necessarily because she gets to have this conversation again, but because she gets to listen to her voice again, and today of all days is a wonderful day to listen to Annick speak. Part of her was beginning to think she would never hear her voice again. And what a voice. She's articulate, but without sounding privileged. And her enunciation is a gorgeous mixed bag of clear crisp sounds melded with loose, sashaying rhythms. It's not easy to explain, and she doesn't know anyone else who has quite the same cadence. It's formal and informal. Smart/casual. It is the ease with which Picasso could draw a figure in his later years:

That only took you seconds to draw.

Yes – but it took me years to learn how to do that.

That's Annick's voice, the way she speaks.

Annick turns the faucet on and runs one of the pads under the water. A light, fluffy foam builds up on the surface of the pad and she rubs it against her skin. She does this like she does everything: completely unselfconsciously, like she's alone on the planet, as though there were no one else in existence to watch her. Annick performs every task like this, with a clean grace that suggests a mastery of the task, like she's executed it 10,000 times before, even if it's her first time. It's something that's always amazed Eldo, because every action is affected by being observed, and that's just a fact. She can't even open a door properly or fork food into her mouth without feeling that she has an audience watching and waiting for her to fuck up.

She turns to Eldo, her face still wearing the foam from the pad.

What do you think? Cleaner? Transformed?

Before she replies someone starts knocking on the bathroom door and when this first happened Eldo was curious who it was, but on this replay Eldo could not give a damn who it is. Instead, she wants the mystery knocker to just fuck off and die. She wants this one moment in the bathroom to go on for the rest of her life. Oh Annick, say something else, say anything.

But she doesn't.

Instead Eldo blinks, opens her eyes, and she's back in Paris, the pharmacy, watching Serge haul his trembling body towards her. Every step is clearly agony. But he's got what he needs from here (presumably, even though Eldo is pretty sure they could get him what he needs from a less legal establishment) and the new lead drama is that Serge is three minutes away from going to the toilet in his trousers and needs to get into a hotel like now, like woah.

Eldo can not believe this shit, but is also a fairly decent person deep down (isn't she?), so she puts the Annick story on hold for another few minutes to get Serge booked in to a hotel somewhere, to let him shit and sleep it out while Eldo runs as fast as she can to the Musée d'Orsay.

They step out of the pharmacy, and as luck would have it there's a hotel right next door. It's the Opera Hotel. And although Eldo doesn't know it, this is going to be the location of one of the most nightmarish events in her life. But right now she has no clue whatsoever, right now it's just a building, and anyway, right now she's only thinking about Serge not shitting himself.

The man at the front desk looks exactly how Eldo imagined he would when she saw the hotel from outside, like this man embodies the building itself: mustachioed, tall, thin, and somehow superior, even though Eldo and Serge are paying him for the privilege. Whatever, get Serge into the room, and get to the Musée. That's all that matters.

There are, of course, forms to fill in, and Eldo completes the task as quickly as possible, and when she hands them back over there's a lull during which the man looks over the sheets without speaking or, more importantly, handing over the key, and not having anything else to do Eldo picks up a Hotel Opera book of matches from a bowl on the counter and places them in her pocket.

Finally, the mustachioed man approves of the form with a nod and a sound that escapes through his nose, and hands over the precious, precious key. Toilet time. Eldo wants to abandon Serge right here right now, to leave him and run, but she knows that Serge is in hell and pity gets the best of her. So Eldo accompanies her friend up to the room, Room 48, makes sure he gets to the toilet in time, and then makes her exit accompanied by an orchestral crescendo of bowel motions echoing from the bathroom.

And now it's:

Eldo.
Paris.
Alone.

Rather than risk getting lost in the winding streets of the city (happens every fucking time she's here, without fail), Eldo takes the Metro. Now, a lot of people will tell you that Paris is dirty, and those people are completely correct, but they're missing something far more important than the nature of cleanliness.

With the layer of dirt that covers Paris comes a kind of similar mentality in the inhabitants, a rule-breaking, louche, insouciance that Eldo simply adores, especially on the subway: people strolling from carriage to carriage, climbing over barriers, and wandering down sections of the underground tunnels that they're clearly not supposed to. You simply wouldn't get this kind of behavior in Eldo's city, or in New York, and our man just loves this distinction. This very Paris-ness. All the same, there's a time and a place to admire moral freedom, and this just isn't it. For inside Eldo has convinced herself that all of the delays she's encountered from New York to here mean she's going to miss Annick again, and her insides are starting to kick against her to hurry the fuck up. To be there now.

To shake off the dregs of the tramadol from the plane (not to mention whatever else she's ingested but forgotten about since leaving the airport) Eldo's put together a steady supply of uppers in her jacket and trouser pockets to keep her sharp and focused and on point, dipping in at regular intervals. Her pupils are now barely discernible black spots at the centre of her irises. There's a chill in the air and most people are wearing woolens and scarves, but Eldo is sitting on the Metro in a thin shirt, sleeves rolled up, carrying her jacket, drenched in sweat. Her sense of smell has gone into overdrive. The variety of aromas she's encountering is astonishing, but she doesn't know if this is the uppers, or simply the high level of anxiety she's undergoing, or maybe just that Paris has so many olfactory notes to offer. Whatever. Got to find Annick.

When she finally gets to the Musée d'Orsay it is with utter dismay that she finds it's closed to the public today, and only today. Apparently, the whole place has been booked out by a fashion house for a photo shoot, or whatever.

Eldo takes a breath – fights against the rising tide of panic that's sitting in her chest and starting to spread throughout her body.

Okay, take another pill and think about this.

It's closed because of a fashion shoot. Now that might explain Annick's alleged presence, but it doesn't explain how she's going to get in. And she gets a ticking noise in her head, and starts to formulate a plan which involves her dressing up as a photographer and worming her way into the building (she's already got the photographer's fake name and accent ready – going for something conspicuously foreign, but free enough of any specific territory that no one would be able to place it geographically) when a hand falls on her shoulder. Eldo turns, and perhaps she shouldn't be surprised to see that it's Frederic. The fat man smiles his big fat friendly smile and says:

What an incredible coincidence

(Eldo doesn't like how he says this word, because something about his tone suggests this is anything but a coincidence)

Frederic goes on to explain that he's here for a lecture on

scent, and if Eldo would like to install herself inside the d'Orsay (yes, that's how he puts it), then no problem at all. He can facilitate.

The rising tide of clock-ticking-anxiety in Eldo's head begins to dissipate, ever so slightly.

There are words and greetings between Frederic and the staff and the next thing Eldo knows, she's standing in a room filled with people and chairs, and a board, but she's not looking at any of this, she's looking out the window. And she can't fucking believe what she's looking at.

The room overlooks the main gallery, and from up here Eldo can see, actually fucking see, Annick down below.

For reals. No shit.

The frustrating part of all this is that she has to play out this scene in the room with Frederic first, the fat man's been clear on this. Eldo grinds her teeth and angsts about Annick disappearing before she can get to her, but Frederic assures her that that's not the plan and that everything is going to be okay.

When Eldo asks him to define *okay* he simply smiles that smile of his and doesn't elaborate.

Whatever.

So Eldo is paying no attention whatsoever to the room she's in right now, and instead is locked on the surreal image of Annick behind glass. All she can hear are the sounds of the murmuring and body/feet shuffling from the other people who are sharing this space with her – Annick is pure visuals, like a character in a film, or someone on TV.

The shoot is being set up right in front of Alexandre Cabanel's *The Birth of Venus*. And Annick's being made up in a body stocking, with a wig, and props, to recreate the image in the painting. The whole look is really working for Eldo, but then the original painting really works for her too. Of all the paintings it could have possibly been, this is surely the only one that you could say is pretty hot at the d'Orsay. Well, you know, as far as a painting *can* be considered hot. Something about the skin tone Cabanel captured, those hips, and those eyes that peer out at you from underneath Venus's arm. And God damn, Annick is wearing this look well.

Eldo supposes that she's going to lie there, supine, oozing sensuality, in front of the original to create some kind of vapid juxtaposition between the real thing and a facsimile re-created with a real person. Yeah, that sounds like fashion, or advertising, or whatever this is. Although deep down she's not really sure what the juxtaposition is supposed to evoke.

From her vantage point she can see Annick's mouth move, and even make out the tiniest of laughs from her at one point, all without any audio at all. Not that she needs to hear her laugh mind you, because she has it recorded in her head already, but oh God, it would be so sweet to hear right now.

And for some reason, even though she's so far away, Eldo is able to see her up close. As though she could reach down to the ground, or to a rug that she was sitting on, and pull Annick towards her, closer. She's far away, and yet she's able to see the texture of her skin and hair as though she were no more than inches away. Or centimetres. And even though she wants to smash through the glass and leap to the floor below, and run over to her right now, and hold her and tell her that she's here for her, she knows that this is out of the question. She has to see this scene to the end first.

So she waits. Stays here, standing, holding a glass of champagne (always champagne) and once the lecture is over, she will amble around the D'Orsay, bump into Annick 'purely by coincidence,' and then the two of them will hang out, and she'll take it from there. And somehow or other this nonchalant, rambling, unstructured plan will result in her preventing the murder from happening, and in some way or another save Annick's immortal soul or whatever from some kind of inter-dimensional demon that looks like a chick from a

Dracula movie.

Yeah.

That's the plan.

And it's going to work.

Eldo's dream state is broken by the light, repeated sound of metal tapping gently against glass, and she turns to see a 40-something lady, brunette, with a sharp bob (again?), well-dressed in black everything, striking the tines of a fork against a champagne flute. With a Pavlovian response, the scattered guests assemble together and take their seats without anyone telling them what to do. And Eldo, reminding herself of the importance of going along with it all, does so too.

She looks around, not sure where Frederic has suddenly disappeared to, and because she's unable to sit next to the only person she knows, she sits next to a lady, well-dressed, wearing something fur-lined, who smiles politely. She smiles back, keeps her appearances up, and then gives her attention to the speaker standing in front of them all.

Eldo's surprised at how easily the speaker's gained the room's attention. How collected and well organised she seems to be. How little wrangling needs to be done with the crowd. As though everyone knows the part they have to play already. More out of habit than anything else, Eldo takes another upper. Maybe that'll get rid of the high-pitched noise in her head. Or the ticking. Sure.

The lady starts talking. Her voice clear, and soft, but somehow filling the large space in a way that something that small and gentle shouldn't be able to do. Next to her is a board with a picture of a triangle (although Eldo prefers to think of it as a 'pyramid' for some reason) separated into three sections:

- head
- heart

- base

And she's explaining the mechanics of how scent works. And yes, it's stuff that Eldo already has some awareness or knowledge of, but it's a whole lot more interesting than she was expecting.

And that voice is no hindrance:

We can enjoy the beauty of a Roman arch without any background in the subject – the mastery of form, the way it catches the light – any uncoached, untrained observation that we make is valid.

But there is an argument that the true beauty of the arch can only be fully enjoyed when one appreciates the genius and simplicity of the engineering. And that is how I would like us to approach scent – from a structural perspective first, so that we can further enjoy the beauty that we already recognise.

Every scent is a molecule. A piece of an object which has broken away from its whole and encounters our bodies no longer as a solid object, but instead as an olfactory sensation. The lighter a molecule is, the faster it evaporates. The heavier, or more complicated, a molecule is, the more slowly it evaporates.

This is elementary chemistry, but how does it relate to perfumery?

The woman pauses here before continuing, and her eyes flit over to Eldo's, and then away. The way she might glance at her if she was a fellow passenger on a train, or a plane, or a pedestrian walking past her in the street.

She's holding a pen in her hand and as she speaks, she often places this in the corner of her mouth, absent-mindedly, as though she were unaware of what she was doing. And every time the pen finds its way into her mouth her eyes find Eldo's again, and then she turns back to the board and starts talking again.

She's wearing a trouser suit, in impeccable condition, and these details, in addition to the way she moves and talks and looks, just adds to her, adds to her whole… femaleness.

These moments and glances are fleeting, transitory, they probably take something like two seconds at most, but to Eldo they put her in a reverie that seems to go on for eternities at a stretch. Damn. Must be the uppers.

Anyway, she continues. And even from this distance Eldo thinks she can hear those gorgeously beautiful eyelashes brush together every time she blinks.

As most of you are probably aware, there are three elements to a scent: head, or top notes, heart, or middle notes, and the base.

Always the base.

The top notes are the lightest molecules. They evaporate fastest, and when first applied, these are the notes that tend to dominate. They're often sharp, distinct. Citrus is a popular top note, for example, whether lemon, or bergamot, or something else.

The way she speaks is animated, her whole face comes alive as she delves into the subject, but particularly those eyes. Her hands dance a tattoo, back and forth, accompanying and underlining the point of what she's saying. And although Eldo is genuinely interested in what she has to say, she's pretty sure she'd have her attention even if she were reading out washing instructions.

Below the top notes is the heart, and the heart molecules are heavier. They evaporate more slowly, and are often only revealed in their truest sense once the head notes have disappeared and given them the space to shine, to come into their own.

Heart notes last longer, can be stronger, and are often either floral or spicy. But it is difficult to talk about the heart without mentioning the base, because the base is constant, subtle, but ever-present.

Her hands illustrate each and every point here: one is sculpted into a fist at the word *heart*, suggesting the weight or solidity of the molecules perhaps, and then it relaxes, her fingers spreading open, like a flower blooming, as she mentions evaporation. In some ways she almost needs no words to accompany her. But of course, there must be words.

And here her voice lowers an octave, and it's not evident whether she does this consciously to build interest, or subconsciously because of the quiet yet majestic beauty of the topic, but this is when she begins to speak about that third layer.

The hushed tones that she moves into remind Eldo of the voice you adopt when speaking in a church: reverent, respectful, cautious.

The base lies below everything, consisting of the heaviest, most complicated molecules. They take the longest amount of time to evaporate, which means they are released slowly, over a longer period of time.

While the Head notes evaporate quickly, the Base burns on, not only taking us into the longer form of a scent, what is often referred to as the dry down, but also, and perhaps most importantly, informing and affecting both the head and the heart throughout. Like the softest, gentlest, quietest section of an orchestra.

She raises a finger here and smiles

And that's not easy. It's hard enough to create a combination of scents that complement each other, but finding a bottom layer of scents that works with two higher layers? Which both disappear to leave only the bottom layer remaining? For all of this to harmonise and create a journey as molecules evaporate? Well, that's a challenge that every perfumer knows only too well.

Those higher notes are perceived, even in the first

seconds following application, through the filter created by the long-lasting base. Their smell is not the same as it would be were they in isolation. And yet each scent is isolated, because each scent is an individual molecule, each molecule is, by its very nature, singular and alone.

She pauses for a moment. Brings her hands together, fingers interlaced. All apart from her index fingers, which find themselves placed against her lips, eyes cast downward. Either she's thinking, or she's letting the last words she said echo around the room to slowly sink into the minds of the audience. It could be either.

Finally, her hands are lowered slightly, and her index fingers come away from her mouth, and she speaks again. Taking small, elegant steps as she does so.

Or perhaps prowling is a better word. Yes, prowling, like a panther.

So, let's take all of this information from the idea of cognitive understanding, and let's put it into practice. Let's look at an example. And where better to go than with Chanel's iconic No 5?

There's a ripple through the crowd here, the soft sound of hushed whispers, fabric rustling as bodies move ever so slightly. A sound that suggests that they too believe this is an excellent place to start.

Eldo considers making some kind of noise or movement too, just so that she fits in with the crowd. But she doesn't know what kind to do, whether it would be best to murmur something or just shift in her seat, and because she spends too long contemplating the options, in the end she simply stays resolutely still and silent, which is its own kind of noise in a way.

The speaker starts talking again the very second the ripple of commotion dies away, or perhaps it's simply her voice which brings the room back to a serene state of paying attention. Either way, this is a master class in public speaking.

She ups her game here, her face and body becoming more emotive as she begins to not only intone the words connected to her topic, but also to feel her topic, deep, deep down, like hands pushing their way through fabrics heaped in a pile: exploring, sensing, being alive and curious. You can see it in her eyes, in her mouth, in her hands, as they dance and contort, this way and that.

And as she starts talking, she passes out a number of long white cards, scent samples, and Eldo feels like a kid in a candy store at this point, because hearing about all this stuff is great, but getting to smell examples as well is just the greatest.

Let's begin at the base of No. 5.

Those notes of woody Mysore sandalwood, the green, smoky earthiness of vetiver, moss, and patchouli and the rich sweetness of Bourbon vanilla. These are the quietest notes, but these are the ones that inform everything above. They are the softest of woodwind sections accompanying the instruments which play in both the Heart and the Head.

But what instruments are those?

In the heart we have a floral bouquet of jasmine, lily of the valley, iris and May rose. By themselves those notes would be bright, and colourful, but the base restrains and transforms them into something else, simply through its presence.

And a selection of the strips gets to Eldo, and she mouths the words *thank you* and takes a handful and passes the rest on to her neighbor and she smells each scent in turn, isolated: sandalwood, vetiver, moss, patchouli, vanilla, and so on. And it's incredible to Eldo that you could break something like No 5 down into its constituent parts and still marvel at how beautiful each individual part is.

And at the top, above everything else, in that first hit we get when the perfume is applied, are sharp, fruity notes, a wild contrast from the floral heart and the woody base. A head composed of, amongst others, neroli, ylang-ylang, peach, bergamot and, of course, the all-important presence of those trademark aldehydes.

At the use of the word *aldehydes* another ripple goes through the room, albeit very brief, allowing the speaker to continue almost immediately. The shortest of pauses.

In fact, No 5 has become so intrinsically connected to those cool, metallic aldehydes that the two almost go hand in hand.

She laces her fingers together as she says:

Aldehydes.

No. 5.

There is almost no distinction between the two.

Eldo is transfixed, and yes, this is largely down to this bewitching speaker, but it's the topic too. It's content as well as context.

And yes, a great deal of her appreciation here is down to Annick, the teachings she's imparted, and the associations that she holds in her mind with Chanel No. 5. And she also doesn't miss that the speaker mentions the presence of a note of jasmine in No 5, and Jasmine, as we all know, is the name of Annick's agent. She smells the Jasmine card again.

That can't be a coincidence. Surely. Can it?

She muses on this, and lets her eyes lose focus, staring into the middle distance as the woman in black continues talking. She bundles all of the cards up into one handful and passes them all under her face and is amazed at how all of these ingredients together somehow don't exactly smell like No 5 and it's right there and right then that her eyes refocus on something close by. On the face of Frederic, ahead of her, turned around, and smiling.

Where did he appear from?

And right then Eldo knows that her plan to meet Annick as soon as this is done is in potential jeopardy. And this creates a feeling inside her that she isn't comfortable with, and the ticking noise in her head builds up again, and she risks making a bothersome noise in order to take out and swallow another upper. And then suddenly Frederic is sitting in the seat next to Eldo, and although the speaker doesn't stop, her words and presence are turned down in Eldo's head by an unseen hand and the remaining space becomes entirely filled by Frederic and his whispers, so quiet that they barely exist.

The first thing Frederic says is that he doesn't intend to interfere with Eldo's plans to meet Annick in the slightest. On the contrary, the matter he has to impart will take almost no time at all.

Eldo watches Frederic's hand slip inside a pocket, and reemerge, holding a cigarette. Frederic holds it up, his thumb and forefinger rotating gently on the filter. Eldo keeps her voice as low as she can, desperately trying not to draw the attention of the speaker, or bother the other people in the audience.

Let me guess - two of three?

Indeed.

Eldo looks over at the window, at the glass, at Annick beyond it. Frederic understands what she's thinking.

You should perhaps know that this one will be quite different. You will be gone for almost no time at all.

But it'll seem longer?

Why, you don't miss a trick at all. Yes, it will feel much longer for you. To elaborate, the chemicals you absorbed from one of three are now assimilated in your body. You will process two of three much faster, much easier. And, like your meeting with Mona in the bookstore, the time duration experienced by those not ingesting the substance is comparable to the blink of an eye.

How do you know about Mona in the bookstore?

Why Miss Eldo, I thought you would have realized by

now. I work for Mona.

Of course he does. And then Eldo says:

Of course you do.

So Eldo takes the cigarette, puts it between her lips, and is about to reach into her pocket for a lighter when Frederic brings a flame into existence somehow, holds it a few inches from the tip of the cigarette. Before Eldo lights the cigarette, she whispers:

I don't think they're going to let me smoke in here.

Of course not. But trust me, by the time they reach you, you will have already learned all there is to learn.

These chemicals could make a lot of money in the right hands, I'm surprised Mona hasn't sold them.

Unfortunately, they require the subject to have something of a strong constitution. Almost unique.

Oh, let me guess: That's where I come in?

Quite. Shall we begin?

Eldo crushes the filter. Leans forward so that the tip of the cigarette reaches the flame.

There's the sound of burning, like a pile of leaves quickly catching light and then smouldering.

Eldo inhales.

She has just enough time to see the woman giving the talk shake her head profusely and wag a finger at her and then everyone in the room freezes and everything clouds over with a red and blue mist as her eyes are closed against her will and she's suddenly somewhere quite different.

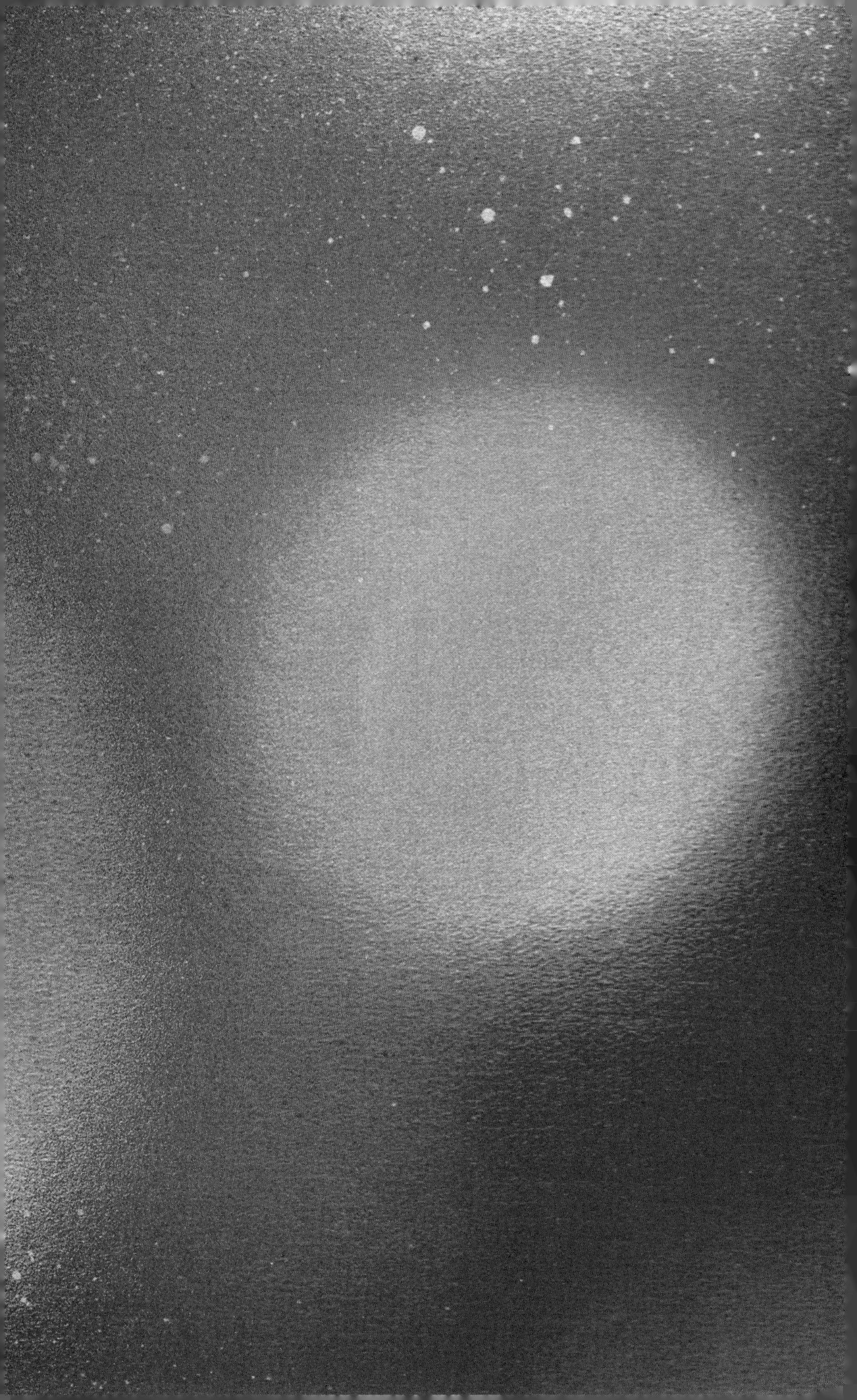

XIV
6th April, 1994
11:52 / All known time
Two of three

Just like the first time, one of three, Eldo notices that if she opens her eyes everything is the same: the room in Paris, the people around her, the window to her right with Annick beyond. Whereas when she closes her eyes, she's in what looks like the same place, the same space, but it's now made of worms, just as it was before. But then everything changes.

The room that she saw with her eyes open slowly dissolves before her closed eyes, like chalk drawings in the rain, until it's nothing more than a rolling landscape, a field of large worms flowing in what might be the wind.

Eldo opens her eyes, it's the room in the museum. Closes them and it's just the heaving vista of worms.

There seems to be some kind of sky above the field too, but even if she were outside there's no way that's a regular sky. It's something very different. More like pools of coloured ink forming shapes on the surface of water, and just like before, these are not any colours that she's able to identify.

The field of grass-like worms flickers gently in a breeze, even though there's no discernible wind that Eldo can feel.

And then the paradox of why there's no breeze and why there's no room and why there's no sky all comes to her at the same moment with beautiful clarity: none of these familiar elements are around her because there is no anything around her, because she's not in a where, she's at a when. At the beginning of it all. This is the way everything started – the nothing is a rolling field of worms that will go on to make up everything there is, and the sky above her is nothing but an illusion – it's there because her mind needs a sky – but there is no sky. There are only the worms at the beginning.

Eldo makes a conscious decision to leave this period and come to the now, to the when that she is familiar with, and for some reason she knows exactly how to do this and as she thinks it to make it so, the worms perform an almighty dance as the universe comes into creation.

The worms grow and shrink and transform the landscape to represent the rapid unfolding of millennia of ever-changing vistas – a vast explosion, matter travelling aimlessly through the cosmos, collecting into clumps, forming worlds, this world, the world she knows.

The world is white hot, the worms moving with a frenzy, slowing as the planet cools, and then slowly forming views that she recognizes: oceans swell, mountains push themselves up through the ocean, the landmass grows, valleys become mountains and back again at such a speed that the worms appear to be in the form of something liquid, but Eldo knows this can't be the case. And slowly, these movements settle as she approaches the now and the landscape becomes recognisable. This is the present.

The speed at which Eldo travels from the time before anything, to the beginning of everything, through the formation of a post-cooling universe, to what we think of as the now, is astonishing. What's unfolding before her eyes is the changing landscape of both the universe and the planet over billions of years, but in terms of time, fourth dimensionality, not in terms of matter. The worms are a representation of tangible time. As physical a property as anything else. Not as a temporal concept, but as a substance.

The understanding she reaches, the crux of this experience, is that it does not relate to space, or the physical. It relates to time.

And it continues.

Bodies of water ebb and flow, a variety of different landscapes replace each other over and over and over again, the land rises up and falls away in increments, as does the sea. It's wonderful.

But where are the life forms? The animals? The plants?

The mammals and reptiles and birds and insects and all of the lifeforms that move and swim and fly and grow are nowhere to be seen. Eldo presumes that this is because she's seeing such vast swathes of time that the existence of a living creature, even if it were to sit in one spot for 100 years, or 1,000 years, is not constant enough for her to see it here.

Life is too small from the perspective of time for her to see it at all.

Too brief.

Too insignificant.

What's more, the flowing worms never form a precise landscape image, they simply hint at shapes and forms. She can't, for example, identify anything at this speed, she simply has the impression of mountains, of lakes.

The idea, but not the photograph.

The suggestion, not the detail.

But maybe you can slow the passage of time?

Did I say that?

Did she say that?

From behind, over her left shoulder, Eldo can feel someone's hand.

Oh, now this is new.

Her previous trip to this... sphere, realm, whatever... one of three, involved no sensation of touch whatsoever, no physicality, and although that's the same here she can definitely feel the presence of someone, can feel their hand hovering over her shoulder.

Or maybe that's not what it is, perhaps it's merely the

heat from their hand reaching her shoulder (does she even have a shoulder here?)?

Yes, that's more what it feels like. There are no fingers on her, it's just the whispered suggestion of a touch that is yet to happen. But it's there. Heat. Warmth.

Eldo guesses that this is most likely the hand of one of the audience members at the perfume event. Reaching out to tell her to put her cigarette out.

Oh wait, that's interesting

She thinks.

Eldo is much more aware of the room she's *actually* in this time. With one of three she seemed to float away from the reality of her physical New York setting, and become a part of the world of tendril spaces that played out in front of her. But here she knows she's actually in Paris, in a room in the Musée d'Orsay, and is strongly aware that what she's seeing is nothing but a slideshow.

I must be getting a grip on this thing. Could sure do without that hand over my shoulder though.

Again, Eldo's not sure if she just said those words, or thought them, or whether someone else said them – as though her life were being narrated by someone from somewhere.

Hers?

Hello?

She ignores these thoughts, ignores the hand over/behind her shoulder as best she can, and focuses on the worms, and then something rushes through her, a realization washes over her, and she remembers that they're not worms at all.

How could I have forgotten?

She remembers the triangles. Remembers that these worms are some kind of simplified, elemental version of what everything is made up of. Matter on a subatomic level.

When viewed from this distance, in detail, with whatever this chemical is that is coursing through her body right now, both time and objects look like this. Like worms. This is the form from which everything is made.

But if you were to zoom in on an object or a moment under the most powerful of microscopes, this is the form you'd see: something akin to the triangle, or a diamond, repeating over and over and over again, vibrating with different levels of intensity, and both of these tessellate together to form something akin to a serpentine whole. The worm. The one worm which flows through everything. It's all so obvious now.

Everything small is just a version of everything big.

And everything in a single, frozen moment, is the same as everything in eternity.

It all makes sense.

Matter and time are both made of the same thing, they can both be grasped and moved, and although she's not sure how this is happening, or how to explain it, she feels sure that there's a way that she can 'reach out' and take hold of both realms: time and space.

Perhaps she'd be able to control both.

I mean... perhaps I'd be able to control both.

Me. Eldo. But how?

Eldo gauges the weight of this task the way someone might walk around a large stone that they have to roll: sizing up how the weight of the boulder is distributed, and how the ground lies around it, where it is highest and lowest. If she were to push this boulder, to get it moving, which side would be the best to push it from, which offers the least resistance, where in all of this madness is the road to awe?

Without being sure this is possible, let alone how she can do this, Eldo lays both hands on the stone in her mind, the metaphorical boulder, the very concept of controlling time and space at the same time, and tries to bring these two planes together.

There's the sound of unseen moving parts, like vast cosmological cogwheels turning.

How am I doing this?

There's a rushing sensation in her mind, a monumental wind, as though she were falling forward at great speed without moving at all, and Eldo finds the colour of her thoughts slowly moving from one hue to another, blending, creating sights she's never seen before, sensations she's never felt, and her hands find purchase on the navigability of the concept she's dreamed up, and before she knows it Eldo is witnessing the binding of time and space under her control in front of her eyes.

It's all too beautiful.

She's not sure how it works.

But it's fast, so fast.

The slightest thought carries her across the globe, through the centuries, it takes a herculean effort to control her mind (*or is it my body?*) to be able to navigate in small increments. But she learns.

I learn.

It is as though she were both the bearer and the water in a bowl, carrying herself without moving, keeping the water as still as she can.

I am the bearer and the bowl and the water.

Eldo plays with time and space like they were toys. Travelling vast distances in moments. Freezing and unfreezing time. Taking it backwards, forwards, faster, slower. She relaxes lets time tick by at a real time rate, at the speed it wants to, as though she were releasing a balloon to the wind, and watches it tick by as she moves from one place to another, as the landscapes evolve and pass by so quickly that they seem to be building and destroying themselves as the vista soars from one to another, breathlessly.

She moves from where she is now, when she is now, in Paris, to the city, and from the city to the Chelsea. She even takes the time to move up into the sky to find airplanes zigzagging the planet high up above the surface, minuscule, like fruit flies travelling in perfectly straight lines.

And now that she has control, understanding of it all, she's able to see the glowing forms of life forms, of animals, of people in motion, and she knows that if she wanted to, she could alter these people, these structures, by moving time. And she could alter time by moving objects.

Simply by exerting my will – by wishing it.

Because moments are objects and objects are moments.

She moves to the city, takes hold of the temporal landscape, pulls it backwards like a toy car to see the wireframe worm landscape of the place she knows so well become the desolate landscape it was when the Earth cooled, and then back again to the present.

With a firm hand, she takes hold of it all and tries to move time forward, beyond where she is already, and far into the future. But there's resistance, something there, a barrier holding her back, so Eldo shrugs and gives up on that experiment.

Instead, she returns to the game of taking a familiar place in the now and moving it to an unfamiliar place in pre-history.

For a while she enjoys this: taking a place and then moving backwards, slowly to begin with, so she can take in all the changes (or try to, at least), and then faster and faster and faster, marveling in the blur of it all, especially when she gets to the part where there is no land mass whatsoever (and it always surprises her how quickly she gets to this point) nothing but ocean, as far as she can see, an ocean made of undulating worms. Liquid and solid being the same matter.

It's an exhilarating experience.

And then she moves forward again, back to the now.

Eldo performs this same routine several times, in many different places around the world, geographically moving around the world at random, until he, perhaps unsurprisingly, finds herself back in the city. She always ends up back in the city.

What a trip.

And the more she does this the more she begins to recognize the world, to see familiar forms. Especially in the city. And especially in the now of the city.

And even though there's no real distinction between a person and the pavement they walk on, between the rain and the shopfront it falls against, even though it is all one and the same heaving mass, she feels faces she knows, places she knows. Not sees, but feels. And then she realizes where she is, and when she is, and then she realizes that this is why she is here.

This is it.

This is it.

She's at home.

Watching herself.

In reverse.

It starts with her coming in through the door, backwards, with the bag she took to New York, in a rush, seeming a different colour than normal, as though something were wrong. And then Eldo unpacks the bag she took and places the meager items inside back where they belong in her room, in the various housing stations they belong in around her apartment.

She brushes a thin layer of dust back onto the cover of *Les Fleurs du Mal.* Places her cigarettes and lighter down, picks up an extinguished cigarette from the ashtray, teases the tip of it from cold ash to a warm glow with her fingers, and brings it up to her face. Inhales that final/first drag.

This movement, this direction all feels so normal to her now that it requires mental effort for her to remember the concept that what she's looking at is unusual.

Eldo watches, engrossed, as she, the central character in her own drama, moves in and out of the apartment: dirtying herself in the bathroom, bringing food up and out of her throat while reading or listening to the radio.

It's fascinating, even when there's no one in the room.

And suddenly, without her even realizing where and when she was going, she realizes that she's there.

This is the place.

This is the time.

The lost hours.

The black spot.

Her apartment.

In the city.

On Saturday evening.

The 2nd of April.

Eldo is at home, with another person, and it's difficult for Eldo to feel who it is because everything is just a swirling mass of tendrils, with no discernible features, and something about this figure is recognizable but different. Something is strange. And details are so incredibly difficult to decipher with two of three.

And what do details matter anyway?

They matter quite a lot here actually, because this is the time period that is a haze to us, and this is the opportunity to find out why.

Oh yeah, of course.

She can tell that the shape in her house is both male and female, that's for certain (although she's not sure how) and appears to be offering her a cigarette. She looks closer at the filter, moving into it, inside it, so that it is everything. And this is when and where she sees the ball in the filter. And even though it's so vast that all sense of perspective is lost, with it being more akin to the night sky than a recognizable object that one can touch and feel, she recognizes it for what it is. And she knows what it does.

So she comes back out of the filter to view the scene as it plays out.

But who's that handing it to me?

But who's that handing it to her?

Not Serge, that's for sure. The vibration patterns they're giving off are all wrong. She looks more closely at that vibration pattern, and not the non-existent features, and she locks onto it, and searches for where she's seen that pattern before, and just as the Eldo-who-is-present takes a drag from the cigarette with an already crushed pod in the filter, the Eldo-who-watches realizes who's sitting opposite her:

Mona.

Shit, that's Mona.

But as sure as she is that this is Mona, she feels like it's also not. Don't ask her what that means.

And as Eldo takes a drag from the cigarette she judders, like her body experiences an electrical fault, and she glows like a beacon, with light coming from her, not reflecting off her, and something crawls out of her, something dark, with a vibration pattern different from anything else.

Wait, almost everything.

And she travels to south-east Asia, to Malaysia. She swoops through the forests until she finds agarwood trees, and moves into them, looks at how their internal work structure vibrates.

She moves from tree to tree, until she finds one that's been infected with phialophora parasitica, and has produced its antibodies as a resin. And although the matter of this resin is not the same, the molecular structure trembles at the same rate as the dark creature crawling from Eldo's body, seven thousand miles away.

Huh.

Interesting.

Eldo moves from the forest to her home, and into her body, and rewinds time to capture the moment the creature first appeared, and she searches everywhere inside the body of the Eldo-who-is-present and she is a cosmos inside a body and eventually she discovers the seed: one single piece inside her, one molecule that vibrates at the same rate as the oud in Malaysia, and it's this piece that the creature stems from, this is both the door that it passes through and the building block that it grows from, the element that it copies over and over again to create its own physical body, and she steps back, slowing time, watching a slideshow of the creature, the thing that's constructed of this one molecule in her body which has the same vibration pattern, and therefore the scent of, agarwood resin, of oud, watches it twist its way through Eldo's body, like she's a door, a gateway, a portal, a birth canal, crawling out of nowhere, out of nothing, and into the space of the world.

This can't be happening, it can't be happening.

But it is. It did. And it will.

Eldo watches all of this over and over again, but there's nothing to glean, nothing to learn. It's just actions. Things happening. There are no motives, no reasoning. So instead she moves out of her body and homes in on Mona, moves closer to her, as though by looking at her features she could decipher the underlying meaning of this moment she shared with her. But there are no features to make out here, no lessons to learn, she's simply a mass of swaying worm-like tendrils, another beacon of light, a light that glows like a star, a light made up of diamond shapes, with those diamond shapes all vibrating.

That's 'all' there is to see.

Eldo looks at the version of her that is sitting with the male-and-female Mona, at the diamonds that she herself is made up of. They're vibrating too, but at a different rate, slower, with a pulsing energy from inside which spreads out.

There must be something here.

Eldo looks back at Mona again, looks closer at her cells, at how they move, she spins herself out of the room and into the city, into the world, moving from place to place, person to person, at the speed of light, comparing the smallest pieces of everyone, the stuff that they are all made up from.

She looks at how it vibrates, looking for a match, a match for Mona.

And even though she can find armies of people who have the same vibration rates, she can find no one, not one person on the planet, who has the same pattern as Mona.

What the fuck?

So this is the lesson – this is what two of three exists for: to teach her how time and matter, how time and geography are interrelated, but more importantly, that on the evening of the 2nd of April Mona came to see her, and she drugged her without her knowledge, and the oud, the thing, crawled out of her, or is made of her, and Mona herself is made of nothing that can be found on this planet. And all of this is knowledge in abundance but somehow Eldo still knows nothing.

Ain't that just the way?

And then there's the gentle stirring sensation of physicality, of her body crying out for air, and she can feel her absent physical form far, far away take an involuntary breath and she feels the landscapes in front of her ebb away, slow to begin with, but then faster, so much faster, and she's falling backwards, through a vacuum, and then she opens her eyes.

XV

6th April, 1994
11:52
The Musée d'Orsay

Eldo's still in the room where the perfume talk is being given, she's able to make out that much as her chair falls backwards towards the floor. And then she thinks:

Damn, this is going to hurt.

No smoking!

Are the words she hears just before her head collides with the cold, tiled floor. There's an explosion of light behind her eyes, and this is Eldo's rude reintroduction to the world of texture and sensation and physicality. She's had better.

She's surrounded by standing and crouching bodies very quickly, and there's a general uncertainty amongst the group as to whether they should be reprimanding her for smoking, or checking to see if she's okay after her fall, but once some squabbling is out of the way, most of it in French and therefore leaving Eldo outside of the realm of understanding, the latter wins out, and all appears to be forgiven.

Eldo apologises to everyone present with a number of *pardon* and *excusez moi* mumbles and then it hits him:

Annick.

She looks at the window. Yes, Annick's still there, still on the shoot, still in the same outfit. It's not too late. And Eldo uses the drama of the moment to excuse herself from the room and make for the exit, vaguely aware of the tube that Frederic is holding, about a foot long, which looks like it's made of carved ivory, but she pays this no mind and tells her feet to keep taking her to the door, doesn't care that everyone is looking at her, but then she catches the eyes of the speaker and she looks devastated that her talk has been halted when it was going so well, or perhaps she's simply concerned about Eldo, about another human being that she barely knows because she has more of a heart than most, and Eldo wishes she could go over to her and apologise and tell her how wonderful she really is, but she can't, she can't stop this thing that she's on, and she needs to keep moving because she simply only has one thought on her mind right now.

What else is new?

And as she reaches the door and places her fingers on the handle there's a spike of pain in the back of her neck, like a bee sting. She slaps at it, expecting to find a bug, but instead her fingers find something that's soft and hard at the same time. She brings it round, opens her hand to see a small dart: wooden body, feather flights, blood on the tip mixed with something dark and sticky. Like curare.

Her head turns as her body moves through the doorway, and she catches a glimpse of Frederic putting the ivory tube away, concealing it, smiling. Eldo's feet keep going, she can't stop this now, and she dashes the dart to the floor (wait, did that dart have legs?), but there's a sudden sluggishness to her steps now, as though she were walking through mud, or treacle. And then Eldo thinks she should open her eyes, but for one reason or another she can't.

She finds herself alone, leaning against the wall when she's finally able to open her eyes again. How long was she out for?

How long was I out for?

But not being able to answer this she just keeps going, through corridors, down staircases, looking for the main exhibition hall, looking for Annick. Her feet made of stone. Her flesh feeling grey, lifeless, cold. And she turns another corner and there it is – the main exhibition hall, and she makes a break for it – except that there are two men here in suits and dark glasses, with wires leading into their ears, and they step forward, blocking the way, hands extended in a universal

Stop right there, pal!

gesture, and Eldo does stop, and they both speak French, no English, and she's wondering what kind of story she needs to tell them in order for them to just let her pass, and her brain simply can't function properly, she can't find the words, and she thinks this is where it's all going to go wrong.

But then it doesn't.

Because this is the moment that Annick sees her, and her eyes grow wide, and she stands, and her face and her skin and her entire body comes alive.

And then she's running.

Across the floor.

Towards her.

And the two men in suits and dark glasses understand the universal meaning of what they're seeing, and they step aside, and there Annick is, yelling Eldo's name, running towards her, dressed as the Cabanel Venus, and everything begins to echo, and there's a light around the edges of Eldo's vision, as though there were a pressure on her retina, and then she's vaguely aware that she's falling, backwards, again, and then everything is dark and silent.

She's in the wings of a theatre, there's commotion going on all around her, but Eldo can tell that the largest amount of sound is coming from an unseen audience, somewhere beyond the stage that she's behind. She's surrounded by hanging ropes and painted scenery and props and people walking back and forth, following the roles that they were assigned to perform, and there's her just standing there doing nothing.

Isn't that just the worst sensation?

It's dark back here, so instead of relying on her eyes she simply follows her nose. The smell of wood is everywhere, a hard wood, something like oak, which permeates everything else. The wood is the base.

On top of that there are other smells: sweat, machinery oil, stale cigarette smoke, but none of these is the one she's interested in.

There's a familiar, exotic richness that she's focusing on, and it's this scent that's telling her who's here and where she needs to go. That richness is unmistakable. She begins speaking before she reaches her.

You're close.

I'm right behind you.

This is where she turns and locks eyes with her, she's wearing a silver wig, a lot more make up than usual, and an outfit that leaves very little to the imagination. She looks like she comes from another planet and would be difficult to recognize if it wasn't for her characteristic aroma.

No, I mean your actual body – it's very nearby, much closer than when you spoke to the other shadows.

That depends, where are we?

At the windmill.

The red windmill?

She nods. Lights a cigarette. A passing man yells at her that there's no smoking backstage, so she carries on smoking.

I've always wanted to come here.

Well, here you are. Kind of.

Not really though.

You're learning, that's nice. Admirable. You people are good at that when you want to do it.

You people?

She takes a long drag on her cigarette, and turns away from Eldo, scratches the back of her head where her real hair slightly sticks out from underneath the wig, does not reply to her question. Eldo decides to move things on rather than to continue staring in silence at the nape of her neck.

So, I know where she comes from.

The shadow smiles at this.

Our Mother?

Eldo says nothing, just nods, even though the oud isn't looking at her. She knows somehow that she'll see this, or register it at least.

It was never a secret.

No one told me.

Oh, my dear sweet Eldo. All you had to do was ask.

That's why she didn't hurt me on the plane.

She nods again. A throaty *uh huh* comes from inside her as smoke works its way out of her mouth to swirl in the stage lights.

She couldn't hurt you if she tried.

She turns and looks at Eldo again now, moves closer to her, wraps her arms around the back of her neck, keeps the cigarette in the corner of her mouth.

One can not harm the seed that one grows from.

She pushes her hips against Eldo's hips, inhales, exhales, one eye half closed as smoke rises up, past it, to keep the irritation away.

That would be some kind of crime. An intergalactic crime. It's a universal truth.

But if she comes from me then why go after Annick?

She pushes herself against Eldo, harder.

Because she means everything to you, and we can't have that.

She brings her face closer. Eldo can feel the 800 degrees Celsius heat from the cigarette that dangles from the oud's mouth, and yet the warmth from her hips, and the breath from her body, is somehow far hotter, far more dangerous. She knows this. She's so close that her whisper, so soft, so hard to hear, is fully articulate to her ears. Every syllable.

Every breath.

Why do you persist? Why do you simply not give in to us? Are we not everything you ever dreamed of?

Eldo is racking her mind for an answer, doing her best to ignore her eyes and her voice and her skin and her hips pressed right up against her own, and then she hears Annick's voice, and she opens her eyes.

And there she is. Standing above her. Saying her name. A white ceiling behind her. How did she get here? Why is she lying on the floor? Why is Annick wearing a wig? Then she shifts and sees the Cabanel in the distance, and thinks:

Shit. The d'Orsay. I'm still in the d'Orsay.

Eldo sits up, plays it as cool as she can, keeps her eyes on Annick's face and smiles, feeling that perfect pearl of her name passing between her lips.

Annick (there's that name again) helps Eldo to her feet and she's checking the back of her head, which seems to be bleeding a little from where she hit it falling to the floor, and when she brings her head back round she says:

Did you get stung by a bee?

And there are trace memories of Frederic and something about something, but Eldo's not piecing things together as clearly as she'd like to be able to and Annick suggests a café, food, sitting together, talking, and Eldo nods and says:

Sounds good.

And she leans forward and tells her how much she's missed her and then they embrace and Eldo is lost in a hemisphere of hair and somehow she manages not to simply weep with joy, because deep down that's all she'd really like to do.

The café they go to is called something like The Blue Angel and it's dark inside, even though one side of the place is all windows, floor to ceiling. The furniture is all made of wood, dark, and stained, and there are a number of older French men scattered around: eating, drinking, talking, smoking. The smells match the sights too – there's food, and wood, but the cigarette smoke drowns everything else out. It's dark tobacco, Eldo would put a lot of money on Gauloises leger brun being the most popular brand in this joint.

Pretty much every square inch of the walls is covered in paintings, and there's one that dwarfs all of the others: a blue woman with wings protruding from her shoulders, done in something like a combination of Picasso and Schiele's styles, and Eldo gets to wondering whether this café is named after the painting, or perhaps the painting was painted specifically to be hung here because of the name of the place. Could be either. Or something else. Who really knows? Anyway, they take a table together right next to the windows and Annick picks up the menu and starts scanning.

So what are you doing here, you never told me.

Do you want the truth?

Always.

Eldo thinks about this but decides to leave it a bit longer.

Let me get to that in a minute. I'm still feeling a bit light-headed.

No problem. *What are you going for? I'm having soup. I mean… that's pretty much the only thing I can have while I'm working.*

You mean food?

Annick puts the menu down.

Yes, I mean food. That's why we're here.

And then she narrows her eyes with a mischievous look, as though she's just remembered something and says:

When was the last time you ate?

Food? Uh…

Eldo searches her memory banks and tries to find a picture of food sitting in front of her, of her eating food.

Chewing. Swallowing. There's nothing that she can recall. Certainly nothing while she was in New York. What about on the planes? Maybe a bag of peanuts? No? No. There's nothing. But instead of telling Annick this Eldo simply says

Two days ago?

Annick shakes her head.

I don't know how you can do it. I mean, hell, I don't eat much, but I need my three squares. Even if one of them is nothing but fruit, and another is nothing but vegetables.

I never knew you were so concerned about food.

I wish I wasn't, but you don't get to look like this without giving it some careful thought and attention.

I always thought it was your genes.

That's sweet. No, it's a discipline.

Discipline's important…

Eldo says as she lights a cigarette, unaware of the paradox, and exhales towards the window as the waitress comes over and starts asking questions that Eldo can't answer. She keeps her eyes on the glass and the view beyond, but she listens. The waitress speaks in French, naturally, so Annick does all the talking. She clearly orders something for Eldo too, even though she didn't mention any preferences or leanings. Eldo waits until the waitress is walking away before she speaks.

Sounded like you were speaking Spanish.

I was. I ordered you a cheese sandwich, but they do them Spanish style here. Bocadillo con queso y tomat.

Nice. Spanish style? What does that mean?

Annick shrugs, also lights a cigarette.

I have no idea.

With a jolt, the waitress is back. Dropping the smallest glass of kir and a cheese baguette in front of Eldo, accompanied by a plate of snails for Annick. Eldo shares her gaze between Annick and the plates and the window. The waitress leaves with a flurry of words all directed at Annick. Eldo never even glances at the waitress. She doesn't even have the vaguest idea what she looks like.

She looks down at the baguette. The first word that comes to her mind is *dry*.

You know, gee, I'm suddenly not sure I'm that hungry.

Don't be ridiculous. You passed out, haven't eaten for two days, although I'm calling bullshit on that, it's clearly longer – and you are eating that. All of it.

Yes dear.

Annick picks up a snail and teases it out of its shell with a small silver fork.

When was the last time I saw you?

I'm not sure, why?

Feels like a long time. I've missed you.

You have no idea how mutual that feeling is.

Eldo smiles, looks down at the baguette. She flips the top off and is surprised to see that the inside of the baguette is coated in tomato seeds, or maybe that's just the juice from sliced or crushed tomatoes. She was expecting actual tomato flesh, slices, but there's none at all. The sight isn't all that appealing, but the scent is wonderful – rich and deep and fragrant.

Spanish style?

I guess. Try it.

Eldo wants to do as she says, but it looks so dry and unappetising that she just sits there, staring at it. She opens her mouth to say something, the feeling of not wanting to disappoint Annick ruling everything, but she seriously doesn't know if she can do this. She gently and surreptitiously grinds her teeth together to see if they're up to this task. There's the slightest pain as she presses her teeth together, which tells her that she hasn't used them for a while. They're getting soft. Complacent. Or perhaps she's just been grinding them like a motherfucker. Could be either.

Annick speaks again.

Eldo. Eat the sandwich. You'll thank me for it.

So Eldo lifts her kir, sniffs it, takes the smallest of sips and swills it round her mouth, puts the glass down, and looks at the sandwich. But then she notices the plate the baguette is on.

Damn.

There's something she just really likes about that plate.

Her mind moves away from the bread, from the concept of food, and takes in the stillness of the sunshine passing her, the muffled sound of the traffic outside, the chatter from the nearby old French men who won't stop smoking and drinking and talking, and the roundness of this plate, and the sound of Annick nearby, and her scent in the air, and the blue circle that runs around the rim of the plate, and the wood that is underneath, and the way the ceramic of the plate and the wood of the table look next to each other, the pale ceramic and the dark wood, the permeability of one material and the resistance of the other, the way they sit together, one resting on the other, one supporting the other, and she looks up and sees Annick, and she means so fucking much to her, and her throat thickens, and tears come to her eyes, and before she knows it she's sobbing and Annick is leaning forward and asking her if she's alright and no, no she's not.

I just never thought I'd see you again.

Annick moves closer, lowers her voice.

Eldo... what's been happening?

And she sobs, and she nods, and she takes a deep breath, leans in, and talks. She starts at the beginning, with the dream, walking on the streets in the city, the conversation with the dream girl, Herman outside the gallery, the exhibition, everything, right up to now. And Annick, God bless her, seems to believe every word.

The waitress comes over to their table and Annick orders coffee for the pair of them on autopilot, and as the waitress walks away Annick says:

Jesus. Do you smell agarwood?

And Eldo, her gaze drifted to the window once more, her mind temporarily off the game, turns to look at this waitress, to see her, but there's no trace of her at all.

Eldo thinks for a second.

That waitress, was she a dark brunette, long hair with a widow's peak at the front, pale skin, red lipstick, thin curved eyebrows, and dark soulful eyes?

I mean... that describes a lot of people in Paris, but yeah.

I first met her on the plane, on the way to meet you in New York. Then I met her a few more times, or shadows of her. In different places, around the world.

You mean...

Yes.

Annick doesn't say a word. The sounds of the café all around them seem louder now. Eldo feels like an ass. Small cups of coffee are placed in front of them. Eldo looks up at the waitress, but of course, it's not the one who took their order. She speaks to Annick.

Ask her where the other waitress went. The one who took your order.

With doubt burning away in her eyes (and who could blame her?) Annick starts talking to the waitress. There are a lot of words passed between them, and Eldo tries to understand, but fails, and she picks up her coffee and it's small and not that hot, but sweet Jesus is it wonderful, and Eldo knocks it back in two quick sips and then Annick says *merci* and the waitress leaves.

Let me guess: there is no waitress here that matches that description.

That's what she said.

Eldo rubs her eyes. Annick picks up her coffee, drains it.

I thought I was going crazy for a while, or thought maybe all... this was just taking its toll.

So what now? What do we do now?

I don't know. Go back to the hotel, see Serge, take it from there?

Why don't I just not go to the gallery on the night?

That's what I was thinking, but I don't think that'll work.

Why not?

The scent of agarwood fills the air again. A hand picks up the empty coffee cups. Eldo and Annick look up at the waitress in unison. She has a lit cigarette hanging from the corner of her mouth, takes a drag and exhales while saying…

Because you always end up at the gallery.

XVI
6th April, 1994
14:13
The Hotel Opera

The walk to the hotel involved a lot of talk, an abundance of questions from Annick, a deprivation of answers from Eldo.

Here's what the main topic was:

Back in The Blue Angel Eldo had reached out and grabbed the waitress's hand and then there was a whole bunch of shouting when, it turned out, she shimmied and turned back into the waitress who was *not* an inter-dimensional vampire, and Annick, who saw the whole shimmy act and was as confused as Eldo, had to talk their way out of her getting a beating from the owner. Or the manager. They couldn't work out which he was.

Anyway, so now they're back at the hotel, and the plan is to pick Serge up as quickly as possible and take it from there – maybe head back to the city, or maybe just stay as far away from it as possible. Even though both of them secretly believe what the waitress said and that arriving at the gallery is unavoidable. But what is certain is that the coffee at The Blue Angel was motherfucking strong and both of them are now walking and talking a mile a minute.

They stride up to the desk at the hotel and the man standing there, smart clothes, a wry smile, greets Eldo in English. Eldo responds with:

Mi llave por favor.

Because her false confidence thinks this is French, when it is in fact Spanish, and the deskman, who doesn't speak Spanish, but is familiar with the word *key* in a number of different languages, doesn't pause, he merely reaches round, grabs the key from the hook and hands it to Eldo.

Room 48.

And as Eldo's hand meets the desk clerk's to take the key she feels a sharp pain in her palm, like she caught it on the thorn of a rose, but she plays it like nothing happens.

Eldo and Annick turn, make their way to the lift and Eldo looks at the palm of her hand as she walks. A tiny swell of blood in the centre.

Did the deskman do this?

The lift door closes and, as Annick asks her which floor and she tells her, she takes a closer look at the palm of her hand. Her eyes are playing that game where they can't focus on anything small, so she narrows them, bringing a haze to her peripheral vision and a slight sharpening in the image of the welt in the centre of her palm, peers as hard as she can at the drop of blood.

It almost looks to her like it's in the shape of a peyote button, but that would be crazy. Wouldn't it?

They reach their floor, the lift door opens, and Eldo nonchalantly wipes the palm of her hand against her trousers and they both start walking in one direction, without even knowing whether they're walking the right way.

What a perfect summary of their time together.

It turns out that they are going the right way, and when they get to the door Eldo knocks before Annick reminds her that this is her room and she has a key and there's a flash, a fleeting emotion, where she feels like a complete ass. But then, as she's fumbling around in her pocket to find the god damn key which the deskman just gave her *(Where the hell did I put it?)* her fingers finding nothing but pills and pills and pills, and Annick and Eldo freeze at the sound of metal on metal in the lock and the door swings open, and they both sigh with relief when they see the gaunt frame of a very unwell looking, very sweaty, Serge standing in the doorway, breathing with difficulty.

Eldo, man, I had the weirdest dream.

Eldo puts a hand to Serge's neck and ushers him back into the room (which smells of sickness: stale clothes, fresh sweat, and something that gives a note of infection, of disease) and when she takes her hand away, she notices a spot of blood on Serge's neck and looks at her hand, at a mess of blood mixed in with Serge's sweat, and she cleans it off on the bed linen.

Now, although Serge is perspiring steadily, he also has a chill, so he's wrapping himself in a luxurious blanket at some moments, taking it off and standing in front of the cold air that comes in through the open windows at others. Outside the sound of Paris seems far, far away, and then Eldo spies the room service order that Serge made, and she smiles both outside and inside.

The bed side counter is covered in a variety of different pills and tonics – some of them look contemporary, the regular kind of blister packs and childproof caps that she's come to know oh so well, but then others seem to have come from a lifetime ago – brown glass, with labels printed in a swirling script, or maybe that isn't printed, maybe that's… handwritten? Could be. Sure looks it.

Eldo goes through the bottles and packages one by one, asking Serge where he got them from.

I no know, man. I pick up the phone, I speak to someone, later a little old person, or maybe it was a kid, come to the door with all this in a bag.

A brown paper bag?

Yeah, how you know?

I didn't. Just seemed apt.

As Eldo scrutinises the pills and tonics she pops open the

odd blister pack that looks like it might be interesting, pops a pill here and there, takes a sip of whatever might have something to offer, and generally behaves like you might at a buffet.

Annick sits next to her.

Anything good?

I thought you were on that healthy kick, keeping clean, eating soup, right?

Annick gives her a look that's pure her and Eldo smiles and passes over a dark brown glass bottle of cough syrup that she just sampled.

Try this, it is not for children.

Annick unscrews the cap, drinks it down, and then coughs. Ironic. And maybe it's bullshit, but Eldo could swear a little cloud of dark smoke just came out of her mouth. Like she was a dragon.

Oh God, is that pure codeine?

Sure tastes like it, but they must have mixed something else in there.

Petrol?

Could be, could be...

Eldo runs her tongue around her gums, getting the residue of the thick brown syrup out of her teeth and swallows it down and peers at the label on the bottle to see what the hell else is mixed into this, but the letters and words on the labels are moving around with a life of their own and she can't get a lock on anything and she pinches the bridge of her nose and closes her eyes and says:

I need to use the bathroom.

And she's up and moving towards it the next second.

And it's in the bathroom that Eldo suddenly realises she's not feeling very well at all, and she's not sure whether it's just the stress and the weight of the last few days, or the mix of pills and syrups she just imbibed, or perhaps even that sharp pain in the centre of her right hand. But whatever it is it's right then that everything begins to change.

She can hear Annick's voice through the door asking if she's okay, but she doesn't reply. She's sitting on the toilet, peeing. And although she has no memory of sitting down, or taking her trousers down, or lifting the seat, she's ever so grateful that she managed it, because she can tell from the stench that what's coming out of her right now is the darkest and thickest of urines, and we're all going to appreciate every single drop of this being flushed away.

Her hands are gripping the toilet seat tight (cold, hard plastic) when it suddenly becomes soft, as though it were padded with something, or made of leather. The shift in its material value is unsettling, to say the least. And then the whole thing veers to one side, like it moved, like she's sitting on something alive.

Eldo jumps to her feet, trousers dangling, spins around. The seat is just a seat.

She reaches out, tentatively, and her fingers make contact: plastic.

Cold, hard plastic.

What the fuck?

And then she looks around, at the room, and is mildly surprised to see that it appears to be filled with small blue lights, hanging in the air, like incandescent snowflakes, or fireflies, frozen in time.

She pulls her trousers up, buckles her belt, and plucks one of the lights from the air. It doesn't seem to be attached to anything. It's just floating. She lets go of it and it stays where she left it, not falling to the floor the way you'd expect it to.

What the fuck?

This has to be peyote.

Did I get spiked with peyote?

And that's when the room begins to swell, to grow. Each wall moves away from her, revealing more and more of the tiled floor until it stretches into the distance, and although Eldo knows that this is not possible, there's nothing about this experience that makes her think it's a hallucination. Not even a little bit. It's all too real.

And then she hears the words:

This can't be peyote

echoing in the bathroom and she can't tell whether she said that out loud, or the words came from somewhere else, or maybe she just thought them so damn hard she actually heard them.

Is there someone in here?

There can't be.

Or can there?

Where could they be?

And then she looks at the bathtub, at the shower curtain.

The curtain is closed. Pulled across, tucked into the bathtub, concealing the interior of the tub and the fittings. It's rippling gently from a breeze that she can't feel. Eldo walks towards the tub, her feet made of obsidian, dragging on the floor. Under normal circumstances this should take about four steps, but it now takes somewhere between thirty or forty, or more. It's one thing to think that the room has grown, but quite another to take so many steps while getting no closer.

Is this peyote? It sure doesn't feel like it.

Maybe not. But now's not the time to think about this.

Now's the time to focus on the shower curtain as her hand makes contact with what she expects to be plastic, but when she touches it she realises it's skin. Wet skin. Heavy wet skin.

Human?

Hard to tell.

She pulls the skin back, bracing herself for what she will find in the bath, but there is no bath, it's just a corridor. She walks down it, and even though the door at the end is miles away, and each step seems to take her a lifetime, the door comes towards her at a much faster rate than it should, and then she's on it, turning the handle, receiving the gentlest electric shock as she does so. It's too bright to see anything on the other side of the door, because as she opens it there's nothing but burning white light.

Eldo runs her fingers through the grass.

Grass? When did I get outside?

She looks around and she's in a garden, somewhere. Could be Paris, but then it could be anywhere. Then there's a voice, and she looks to her side and Annick is sitting near her, smoking, and talking about sobriety.

It really is its own kind of high. The first day is always a drag, because it's a fragile, itchy bastard. And you know full well that all you need is the tiniest taste and you can get that uncomfortable feeling to go away.

She thinks for a second before continuing, her eyes looking up and to the right, visualizing.

It's like being dry... it's so easy to undo it, to become wet, but once you're wet it's so much harder to get dry again. And, of course, this is the conversation going on in your mind all the time.

Wait... Its own kind of high? What does that mean? Like exercise? Endorphins? What, are you healthy now?

Dear God no. I'm not an asshole or anything like that. I'm just using sobriety in-between periods of decadence, mix and match, don't worry. All I'm saying is that the periods of sobriety have a real impact now. You become so aware of everything. You sharpen up. Everything clears. Feels easier. But I have the feeling that it wouldn't be that wonderful if it was permanent.

So you still indulge?

Fuck yes, I'm only human, but I like to try and space it out a bit. It feels like I enjoy it more that way. Enjoy everything more. The sharp times and the fuzzy.

Eldo knows what Annick means, but acknowledging that she might be right means acknowledging that she hasn't spent a day sober for the last… shit, what is it? Eight years? Maybe longer?

She remembers that she was sick a while back, some kind of viral infection or whatever, and the beginning of that was officially the last time she managed to get through a single day without drugs. Of course, the virus itself was a kind of drug, leaving her foggy and confused by the simplest of tasks, so some might say that doesn't count, but those people can go fuck themselves.

Anyway, instead of letting Annick into this train of thought she simply looks around and mutters:

Where are we?

Without really looking at Annick.

The Tuilleries?

Eldo sits up and looks around.

That place that Manet painted? How did we get here?

Annick takes a drag and furrows her brow, looking concerned.

We walked here. Are you feeling okay?

Eldo scratches her neck. The answer is no, but she doesn't want to say that, so instead she comes out with:

Yeah, I'm fine.

And she then turns her attention back to the grass.

It's so green.

Annick smiles at this.

You want to know a fun fact? Grass is not actually green.

What?

It's true.

So what colour is it?

It's every colour but green.

Eldo's confused face is the only reply Annick receives, so she elaborates.

It's true. There are wavelengths in daylight, and that's where colour comes from. The grass is every colour but green, and it absorbs every colour that isn't green: red, blue, yellow, and so on, every other colour in the rainbow. But because it doesn't contain any green it reflects the green wavelength, and that's why we end up seeing green when we look at it. We do that with everything. All we ever see is a reflection of the colour that things aren't. Grass is not green, elephants are not grey, blood is not red.

Where did you hear that?

Nowhere. I read it. In a book.

So what colour is grass?

I told you. Every colour except green. All at the same time.

Eldo turns her attention back to the grass. It almost looks like a field of worms, waving in a breeze. The blades are broad, waxy. They have a subtle smell that grows in intensity when she plucks one from the ground and tears it in half, releasing a small amount of liquid that is heavy with the scent of something wonderful.

What was that address in the match book again?

Which match book?

Eldo goes through her memory banks. Huh. Which match book is she talking about? She has a memory of finding one somewhere, or being given one, of it having an address written on the flap. Of her thinking that this must be important. Something to do with Paris. With Mona.

Weren't we in the hotel before?

The hotel?

Yeah, the Opera. With Serge.

Annick just looks confused and shakes her head. Eldo's

hands go to her pockets, she rummages around.

I could have sworn...

But she's stopped mid-sentence as she finds something square and flat in her pocket, takes it out. A match book.

This is the match book.

Annick leans closer as she flips it open,

Where did you get it from?

I don't know. I want to say New York, but I can't be sure.

Does it have anything written in it?

Yup. Oriza. 47 rue de Coty.

Eldo knocks on the ornate wooden door with the number 47 on the front. Annick is with her, but she seems uncomfortable about being here.

You sure this is the right thing to do?

To be honest with you, Annick, I really don't know what's happening any more.

Several bolts are unlocked from the other side of the door, and Eldo and Annick go quiet. The door opens a crack, has a chain attached, preventing it from fully opening, and an old woman peers through the gap. Her skin so densely wrinkled that it looks like there are secret messages written in her flesh. Her eyes so milky white and watery that for a moment Eldo thinks they belong to a walking corpse. She keeps the chain on the door, says something in French. Annick looks at Eldo.

Well?

I don't know. Tell her that I need to talk to her.

Annick says something to the old lady in French, who then replies, and Eldo waits impatiently for the translation.

She doesn't see why she should let some 'like the boys' woman in when she doesn't know who you are.

Seriously? She said that about me?

Uh huh.

Charming. Tell her I'm a friend of Mona's.

Really? Isn't that a bit of a reach?

I think this is important.

Annick doesn't say anything.

Try it.

She sighs and turns back to the old woman, says a lot of French words which fly past Eldo so quickly that she almost doesn't catch the word *Mona* in the middle, but the old woman certainly does.

She gasps when she hears the name.

The chain is released.

The door is opened.

Eldo and Annick are in the house, listening to the monotonous ticking of a clock which they can't see, while the old woman, whose name it turns out is Oriza, is making tea in the kitchen. Perhaps that's where this monstrous clock is.

The place is like a museum of everything Paris used to be, as well as a tribute to dust. The room is thick with it. Covering every surface. There are two windows, and Eldo approaches one of them, takes hold of the heavy curtains and rubs her thumb against the velvet drapes, creating thick ropes of dust which fall to the floor revealing the richer red of the material underneath. She looks over at Annick who is watching her hand. Their eyes meet and she raises her eyebrows, Annick asks her a question:

So she does know Mona?

Apparently so.

And why are we here?

Oh, I have no idea. I have no idea why anything's happening anymore. I don't even know how we got here from the Tuilleries. Last thing I knew I was in the bathroom in the Opera.

Which opera?

The hotel. You and Serge were outside.

Outside the hotel?

Outside the bathroom.

Eldo looks out of the window, it's facing a well of rear windows, a triangular common parts area on the ground far below, all the windows she can see displaying the abundance of unseen life that the building is teeming with, but which can only be pieced together from visual and aural clues: voices, mess, clothes, music. There are many people living here, you can tell, even though there is no one in sight.

And then Oriza walks in, holding a tray with three cups, all on saucers, and a teapot, everything tinkling gently, and Eldo brings her head away from the window, either because she doesn't want her to think she's snooping, or because she wants to be, or at least appear to be, polite – she's not sure which one is driving her right now.

Everything on the tray looks antiquated and expensive. Chamber music is playing from somewhere in the apartment. Has that just started or was it playing the whole time? Oriza sets the tray down and pours the tea. She's talking the whole time, but as Eldo has no idea what she's saying she simply assumes the facial expressions of someone who is listening attentively, while in reality her words are merely musical notes. Annick and Eldo both sit down opposite Oriza, and Annick lets the ancient woman finish, turns to Eldo, and says:

She wants to know why you're here.

I think I'm looking for Mona. Does she know where she is?

Annick and Oriza spend some time talking here. And although Eldo doesn't understand what they're saying she feels pretty sure from the tone of it all that Oriza doesn't know where Mona is. Turns out she was kind of right, but it's more complicated than that.

She says she knows where she is, but that it's useless to tell you because you can't reach her and you won't understand, and then she added that she hasn't seen or heard from Mona for around three years.

What does that mean?

As Annick is about to reply Oriza starts talking again and Annick divides her concentration between a waiting Eldo and a talking Oriza.

Okay, so something she forgot to mention, which is important, is that most of the time you can only see Mona when she wants to see you. There's something else she's saying about a way to see Mona, but I don't understand what she means.

What are the words?

She keeps saying trois sur trois, three out of three. But I don't get it.

And Oriza leans forward, revealing a grace you would not expect in a woman of her age, locks eyes with Eldo, opens her mouth, and lets that ancient voice intone in English. It sounds like history speaking.

You think you're here, but you're not here.

Eldo's shocked, but, as ever, she plays it cool. So cool in fact that you'd think she wasn't surprised at all. She looks over at Annick to play a game of *What the fuck?* eyes with her, but she's not looking at her, instead she's staring down at the table in front of her, like a bored teenager. Finding no camaraderie here she looks back at Oriza, and she continues.

She says nothing because she is not here either. You are in the hotel, n'est pas? To be more precise, you are inside your own mind.

Apart from thinking the words:

Aren't I always?

to herself, she notices that the room is completely silent now, gone are the noises from outside and elsewhere: the shrieks of children, the radios, the dogs barking, the ticking clock, the chamber music, the traffic. Everything.

Those sounds were the sounds you believed you would hear in a place that looks like this. The dust is dust you would expect a woman of my age to have in her apartment. Go beyond what you expect.

She stops talking, her words echoing around in the hermetic silence of the room. Eldo focuses on that silence, on the lack of sound, and starts looking for noise in the way that you might look for a missing key, or a lost glove. And the sound of a gentle humming comes to her. Is that traffic she's hearing? No. It can't be. It's too monotone. Too mechanical. Too small.

And then it comes to her.

It's a fan.

An extractor fan.

The hotel bathroom had a fan in it that turned on automatically when she turned the light on.

She gets to her feet. Annick keeps her eyes on the table, doesn't move. She's like a dream character without any motivation now. Like a… like a…

But her insight goes nowhere, because suddenly the thin man with the moustache and the taxi driver are standing in the room too.

What are you doing here?

Eldo asks.

They answer as one.

We are composites, approximations of how you believe men in our positions should look.

Uh huh. That makes sense.

The two men cock their heads to the side in unison and say:

The real question is whether we've been projections the entire time, or whether your attention to detail has been lacking, presumptive – perhaps when you looked at us you simply saw what you wanted to see.

And then Eldo blinks, and it's just her and Annick and Oriza in the room, the old woman wearing a gruesome mortician's grin fixed to her face.

Eldo moves towards the other window in the room, the one she hasn't looked out of yet, expecting to see traffic, or trees, or anything, but when she gets there and looks out, it's not what she expects.

Instead of a view of cars passing, or trees swaying in the breeze, or neighbours looking out and seeing things, Eldo is met by a wire frame grid. Almost as though the image here is unfinished. Oriza speaks again.

You've been infected.

Infected?

The door man at the hotel, the fever that Serge is suffering from.

Eldo looks at the palm of her hand, the scratch is there, but now it's thick with black and green pus. Infected.

You're being primed for trois sur trois. This stage you're experiencing is unpredictable. You're moving through distance and time, but without control or goal. It's sloppy work and will create gaps.

Gaps?

Like the one outside the window.

Eldo glances over at the wire frame outside, then back into the room, at Oriza.

Uh huh, I see.

You can regain control, take yourself anywhere, any time. Where do you think you should go?

Eldo thinks about this, where should she go? She could travel straight to the gallery, confront a moment that has grown in size and importance for her, but Oriza shakes her head.

You are not ready for the gallery. There is much you don't understand.

And as she opens her mouth to reply she finds herself moving somewhere else, and when she arrives there she realises that this was the only place she could have gone to.

Her apartment. In the city. On the 2nd.

From the way the light falls through the windows she figures it must be sometime around noon, but she can't be sure. What she can be sure of is the fact that no one is here.

God damn it, right place, wrong time.

And somehow, she shifts the when of the now, and the light in the room moves from soft and natural to harsh and electric. And when she stops everything, she is pleased to see that it is night, and the room is now populated. This is the night of the 2nd. The night she can't remember.

There are two figures here, one of them is Eldo (who we shall call the present Eldo, she's heavily inebriated, and it's a super strange experience watching herself, especially in such a state) and the other appears to be Mona, but while the inebriated present Eldo can't tell, it's clear to the Eldo–who's-watching that this figure is simply someone wearing a Mona mask.

It's not even a convincing mask. It's made of hard plastic, shiny, held on by a string around the back of the head. The body of the person wearing the Mona mask is also much larger than Mona. The whole thing would be farcical were it not for the fact that present Eldo is falling for it, hook, line, and sinker.

The Mona-who-is-not-Mona leans forward and proffers a cigarette. Present Eldo shakes her head.

No, feel kinda… sick.

This isn't a regular cigarette.

God damn it, even the voice is wildly unconvincing, that's clearly a man.

Oh, an el zumo? You should've said.

The Mona-who-is-not-Mona holds the cigarette up and

points to the filter.

You squeeze it here, pop the capsule inside, light it, inhale, and that's when you get the hit.

Hit of what?

It's a flower, a flower that only grows in Aulnay.

Ornay?

Aulnay. It's in France.

What does it look like?

It's just a town.

No, not... the town, the flower. What does the flower look like?

What does it matter?

What does it matter about what does it matter? Just tell me what the fucking flower looks like, Mona.

Touché. It's small, blue, easy to miss.

The Eldo-who-watches steps over to Aulnay, France, to check this out.

Turns out Aulnay is rural, quiet, and dark. Pretty nice. She shifts time and brings the Sun up so that she can see and looks around for a flower that fits the bill, finds a patch of them growing outside a church: small, blue, inconsequential.

The apocalyptic relief carved into the stone on the exterior of the church that overlooks the flowers does not go unnoticed by her either. It's a parade of the damned being tortured by demons: creatures which have human bodies and animal heads, or animal bodies and human heads, armed with pitchforks and spears, penetrating and holding aloft the screaming bodies of the eternally suffering.

It has nothing to do with the flower, but it's chilling that these two things are in such close proximity. Looking at each other.

And then with one step she's back in her apartment, and

picks everything up right where she left off, which was with the Mona-who's-not-Mona saying

...small, blue, easy to miss.

And it's inebriated present Eldo's turn to talk.

And what does it, like, you know, do?

Try it and you'll find out.

The Mona-who-is-not-Mona keeps the cigarette held out until Eldo breaks (or perhaps just gets bored) and takes it from her... him... whatever. And with eyes that are having difficulty focusing, and losing interest in trying to show that she has little to no faith in the claims made of the cigarette, she lights it, crushes the filter, and inhales.

And then everything gets pretty wild.

Present Eldo freezes, but not like you would in real life if you just stopped moving. No, it's more like how you would freeze if you were a recorded image, paused, juddering ever so slightly, but in the real world, not on a screen.

The Mona-who-is-not-Mona also freezes at this point, but not like an image, merely like someone who is keeping still. Like someone pretending to be a statue when the music stops.

The Mona-who-is-not-Mona puts a hand to the mask and lifts it, and, to no real surprise from the Eldo-who's-watching all of this play out, it's Frederic underneath.

The fat man peers closer at present Eldo, waves a hand in front of her unmoving face, and then relaxes a little. Something shifts in his shoulders and neck, almost like he'd been tensing himself, preparing for something to leap out at him.

And then it does.

A thunderous sound roars through everything, as though the universe cracked, as though all matter was breaking in half. From the noise you'd expect the earth to be shaking, the building to fall, but there is no movement in the room at all, even the glasses and cups of liquid in here show no tremor at all, they're perfectly mirrored pools.

And then Frederic falls over, onto his back, arms and legs bent, like a bug. He rolls from side to side and onto his front, crawls away from Eldo, scuttling like a crab, like a cockroach, edging himself closer to the door all the time, getting the fuck away, a look of desperation in his eyes.

Something's clearly wrong.

Present Eldo still isn't moving, she's frozen, like something preserved in amber. And the Eldo-who-is-watching suddenly understands that the frozen body of present Eldo is the source of this apocalyptic sound.

Something is happening.

Something is coming through.

Tearing its way through, from somewhere else. And then a wave of scent hits her, so thick it's palpable, you could cut it out of the air: the now unmistakable oud.

Eldo-who-is-watching remembers the molecule inside her body, the kernel that the oud uses as a portal. What is it? A thought? Cancer cells? A piece of oud from yesteryear that lodged in her body and then just stayed there? Does it even matter what it is? Probably not.

And then she watches the oud crawl out, or grow from, the body of present Eldo like a spider, like a slime mould, like hatred. It's a conjuring trick like nothing she's ever seen, Eldo simply can't tell how it's coming through her. Is she a door? A seed? What is this sight unfolding before her eyes?

And then Frederic takes a folded piece of paper from his pocket, coughs, and reads it out loud:

Eldo – I am reading these words not to the Eldo-who-is-here, but to the Eldo-who-is-not-here. The Eldo-who-watches.

The man has Eldo's attention.

This message is from Mona. She wants you to know that she is sorry, but this is unavoidable, in fact, it has always been unavoidable. Mona does not expect you to understand everything at this juncture, but she asks you to look into your heart and forgive her. Mona says that you do not have that capacity right now, that you never do at this point, but that's okay. Mona then closes by saying that you should leave now. There is nothing more to ascertain.

And Frederic goes quiet.

Eldo waits for more, but Frederic's eyes fall and his mouth closes and he folds the slip of paper in half, places it in his pocket, and leaves, escapes, closing the door behind her. Leaving present Eldo behind, with the oud swelling and swirling and becoming mass, and the Eldo-who-watches knows that it is time to leave, and she closes her eyes and feels the wind of space and time lift her up and take her far, far away.

When she opens her eyes again, she's back in the perfume store in New York. It's dark outside. But it's not the night that she and Serge were here, that's obvious straight away, although don't ask her to explain how she knows this.

Serge… damn… is he back at the hotel? Is he okay? Am I okay?

The sparkly well-dressed assistant comes over to Eldo and says:

Nice to see you again.

And it's only now that Eldo realises that she's in the world, a part of it, that she can be seen again. And she breathes a little easier because she'd forgotten how nice it is to be seen, especially when it's by a young, pretty woman. Wait… Miss… Barberry, was it?

So nice to see you too.

Something judders in her body, there's a tremble, an

unpleasant sensation. The lady doesn't notice this at all and says:

Are you looking for anything in particular?

Eldo just shrugs and gives the universal gesture for suggesting *nothing* and doesn't say anything at all. Miss Barberry smiles.

Well maybe you're here to see this.

She reaches to one side and brings a metal tray over with two antique looking bottles on.

What do we have here?

Two scents that I think you're going to enjoy: oud and a variation on Iso E.

I feel like we've been here before, done this before.

If so, then you'll be able to tell me all about oud.

And so Eldo launches into the story about agarwood and the disease and the protective reaction and then Miss Barberry stops her by reaching out and placing a finger on her lips (*there's that judder again, what the fuck is that?*) and then says:

But tell me this:

What is it that humans find so enchanting about oud? What is it about the aroma of agarwood producing a protective resin to fight an infection that they like? Are they responding to the scent of protection, or attack? Or is it the very stench of conflict, of dominance, of one thing exerting its will over another, that they are drawn to?

These are heady concepts.

Scent is a heady topic. Here. Give me your hand.

Eldo does as she's told, lifts a hand, and Miss Barberry takes hold of her fingers with one hand, removes the lid of one of the bottles with the other.

By the way, am I still in the hotel?

The Hotel Opera? In Paris?

There is a glass rod attached to the lid and Miss Barberry holds it over Eldo's hand, a sphere of liquid falls onto her skin.

Yeah.

How would I know? I'm in New York. Okay, tell me what you smell here.

She brushes the droplet into her skin with her thumb, there's a small electric charge that runs down Eldo's spine as she does this, which hits something sensitive inside her body and then the judders take hold again for a moment.

What is that?

The judders or the scent?

The scent. Wait, how do you know about the judders?

Uh uh uh. No cheating. Tell me, what can you smell?

She ignores her knowing things she shouldn't know, breathes in the scent from the back of her hand, she knows that scent so well now, has picked it up so many times that when she smells it, she gets flash after flash of that thing, that woman:

Inhale

Her. Walking down a stone staircase, wearing only a fur coat.

Inhale

Her. Sitting at a table, in front of a mirror, smoking, her feet on the table.

Inhale

Her. On a beach, her clothes and hair wet, and she's smiling, laughing, turning.

It's her.

She says. And then:

How is this working?

You don't remember? It releases your own smell, your own scent, it raises it up above everything, brings it to the forefront. It's the ultimate product for individuality, because what it unlocks is you, and only you.

And what's it made from?

This strain is isolated from a small blue flower that is only found in Aulnay, in France.

I've heard of that flower before.

Probably from Mona, right?

Yeah, that sounds about right. Why is this scent so important?

Why do you think? What does your scent mean? What does oud mean? Where is the conflict? The dominance? For you, not for anyone else.

I don't know, help me, Miss Barberry.

She smiles.

Now, I can only guess, but perhaps what oud means for you is your own obsession, circling around and around and around a heavenly body, a body that you call female.

What now?

Consider it. Your obsession, which you think is liberating, exhilarating, of your choosing, is completely out of your control. You think it's cute. But it's anything but that. Your obsession with women is fighting you now, that's what those judders are: your conscious body rebelling against the unconscious cognition of your mind. You want to know how to save Annick, but it's your obsession with women that is driving this, you are trying to protect her from a creature of your own making, something you gave form to, it's you who destroys her, but you're too dumb and lovesick to realise this. You're the monster, Eldo. It's you. It's always been you.

And it's as the assistant says these words that everything seems to freeze: someone is coming into the store and the bell above the door rings but the moment is caught mid-ring and the cheery sound of the bell does not stop, it continues, becoming a gong, a wind tunnel, and no one in the store moves, and Eldo takes in the deep, deep blue of Miss Barberry's eyes, and the judder runs through her again and suddenly everything begins to make a lot more sense.

Eldo thinks back to Frederic's words in her apartment in the city, how he knew she was there. How did he know that? Is she really the monster? And what does all of this have to do with a flower from Aulnay? Jesus. So hard to think straight. But now she remembers something she wanted to ask Miss Barberry, and as luck would have it the ring of the gong fades away and time picks up again, so she says:

How did you know I'm staying in the Hotel Opera?

But Miss Barberry doesn't say anything, just smiles, and there's something so terribly wrong with her smile, and fear creeps into Eldo's gut, like a disease, like arsenic.

And just like that the perfume store is gone and Eldo is somewhere else. Somewhere where the walls are made of flesh, breathing. The floor is sticky and wet. The stench of sour milk fills the air. Serge is screaming. Serge, man. Apart from the hell of where she is and the blood curdling screams that fill the air, it's good to hear Serge again.

And although it might look like she's in some kind of living nightmare Eldo knows exactly where she is, she's in the Opera, back in the hotel, although it's also entirely possible, in fact extremely likely, that she's been here the whole time and simply never left, and this realisation brings familiarity to her surroundings once more. Normality regained. Sort of.

She's in the harsh electrical light of the bathroom, the fan whirring in the corner. And Serge is in the other room, and he's scared, screaming. Eldo opens the door.

Serge, you okay man?

Serge continues screaming. Eldo takes this to mean that he's probably not okay.

Have you seen Annick? Do you know where she is?

The wall of screaming continues. Eldo draws up right next to Serge and puts one hand on his shoulder and the other on his back, making gentle, circular motions, leans close, and intones:

Shhhhhhhhhhhhhhhhhhhhhhh…

And the sound that comes from her lips rattles her teeth as it fills the air, becomes all sound, the only sound, reverberates, builds, and slowly but surely this one note takes on the resonance of a passing freight train, of a chorus of angels. It fills the room, and Serge's screams slowly die away, and then Eldo whispers:

It's okay man, you're going to be okay.

Serge still doesn't say anything, and although his breathing is rapid, jagged, Eldo can tell from his eyes that her friend is back, whether he's going to be okay is another matter.

Now, Serge. I'm talking to you. Listen to me and try to answer. Do you know where Annick is?

Serge nods.

Where is she?

You know where she is, hombre. She's at the art gallery. Dead.

This throws Eldo, her body quivers.

How do you know this?

Because we're there now. We're at the art gallery, and we're at the hotel. What the fuck is going on man? How are we in different places at the same time?

Eldo looks around, but as far as she can see this place looks nothing like the gallery.

You sure about this one, Serge old buddy?

The next words are difficult for Serge. He takes several gasping breaths before they come out, like the mere thought of saying them is giving him nausea.

I think we're in your head, man.

Eldo's about to say:

That's insane, man

But then she lets Serge's words sit with her for a moment

and she knows that what her friend is saying is true. Tears well up in Serge's eyes and run down his face as he says…

Am I even real? I feel like I just a character that you made up. Like there no Serge. No me.

Don't be so silly, man. Of course you're real. Of course you are.

But how I know?

Hey, how do any of us know?

The two friends stay in the same position, Eldo keeps rubbing a hand against Serge's back until little by little his breathing slows down and becomes normal again. Whatever normal means these days.

We need to be at the art gallery. I mean, so that we can see it.

So let's go there. Let's finish this thing.

Well okay then.

And Eldo lurches herself and Serge, and where she ends up is inevitable, it's exactly where she needs to be. So much so that she doesn't notice that Serge has completely disappeared when she arrives there.

XVII
8th April, 1994
20:45
The Gallery

Everything around her is white, clean, familiar, but that's not the first thing she notices. The first thing she notices is her body make an involuntary gasping breath, an inhalation, and the scent of paint and sweat and a hundred different colognes and perfumes fills her body and Eldo can not for the motherfucking life of her remember when she last smelled something real.

What the fuck, man, what the fuck?

It feels like she hasn't taken an actual breath for the longest time, like she's been underwater, holding her breath, until now. But that can't be true, can it?

The sounds of her surroundings, the art gallery, slowly builds to match the visuals, as though someone were turning them up from nothing. The voices, the soles of shoes moving against the hard floor, polite laughter, glasses being filled, bubbles breaking against the surface of champagne. Everything is audible. Everything is aligned. Everything is harmonised. And that helps a lot.

Eldo's got that nagging sensation at the back of her mind that none of what she's going through is real. She's not sure where or when this sensation began, perhaps with the mosquito in the hotel room in New York, or perhaps it was something else. Either way, what's important now is that there's no way that any of this, the art gallery, the place, the people around her, any of it, is not real. There's a solidity and a physicality and an actuality to all of this that is simply undeniable. And although she has no idea how she got here in the first place, she can be sure that all of this is quite real.

And what happens here happens for real.

Her attention is taken by the walls, by the pictures on the walls, and Fougére's whole working practice comes back to her. What a prick. Having said that, the harmonies and sense of balance that the canvasses hold are quite something. And for a moment she thinks about going outside and saying hello to Herman because damn if it wouldn't be good to see Herman again, but then there's a hand on her shoulder. She turns, and is mildly surprised to see Frederic, the fat man.

My dear, fancy seeing you here.

Frederic, you conniving bastard. Remind me again when we last saw each other?

The timelines you've been experiencing are not my speciality, dear lady, but I believe the last time we saw each other, so to speak, would have involved me not seeing you at all.

My apartment? You wearing a mask?

Indeed. The Eldo-who-watches. You probably have quite a few questions for me.

Sure, you could say that.

But, unfortunately, I have no answers for you.

That's not really much of a surprise.

But I do have something, something that will help immeasurably.

Three of three?

The fat man smiles, a hand goes to his pocket.

Indeed. Because this is quite a public venue, we've given the cigarette the appearance of a brand. It's the little things.

Frederic carefully removes a silver case from his pocket, presses an unseen button and it flicks open to reveal one cigarette. Eldo's fingers take it, and she holds it closer to her face, rotates it until she sees a word printed on the filter, the word is *Eldo*. She laughs.

Oh, isn't that just adorable?

Quite. A singular branding for a singular woman on a singular occasion. We've taken the idea of mass production and made a mockery of it.

Eldo catches something on the air and sniffs at the cigarette. Ooh…

What's that scent?

I'm glad you asked, it's something of my own concoction. I felt that today was quite the event and that three of three demanded to be shrouded in something appropriate. Sprayed and then left to dry. It was quite the fashion in the past for ladies to perfume their cigarettes, don't you know, to create their own unique scent profiles at events.

So thoughtful of you. What am I smelling here?

It's a floral, amber, and musk arrangement – a number of notes: lily and honeysuckle in the head, jasmine and mimosa in the heart, along with a number of fruit accords.

And the base?

Amber, vanilla, and myrrh. To name just a few. It complements the tobacco rather well.

Eldo breathes it in. The picture that comes to mind is Annick, pure Annick.

I've managed to conjure her up quite well, what?

Eldo opens her eyes, and tears fall.

You really have. I'm not sure how I feel about her anymore.

Quite. That's all part and parcel of the journey you've been on, a journey of discovery which forces one to question basic assumptions about one's life, one's philosophies, how one feels about the world around them.

I don't think I'm good for her.

Is anyone ever good for anyone? There's a question for

you. One which none of us knows the answer to, but once all this is over, you'll be able to answer it better than any of us.

And as Eldo opens her mouth to reply there's a sound which stops her in her tracks: the sound of a long-stemmed glass hitting a tiled floor, a woman crying out, a flock of birds taking to the air. All standing and talking to Frederic, and she forgot about the time, about the importance of why she was here. And as she runs in the direction of the sounds, she doesn't hear Frederic call after her…

It always ends this way.

The gallery room is as it was before. Filled with crystal clear statues of women wrapped in towels, standing on plinths. Annick's body lying on the ground. But this time there is something else. The oud. Standing in front of Annick's body, smiling. And although she looks for all the world like a she, Eldo knows it's an it. You can almost hear 'it' in its voice, something inhuman, otherworldly.

Did you think any other ending was possible?

I'm too late.

You are always too late, you will always be too late. No other ending is possible.

Why are you doing this?

I have no choice. I came into this place, unformed, undefined, and you, my creator gave me shape. The figure of your true obsession was taken, occupied by this… person.

The oud gestures to Annick's body on the floor. Eldo's eyes tear up.

Don't talk about her, you don't deserve to use her name.

Please. I know everything about you so well. You gave me shape with an obsession that formed in an instant, you gave me this face, this body, you invited me here, to this space, to this time. And now that she is gone, I am your only love, your only obsession, and now I will tear this realm to shreds.

And Eldo believes that she understands what she is here to do and so she grabs hold of everything, somehow takes hold of this moment, and drags it back, and back, and back in time, back to before Annick dies, back to a point that she can save her and stop this thing.

But she can't do it.

Something is blocking it, something is in the way.

And as she tries, over and over and over again the oud is somehow able to be rewound, but also to stay outside of the control of time, to taunt Eldo, to task her.

You do not save her. You never save her.

And Eldo ignores the stinging tears of rage and sadness in her eyes and asks:

Where are you from? What are you?

Another place, a different place. I am a different thing. Something that was never meant to be here.

And Eldo keeps rolling everything backwards, but the furthest she can take it to is the moment when the waitress comes in, and then it plays out in the same awful way, over and over and over again. And Eldo is unable to stop it, unable to interfere with the steady motion of this inexorable machine that has been created to destroy Annick, to destroy everything, over and over again, and she releases her grip, gives up, and lets it play out for a terrible final time, and Annick's body falls, the waitress comes in, screams, drops a long-stemmed glass and the champagne from the glass somehow splashes up high, far higher than you'd think possible and Eldo follows the trajectory of a single drop of champagne and then the droplet hangs in the air, frozen in time, and that is when she realizes that Mona is about to step out from somewhere, so she turns, and she's there, and she smiles warmly at Eldo, and speaks:

It's always like this, and that's the rub. No matter what you do beforehand to change the outcome, this moment always plays out the same.

Mona? The real Mona?

Sort of. I'm not here, of course, but I'd like to see you, face to face, at least one more time.

Why bring me here if I can't change it?

You brought yourself here. You always do. My involvement is... key, related, but I did not bring you here.

Why is this happening to me?

It wasn't my plan. I want you to know that. It was never my plan.

Frederic? He one of yours?

Of course.

And what did your goons hit me with back at the hotel?

The cut in your hand? That was a primer – in order for you to survive three of three and to continue in the physical realm you had to be infected – Serge was infected in New York, it incubated, developed, and then you were given an open wound in Paris to receive his infection. Comme ci, comme ca.

Risky strategy.

Oh, not at all, I assure you.

And the dart at the d'Orsay? The one Frederic shot at me?

Mona laughs. And although this isn't really the time for levity, it is kind of nice to hear her laugh again.

That was a bee sting. You never realise that was a bee.

Never?

I've seen this moment an infinite number of times, there are subtle variations, but the threads always remain the same – you are always here, Annick always dies. But this thread, this one that we are experiencing now shines bright, something is different this time, something exciting.

Enough of the talking in circles. I want to speak to the real Mona, face to face. And I want to know what all this shit is about.

There's only one way that you and I can see each other

again. Only one way for you to get all the answers.

Mona gestures to the cigarette Eldo is holding.

So what is this? Is this the same stuff that the Frederic-playing-Mona gave me back in the city the other night?

Sort of. It's a variation. A compound made of different elements. A key one coming from a small flower, found only in...

Eldo finishes the sentence

...Aulnay. So you spiked me?

Spiked. Such a leading word. Think of it more as a learning exercise.

I'm pretty sure I haven't learned enough yet.

That's because we're here. You simply wouldn't understand in this realm. Crush it. Light it. Smoke it. Then you'll be where I am. And then you'll understand.

And where are you?

Somewhere wonderful.

Mona smiles coyly, like she has a secret to tell, but won't divulge it right now.

You have no idea how far I've taken things Eldo, no idea the sights I've seen.

Mona puts a hand to her mouth and tears well up in her eyes. Her other hand finds Eldo's shoulder and lays itself across her tenderly, but Eldo can't feel it. She has no weight. No physicality.

But soon you'll know.

Mona steps back.

I know you can do this. It'll be nice to see you face to face, without these avatars.

Eldo doesn't really know what an avatar is, but she doesn't want to seem stupid, so she says nothing. Besides, she's too busy exhaling completely, emptying her lungs.

Then she crushes the filter.

Brings the cigarette up to her lips.

Lights a match.

Puts it to the tip.

And inhales.

And then there's the sound of a multitude of wings from inside her body and now she realizes what that third sound was.

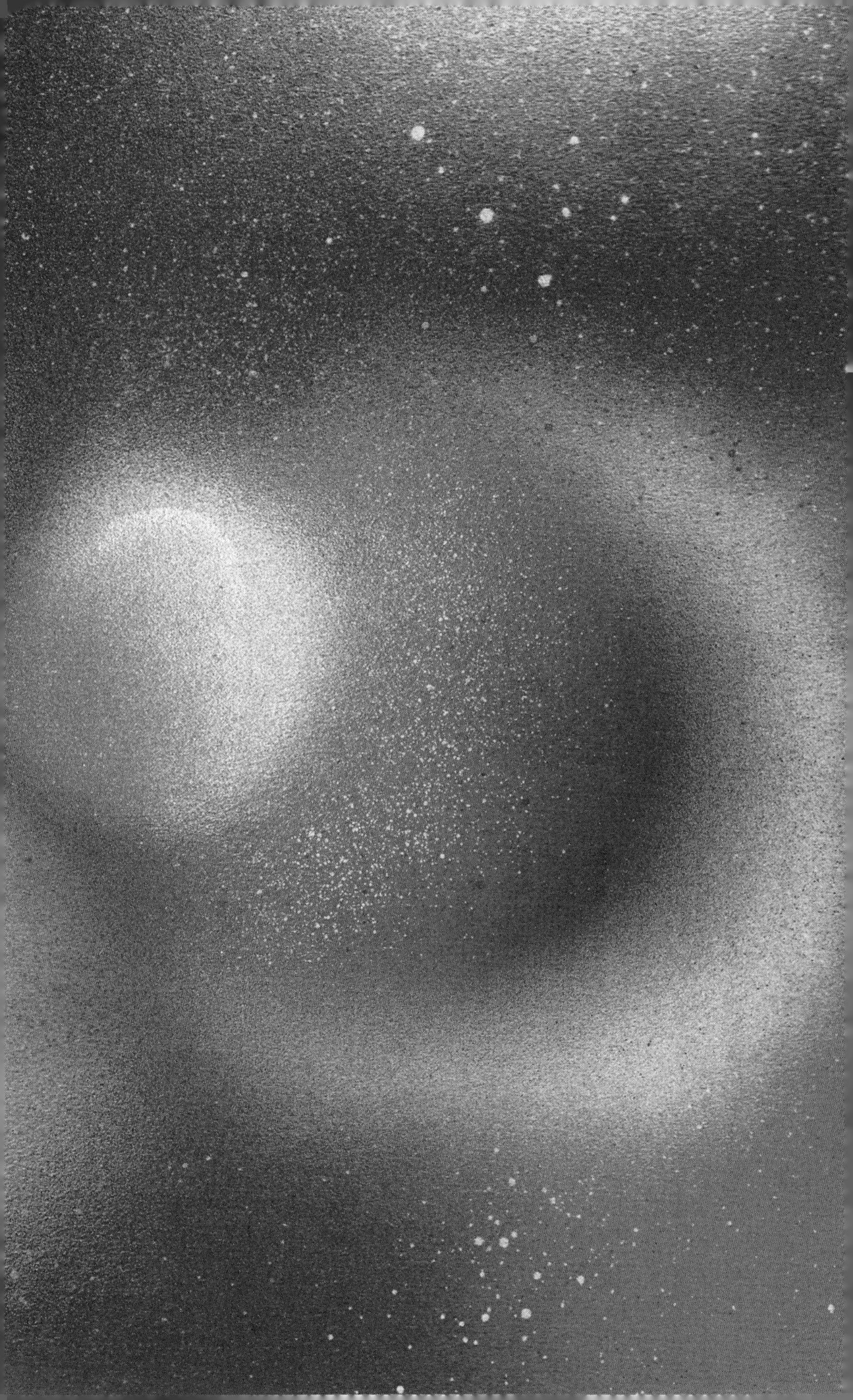

XVIII
All time
Three of Three
Everywhere

All she can see is a field of mandalas, all spinning, all intricate, an impossible sight, but here it is. She can tell just from a glance that the mandalas go on forever, that you could move in as close as you wanted and the field would look the same, pull back as far as it is possible to pull back, and the field would look the same. This sight is a constant, a chaos pattern. And just as the word cliché runs through her mind all breath leaves her body and the mandalas are torn away as though they were printed on a curtain, a material that is both gossamer thin and as heavy as velvet, and the universe lies behind this curtain, and before she knows what's happening, she's moving through the cosmos, fast.

Where am I?

When am I?

Am I?

Eldo is moving at such a speed that the stars' usual appearance as a singular point of light has gone, they're more like a sparkler being swung through the air by a child, and because there are so many of them, all moving past her, they form what looks like a tunnel. A tunnel that she is moving through at a pace so great she doesn't know a word for it.

But if she turns and looks to the side she can see each individual star, planet, body in incredible detail. Weird. And although it makes no sense at all considering how fast she knows she's going, everything seems to move past her in slow motion from this vantage point. So slow that she feels like she could reach out and pick a star or a planet up and hold it in her hand. And she's unsure whether these celestial objects are moving of their own accord or whether someone has set them in motion. And although that second option might sound crazy, it really seems like someone has pushed each object individually, setting it off, leaving it to make its way somewhere else.

But how the fuck can that be the case, Eldo?

I'm able to see all of their features, to study them, even as they pass me at a speed greater than the speed of light.

How is any of this possible?

How is any of this real?

And Eldo's wondering whether she has a physical form anymore, when suddenly her flight begins to slow, and somehow or another she breaks through the atmosphere of something that looks like a planet but can't be and she alights on the surface.

But keeps moving.

She's not sure whether the surface of this planet-which-is-not-a-planet is actually solid, because it seems to behave strangely. What form she has (physical or intangible) makes no contact with the surface. Or does it? The physics are definitely off here, that's for certain.

I'm moving forward, but it feels like with every step the planet rotates underneath me, the surface passes below me as what I call my body carries me forward, the experiential impact is that each step takes me immeasurably far.

But she's also getting the sensation that each step only carries her a distance that is a fraction of the total surface of this planet-which-in-not-a-planet. That would make this thing... Jesus fuck... how big is this place?

And then they come. And they welcome her.

Figures made of light. A handful of them, or thousands of them. She can't be sure. What she is sure of is that all of them are female, and they guide her along as she moves, touching her (do I have skin, a body?) gently, nudging her this way and that, whispering…

This Way and That Way

Over Here and Over There

…as she and the figures move through the landscape at a speed that can not be understood, as she moves over distances which are impossible, and all the while the landscape changes, is changed, is grown and shrunk, built and destroyed, or perhaps it's simply the way a landscape changes over impossibly long time periods, perhaps this is nothing more than the creation and erosion of vistas reduced to a time frame of fractions of a second instead of millennia. It's all so hard to tell.

What she does know is that she was expected, the figures tell her this.

How do I know that you're all female?

And they answer me simply by touching.

Each touch is pure love.

There's an explosion on my body as the hands touch me and the touch contains energy, questions, answers, all at once. So much information. And all of this can be understood in a moment, without words. Or perhaps they are speaking to me and I'm only interpreting their speech differently? Understanding it as a sensation instead of cognitively?

Wait. Did I think that, or did I say it out loud?

And then a thought: Perhaps I'm neither thinking this nor saying it out loud. Perhaps there is someone else saying these words, a narrator. Perhaps I'm not even real in any of this.

Thoughts like that will drive you crazy.

As Frederic might say: quite.

And that's when she catches a minor detail that might have seemed insignificant to others: a single drop of liquid on this otherwise arid landscape, hanging in the air, pregnant. And she's reminded of something. And the drop of liquid moves with her, remaining at the same height, matching the same speed, with them, with us, it's moving at the same speed as we are, travelling impossible distances, but just hanging there, and we are moving over the landscape and through tunnels, and watching mountains form and fall away, and all the time the figures around Eldo are talking and saying things, or touching and making her feel things at the very least, and the drop of liquid is following us every step of the way, staying with us, moving with us, but not moving, a constant, everything is a constant, a universal constant so small and insignificant that it would be easy to miss if it were not for the fact that everything is vast and significant, and this is when Mona appears. Her form is the same as the others, a being of pure light, a colour she's never seen before.

Eldo. Thank you. Thank you for being here, for seeing me.

Mona? Is that you?

No. Yes. Everything is quite complicated now, but when you're in this place it all makes so much more sense.

And Mona touches her and there's a spark, a minuscule explosion in the cosmos, and so much energy and information is contained within that explosion, a slow explosion, and Eldo understands everything.

It all plays out like a storybook. Its unrealness highlighted.
This is just a story.
I did not say this.
I was not here.

But not so much a story told in words. Rather, it's a story told in feelings – in how Mona felt at each step of the way. With the distancing effect that these feelings don't mean to Eldo what they once might have meant. Now that she's in this place, the thoughts and feelings she experienced in the physical world seem far away. With every passing second, she understands them less and less. Like the memory of something explained by someone else that was told to you as you stepped into a car, and now that you're warm, and safe, and driving away you find that the memory of those words is fading fast.

So although she can understand the idea of a feeling, all immediacy is lost. Behind glass. All the same, this is Mona's story, this is what happened:

Lack of motion means death.

Mona must keep moving, keep finding, keep selling. And her search for something new, something bold, something that she could use to make more money, led her to Aulnay, to a small patch of blue flowers (what is blue?) and the possibilities that they contained. Her own body was the testing ground. It started small – trembles in the architecture of the universe – but it grew quickly as her quest for something profound deepened, as she used her body and mind to carve out new experiences – to find new products to sell (what is sell?). But something goes wrong, and the balms or tinctures or powders she creates from the flower make her less and less here, both mentally and physically, until finally there is no more Mona, and she ceases to exist in our world in the way that we understand existence, and now she is here, only here.

All of this is transmitted to and understood by Eldo in the blink of an eye. But the blink of an eye is a time reference that makes no sense here, is far too long here. The blink of an eye is enough time for worlds to be created and destroyed by nothing other than time itself. These references are not useful.

So Mona is trapped now, whatever now means. Stuck on the surface of a planet-which-is-not-a-planet. Alone. Except that there are other figures here, divine figures, but I guess what matters is that she is separated from those she knew as people in the physical realm.

But then she discovers a way to reach those she left behind. A way that allows her to refine the experiment, to hone it, to try it on someone else, someone who could help her: Eldo.

She's the only person she knows with a constitution that could withstand the blue flower, the only one with the mental strength for the journey.

But in her haste Mona makes a mistake.

She finds a crude way to bond with Frederic, uses this body which is a fusion of herself and whatever Frederic was to get back into the lab, to create a different blend from the blue flower, and then she goes to Eldo's apartment in the city, has her smoke it. But something goes terribly wrong.

Instead of bringing Eldo to Mona, the modification brings something into the physical world. Something that was never meant to be here. Something terrible. Something which uses a piece of Eldo to manifest itself as the oud.

What is the oud?

The oud is Eldo's obsession taken to the extreme. An obsession that takes what she loves above all else and destroys it, twists it. And this paradoxical outcome: something which should not be, an act that was never meant to happen, the murder of the physical being known as Annick – introduces the concept of destruction to the oud, and being that it is a creature made of obsession it quickly falls in love with what it can do, enamoured with its own power, and it tears everything in our realm apart.

So Mona needs a new plan, something to stop the oud, something that alerts Eldo to the danger that she's manifested, and so she fuses with Frederic again, goes back into the lab, and creates a three-part system, one which allows Eldo to maintain her connection to the physical realm, but also teaches her what she needs to know in order to stop the oud.

The only problem is it never works. Over multiple timelines Mona sees everything crumble time and time again. And Annick always dies. And the physical realm is always destroyed following her death.

There are a countless number of threads of realities in which Mona has brought Eldo on this journey, and each thread is the same: the physical realm destroyed by the thing that crawled out of her.

But there's something different about this singularity, this lone thread that they are experiencing now, something exciting, something that offers hope.

Wait wait wait, so you wanted to bring me here to rescue you, but in doing so you created a thing that brought about the end of everything? And this is happening in countless numbers of alternate realities, or dimensions, or threads, or whatever you want to call them? Is that the gist of it?

It's complicated for you to understand, but the longer you spend here the more it will all make sense. Explanations are not necessary because you know.

And between the 'n' and 'w' sounds that the-thing-that-used-to-be-Mona makes Eldo wonders whether she's moving at all. Perhaps she is standing completely still, and time is moving around her, the way wind moves around a tree, or water flows around a stone in the physical realm that she once inhabited? Perhaps her position in the universe, on the surface of this planet-which-is-not-a-planet only appears to be changing because the very cosmos is changing and growing and moving around her. Yes. Yes, that's possible. Very.

And Eldo looks at the sky-that-is-not-a-sky and she looks at the Mona-who-is-not-Mona and the figures of light that touch her with bursts of pure love, and she understands everything.

All of this makes sense.
I know.
Mona…
Yes?
Who are these figures around us? Am I dead?
No. These are those who have been, or will be. This is an eternal place. The before and after point. It is the physical that lies in between.

And in a flurry of further feelings, in a roadmap of emotions, Eldo communes with Mona and herself and with everything.

She started a journey some time ago as Eldo, a journey that has provided her with a greater understanding of time and space, and she now finds herself thinking differently. And what she needs to do now is manipulate time and space in a manner unique to the singularity known as Annick, so that she can save her, and there's only one way she can do that. And now she knows what that is.

But what does save mean?

Hello? Did I say that? Is there someone there?

Annick's death means nothing. This is an eternal place. Everything exists here, both before and after the physical. Annick continues, but in a different form. Are you saving her for her sake, or for yours?

I don't know.

It is your obsession which chokes the life out of her. And now you think your obsession should prevent this. You are failing to recognise that it is your obsession which is interfering with what you consider her life.

With what I consider her what now?

Eldo doesn't know if she's talking to herself or someone else, but she understands the point. She has her own ideas about what Annick is, and that understanding is that Annick is a figure in the physical world that she came from and that she wishes to continue its existence in that form, in that realm. But who's to say that this is the goal? This place here, beyond the physical world, is where Annick will come once she ceases to exist in her world. And what's wrong with that?

And if she too will enter this space once she is finished with the physical world then what harm is done? What does any of this matter?

A cube is moved from one room to another. The cube only experiences one room at a time. The cube always exists.

So what difference does Annick's death really mean?

It means if your core meets her in this realm all memories of the time you shared together in the physical plane will be gone.

Is that so bad?

Oh, and did we mention, Annick's death means the end of the physical realm as we know it.

Oh yeah. Well fuck that.

So let's do it then.

And Eldo moves up. She rises up from the surface of whatever this place is, moves through the universe again. Going back the way she came. The return journey is hazier than her journey here, much of it is a blank, no sights, no memories, and then her epochal journey begins to slow, and she approaches a blue orb, and flutters down to the surface so gently, like cotton, like something impossible.

And then she's moving through the recognisable place that is the art gallery, so slowly. And there, below her, is the body of Annick lying on the ground. And whatever form Eldo is in right now separates, comes apart, and moves into Annick's form.

And then things get wild.

Eldo feels the distinct 7,000,000,000,000,000,000,000,000,000 parts of her body separate. They stretch apart without breaking. Opening her up. Allowing her to merge with the 7,000,000,000,000,000,000,000,000,000 parts of Annick's body. The idea of them as people ceases. The idea of them as places is born.

The parts dance around each other, moving in an elliptical pattern. One piece of Eldo - and she's not sure if these pieces are cells or atoms or molecules or elements or what - is its own universe. Its own heavenly body. She moves inside one of these pieces, itself so small that it defies understanding, and inside she finds a vast space, a universe of parts, working together independently of each other, but with one goal: maintain the individual piece.

And then she moves out again, to see all of the pieces at once, and each piece that belongs to Eldo finds a complimentary piece that belongs to Annick, and they combine, like two drops of water becoming one, to build a new whole, and a cosmos is born of their parts swirling together, orbiting each other, creating their own gravitational pulls. A cosmos where each piece contains its own cosmos. A body that is a universe made of two forms, two consciousnesses.

Lean all the way out and they look like a person, lean all the way in, and they are a multitude.

This is how everything is.

All the time.

Eldo and Annick understand this now.

Eldo and Annick are one. Their minds are one. Their memories one. There's a nanosecond in which each person they were becomes aware of their new bi-part identity and explores the mind and memory of the other with a delightful curiosity, like children running around a large house, opening drawers and cupboards to see what's inside. And this nanosecond is long enough for Eldo to see and experience each and every memory Annick has ever had: from the pre-linguistic birth and infancy memories, all the way to the present day, and far beyond.

She's crying, the light is so bright, so very bright, and there's a sensation in her body of discomfort, causing her pain. But she doesn't know the words for any of this.

There's a breeze on her face, and she's walking through grass, long grass, holding the hand of a figure that's much taller than her, stronger, secure, filled with love, a rock for her to lean on and trust. The grass clears and Annick and the figure find bones, the skeleton of an animal that lay down and died, its body picked clean, and the infant that Annick is runs her fingertips across the bones, surprised at how they manage to be rough and smooth at the same time.

She's inside, no breeze, in a stone building, and she sees something and climbs it. The something leads up to a flat platform that slopes down, and she delights in the pure joy of pulling herself up the slope and then letting go and feeling her form slide back to the ground, over and over and over.

She's standing on sand, looking at the sea, at the waves. Suddenly a wave crashes into her. She's startled, knocked off her feet, tears spring to her eyes and the taste of salt fills her mouth.

She's walking on a dark street, the streetlights hum orange and seem to drain all of the colour out of the objects she knows differently when the Sun is shining.

She's surrounded by people, her sense of balance wildly off, and there's a male figure imposing itself on her, pushing into her, mentally and physically, and she shoves it away both from her mind and her personal space, and the regain of her solitude and the music that fills the air is just enchanting.

Her body is weak, aged, her breath rasping, difficult, but the joy and love she feels inside as she watches another person walking towards her, as she looks into their eyes, is epochal.

On and on and on these memories go. All of them threaded together by the chain that is Annick herself. All of these moments, these memories, meaning nothing individually, but they add up to create the whole that is Annick.

Meanwhile, Annick also explores all of Eldo's moments, all of her memories. It takes no time at all for both of them to experience everything the other has to offer. And then the distinction between I and You is gone, and then there is only Them and They are one thing. One entity. One cosmos.

They are formed of spiral galaxies, of planets, of molecules, of atoms. Their parts harmonise as one, formed of complimentary segments – creating their own head, their own heart, their own base.

They are made of matter which is formed and appears throughout the universe with great regularity, but in this instance, with this composition, this structure, they are unique.

They move backwards, or forwards, it's so hard to tell,

but they move so that the Them as a cosmos becomes smaller - or bigger - and the Them as a person, a physical entity, in the world, suddenly becomes visible. They are a person now. One person.

They are in the art gallery. Dead. The absence of life creates its own sound. And then They grip the cosmos, and roll it back...

Peace is disturbed by pain, stillness is disturbed by breath, Their breath. They inhale as one for the first time, a death rattle in reverse. Electrical impulses run all over Their form, inside and out, one by one lights are re-lit. One by one synapses are re-bridged, and as it continues everything becomes much, much easier.

And
They
Are
Lifted.

Into the clenched hands of the oud. Its grip is tight at first, horrifically tight, but slowly, ever so slowly, the grip becomes looser, breathing becomes easier, everything comes back to life.

And then They freeze time.

Here. Now. In this room. It's Us against you. You are made of what is now part of Us. You are an obsession made flesh, your very flesh is part of another obsession. Spirals within spirals.

And what now, little thing?

What now?

They unfreeze time and the difference can be felt immediately. The oud's grip is immediately weakened. As though its body had received an electric shock, as though touching Them hurts.

It tries again, she tries again, and her hair and her face and her eyes look so pained. So confused. She doesn't understand why this is happening.

This never happens.

She has been here an infinite number of times, in an infinite number of threads, and every time she has been here she has left this place leaving a body on the floor.

But not this time.

This.

One.

Time.

The oud steps backwards, brings a hand up to its face, fearful for the first time in its existence, fearful for the first time in any of its existences. Something has gone wrong. The individual it needs to destroy is not the same as it was a moment ago. And the look in its eyes is so lost, so confused, so frightened that They almost feel sorry for it. They know that it is a creature from another place, another time, and that it does not belong here. And yet they still remember loving the form it has taken, and the inevitability of its destruction fills them with something They think is called regret, but despite this sensation They know they must end this thing and They swing Their arms as hard as they can.

Their hands hold a bag.

In the bag there is a bottle – large, glass, filled with something They know is very special to Them, but ultimately less special than Their existence.

The bag hits the oud in the face, but more importantly the bottle in the bag hits the oud in the face, through the material of the bag, and there is an almighty crack, and the creature falls back.

Falls.

Back.

A burst of molecules escapes from the shattered bottle and fills the air, envelops everything, and the oud and They experience this scent on a level that They have never experienced before. Chemical. Memory.

So.

Many.

Memories.

This moment is frozen, this moment contains everything. And They will be able to go back to this moment at any point and lift the veil to see how everything is. The oud falling back, the cloud of scent in the air, Eldo and Annick as one.

And then there is the sound of dry meeting wet. Of hard meeting soft. Of the oud's head making contact with the corner of a plinth which supports a glass sculpture of someone called Annick, and a perfectly spherical cloud of plasma appears around the oud's head, and the plasma melds with the scent of the liquid from the broken bottle in Their bag and although everything is its own distinct piece, all of these pieces are linked, interrelated, like fingers interlocking, like a zip being closed, and the oud finally knows fear, knows hurt, knows mortality, and its physical form takes one final breath and lies still, and They know that now it is time to part.

Their universe cracks, the galaxies spiral out and away from each other, the cosmos unzips, and Eldo becomes Eldo and Annick becomes Annick.

Their individual bodies lie on the floor, still and lifeless, and then there is a rush of air as they both take their first breath in what feels like an eternity.

XIX
8th April, 1994
21:40
The Gallery, and Beyond

That was a hell of a thing.
And now, the real world.
There's a lot of shit going on.

People everywhere, some of them calm and controlled and taking care of the situation, and some of them basically freaking the fuck out and making the entire thing much more difficult for those who are trying to deal with everything as calmly as they can. So much noise. So many people.

Eldo is consoled to the very bottom of her being by the physicality of the world she awakes into. Her eyes are closed, but she can feel the hard surface she's lying on, can smell antiseptic, and petrol, and some kind of cotton or wadding, and when she opens her eyes she is not even slightly surprised to see that she's lying in the back of an ambulance.

She sits up, but a hand goes to her chest.

Lie back. You shouldn't be moving yet.

Hey, it's alright, I'm okay. What a trip.

Trip's the word. What the hell had you been taking? We had to pump your stomach.

Uh… it's probably easier if I tell you I didn't have any ketamine. Not a speck.

The voice doesn't say anything, but there's a sound, too small for most to catch – cogs are whirring. The message is being received.

After some time, and a bunch of cognitive test questions

from the paramedic (*What's your name? What year is it? What colour is the sky?* Questions that she was slow to answer, but, I mean, come on...) Eldo is allowed to get up and go back into the gallery.

Francis is there with an army of police, asking what the fuck happened, and not really buying Eldo's *search me* act, but going along with it all the same, because, hey, who really knows. The easiest way of explaining the whole thing is probably just as a case of self-defence, a fight gone wrong. Shit happens.

And then this line of questioning is interrupted by a commotion near the body of the oud, as two police officers are raising their voices in disagreement over the appearance of the body. One says she's a brunette, the other says she's a blonde, and the argument is added to by more bodies and faces and voices joining in, until it quickly comes to light that no one in the room agrees on what the body lying on the floor looks like.

Some say the dead body is male, some female. Some say pale, some dark. It proves impossible to reach any kind of consensus at all. And then photos are taken, polaroids, and when people look at the photographs they are quietly alarmed to see that the image in the picture doesn't look the same to them as the body lying on the floor. And at that point everyone is suddenly more than happy to go along with the mumbled self-defence story Eldo and Annick are giving. And even though their stories don't completely tally with each other, this is far more preferable to the story where the dead body has a constantly shifting physical form.

And so Annick was saved. Which kind of makes this a happy ending. But then something happened that no one was expecting.

After fusing together, after becoming one, Eldo was distressed to find that she could no longer look at Annick without feeling ashamed. And the same was true for Annick, she couldn't look at Eldo without experiencing an over familiarity that forced her gaze away, down, anywhere else. Something about being the same person, sharing the same memories, the same emotions, the same body, meant that they knew too much about each other now. And not just the past – they had danced together far into the future, fused together as one, and had seen multiple timelines of possibilities for themselves, threads that took them all the way to the end. An infinite number of threads. And now they knew not only their individual possible deaths, but also each other's. Every possible end. In detail. An intimate knowledge of every step and feeling that the other would experience as they travelled to the end. There were no more mysteries to conquer. And whenever their eyes caught the others', even only for a second, they were filled with a burning embarrassment at the excess of knowledge. The over-knowing of another soul.

And it never went away.

No matter how long the gap between them seeing each other, this over-knowing remained. Years could pass and if either one of them even thought of the other (which happened very regularly to begin with, and then less and less over the passing years, hey, you kind of know how it goes) they would blush to the tips of their toes, so great was the knowledge they had on each other. Everything frozen. All secrets revealed.

If there was one positive to all this it was that Eldo was able to extrapolate the lessons she'd learned about the way she thought about Annick, hell, the way she thought about all women, and to take these to heart in the way she moved forward. Perhaps there was something diseased in the way she interacted with women, with the way she looked at them. And sure, there was always a conversation ready to start up in her head about how the hell she is ever supposed to react to or think about a woman she finds attractive, but whenever that happened Eldo would invariably think:

Well, hell, at least I'm considering this, right?

And I don't know, maybe that was a start?

And Annick?

Annick continued being Annick, keeping people at bay for several more years before she decided to make a break from the routine and take a chance on intimacy, and she ended up finding herself in a relationship that went pretty much more or less exactly where you might have expected it to go if you were watching from the outside. And for her it was simply tracing a single thread that she had already witnessed when she and Eldo were one, following it all the way to the end, encountering no surprises along the way, but enjoying the experience.

And Eldo continued being Eldo, for what it was worth. Until a cold dark night in the city on the 31st of December, 1999, where, seeing in the new year, the new millennium, her body suddenly decided that enough substances had been thrown at it and it gave up, waved a white flag, and she slept the good long sleep.

At least… that was one of the possible eventualities she'd seen. While travelling through time and space, while being one with Annick, she had seen so many possibilities, so many threads, myriad endings to her story – some long, some short, but the one that took place on the 31st of December 1999 was the one that she saw most often. Perhaps she would consider doing something to alter that outcome, or perhaps it was meant to be – it's hard to say how she felt about it.

And Mona never did come back from the other realm, whatever that place was, but she would visit Eldo from time to time, using vessels like Frederic, or just doing the whole hummingbird thing whenever she could. But as time went on this happened less and less often as she simply found herself far and far less interested in the dealings of flesh puppets in the physical realm. And who could really blame her? After all, we are an enormous drag.

And Serge? Well, he did alright. After the dust had settled Eldo found Serge sweating to death in the hotel in Paris, and to make up for all the shit she'd put him through, and for just being an overall good guy, Eldo gave Serge the betting slip with Kurt Cobain's name on it.

Once he was well enough to walk and talk, Serge cashed the shit out of that slip, which was a hell of a lot of money, and he went on to do what felt right: he went back to Berlin, found the girl at the cinema, and spent a lot of time, and a little of the money, on winning her over.

Turns out she wasn't really much for city living, and one day, while sitting outside a convenience store in a square in Berlin, they found a map and stuck a pin in it and decided to move wherever they made a hole. So Serge and the girl from the cinema ended up living in a small, rural town in France. The language was no problem, and money was no problem, and the climate was mild, and life was easy.

One day the two of them decided to have a picnic near a local church. They took saucissons, canard, moutarde, pain, ate well, and had one of those conversations where it feels like you and the other person are so well connected that you can feel the emotion in each other's words as they land on you and fall into you and become a part of you.

She falls asleep with her head resting on Serge's chest and he idly picks at the grass, scattering the blades, reflecting on the appearance of this field of grass waving in the breeze, until his fingers find, by chance, a small blue flower and he marvels at the intricacy of the colour in something so small and insignificant. The various azure hues seem to dance before his eyes, as though it were not merely a plant, but more like jewel, or an exotic beetle, or a star. And the planet rotates and a tree that was blocking the light from the Sun has now moved just enough to allow a shaft of light to hit him in the face, to dazzle him, and he closes his eyes, and this is when Serge realises that once his eyes are closed and everything is dark, he can still see the image of the blue flower shimmering in front of his face. He opens and closes his eyes to check, just to make sure he's not going crazy, and there it is – a field of night, with the electric image of a small blue flower burning its way through, clear as day, pensive, coiled tight and waiting for him to drop his guard before it makes its move.

About the Author

Ben Woodiwiss lives and works in London, UK. He has written articles, reviews, and screenplays for several years. He is the Writer/Director of the hit indie film *Benny Loves Killing*. His favourite scents are cigar smoke, frankincense, and the air on crisp snowy days. This is his first novel.